Waterline

Waterline

a novel by
Elizabeth Roberston Huntsinger

Holladay House Publishing

Holladay House Publishing

Holladay House Publishing
1120 Bancroff Lane
Manning, SC 29102

This book is a work of fiction. Names, characters, places, and incidents either are products of the author's imagination or are used fictitiously. Any resemblance to actual events or locales or persons, living or dead, is entirely coincidental.

First edition, first printing 2014

Jacket design by Abby Sink
Author photo by Lee Huntsinger
Manufactured in the United States of America

Hardback edition ISBN 978-1-941980-03-3
Trade Paperback edition ISBN 978-1-941980-04-0

Acknowledgments

I owe a tremendous debt of gratitude:

to Holly Holladay for her uncannily accurate editorial direction and to Abby Sink for the cover that so very well defines *Waterline*;

to Lee Huntsinger and Alasdair Robertson for their expertise in getting us out of cliff-hanging maritime escapades and turning them into—in retrospect—breathtaking, serendipitous adventures;

and to the Georgetown County Library, the Charlestowne Few Pirates, the Arthur Manigault Chapter UDC, the Pee Dee Light Artillery, *The Georgetown Times,* and the Scribblers for illumination and friendships.

Dedication

To Alasdair, Lee, and Virginia Lee

"Please would you tell me," said Alice..."why your cat grins like that?"

"It's a Cheshire cat," said the Duchess, "and that's why."

—Lewis Carroll
Alice's Adventures in Wonderland, 1865

"People can die of mere imagination."
—Geoffrey Chaucer
The Canterbury Tales

Chapter One

Labor Day

D ownshifting into third gear, Virginia turned her old, low-slung Porsche off Ocean Highway 17 onto the narrow, sandy, two-lane track. She switched off the headlights, driving slowly through the dips and ruts she knew by heart. Mindful of the fast-approaching storm, she cast her eyes upward when a distant bolt of lightning illuminated the low canopy of swaying live oak limbs waving long tendrils of Spanish moss above her windshield.

Keeping the engine in third gear, she concentrated on holding an even pressure on the accelerator. The engine would lug if she slowed even a little, but shifting down to second was way too loud and must be avoided.

Nearing the house, she saw her stealth was not necessary. Just as she hoped, Gordon was gone. Despite the humid, early evening heat, she shivered. In the gathering gloom, the tall, white-columned house looked even more cold and remote than Gordon had been during this past year.

She drove around to the back of the house and parked behind the canebrake. In antebellum days, when the house was already over a century old, this thick growth of bamboo served to separate the main house from the slave cabins and farming equipment. This evening, the canebrake was a good place for Virginia to park her roadster out of sight.

Gordon always parked in front of the house and entered through the front door. If he came in while she was here tonight, she could slip through the back door and drive out the overgrown back lane. After driving over the old earthen dike across the abandoned rice field, she could then take the dirt road leading back up to the highway.

Like a thief, she crept up the steep back steps of her former home, reaching the tall, first floor porch just when huge raindrops began splatting noisily on the ground below. The storm was blowing in from the south and most likely already pummeling the marina, her new home. Even after the impending divorce, she knew she would never want to live in this house again, with all of the memories of Gordon's self-righteous, self-centered, adulterous self lurking in every corner.

Tired of waiting for his latest girlfriend to become fed up with his faithless ways and shoot him, Virginia was finally divorcing him. Right now, she was on a time-sensitive mission.

She unlocked the heavy back door and slipped inside the darkened house. Glancing furtively around, she half-expected Gabrielle to run meowing around the corner, but that was not going to happen. She and Gabrielle lived on the boat now, and Gordon was left to his own devices.

Virginia pulled her yellow underwater camera out from the pocket of her windbreaker. None of tonight's photographs needed to be taken underwater, but years of living close to the river and the ocean made her appreciate anything not susceptible to dampness.

Down in the large attached garage, she photographed every one of Gordon's expensive offshore fishing reels, as well as the boat-truck-and-trailer rig facilitating them. This done, she headed to the top of the house to photograph the contents of his gun room. She knew he planned to hide all the marital assets she was preserving on film tonight.

So far, she had not turned on any lights. She knew her way blindfolded around the house, and the lamp on the telephone pole outside shone enough light through the windows to give her bearings and footing.

She started up the stairs to the second floor. On the landing, she paused outside her old bedroom—the bedroom she and Gordon shared until the weekend she was away on a buying trip and he had entertained that *woman* right here in their queen-sized rice bed.

She glanced in the full-length hall mirror outside the bedroom door. Every morning she used to stop at this mirror for a quick check before heading off to the shop. This evening, in the distant glow of the outside light, her slender and coltish reflection, topped by her luxurious long mop of auburn curls, was backlit, leaving muted light on her face. People had been telling her for years that she favored Julia Roberts, but she had yet to see the resemblance.

She turned away from the mirror. Gordon always said, smirking, that she could not pass a mirror without looking, not even in the dark. *Gordon*, she thought, *could not pass a woman without staring—and soon he was going to pay for it.*

Opening the attic stairwell door, she switched on the light, knowing it could not be seen from outside the house. She began climbing the tall, steep, unpainted cypress steps, every one of which was worn in the center from centuries of feet climbing up and down.

The sound of rain pounding on the slate roof above her head echoed through the cypress-framed attic as she stepped onto the highest floor in the house.

Looking around her at the contents of the attic-wide gun room, she squared her shoulders.

What an arsenal! Gordon had gun cabinet after gun cabinet of period long guns, from early matchlocks and wheel locks, to flintlocks and percussion cap models, to modern shotguns and assault rifles. His collection of World War Two Mausers alone took up three cabinets. His vast array of period and modern pistols was up here, too. She had a great deal of photographing to do in order to document her soon-to-be-ex-husband's entire collection of firearms.

She opened the first gun cabinet's glass door, to avoid a flash bounce-back from the camera's strobe, and took a photograph of the very full interior. *Fully loaded*, she thought with a half-smile, no pun intended. Now came individual photographs of each of the dozen rifles in the cabinet. She reached inside for the first long gun.

The sound of a car engine stopped her abruptly. *Oh no*—she had barely begun.

She tiptoed down the steep attic steps to the second floor landing, then held her breath and tiptoed down three more steps. Leaning down, she peered out of the upper edge of the oval, beveled window overlooking the drive just in time to a see a crooked rear windshield brake light go off. Then the car, which had apparently already backed up and turned around, went careening down the lane.

Virginia strained to see more through the driving rain and tossing live oak branches, but all she could make out was the faint glow of red tail lights disappearing into the darkness.

Whoever that was, at least it was not Gordon. More than likely it was some woman checking to see if he was here—and who might be with him. She headed back up to the attic gun room to finish her work.

One by one, she photographed each cabinet, then laid each long gun, then each hand gun, on the floor and took a picture. Gordon had collected more antique firearms than she had ever known.

Standing before the last gun cabinet, she hesitated, resisting the pull of memory. Behind this glass door were replicas of Civil War firearms, the fully-fireable guns Gordon collected during their years of reenacting Confederate and Federal cavalry. She smiled, remembering how Gordon always called it 'calvary.' But he had tired of reenacting and horses, just as he seemed to tire of everything he loved. Selling the horses, the horse trailer, the period wall tent, the folding wooden campaign furniture, and his uniforms, he shut the once-beloved guns up here in this dust-free cabinet. Thank goodness he had not sold *her* reenactment clothes.

Taking a breath, she opened the cabinet door. If these replicas had been original pieces, as the rest of Gordon's collection was, they would be worth a small fortune. She glanced at the luminous dial on her watch. She had been in the house for twenty-seven minutes, and needed only a few moments more. One group photograph of all of the replicas, then individual ones of the replica Remington cattleman carbine and the much larger Colt revolving rifle, the Springfield musket, the musketoon, the Henrys rifle, the Enfield, the Spencer, the Sharps, and several other replicas she did not recognize.

Opening the drawer beneath the glass door, she drew a rapid breath. There lay her beloved forty-caliber derringer, in the little holster custom-made to wear with her Civil War dresses. Gordon had been keeping her derringer in this drawer with the black powder. She frowned. *Where is the rest of the black powder?* Only one lone, nearly-empty canister of Pyrodex remained, with empty spaces where half a dozen more canisters had been after the last time she and Gordon fired weapons at a reenactment. When had Gordon been shooting black powder since then? Tucking the derringer into her belt, she closed the drawer.

Finally finished, she closed the last gun cabinet. She headed downstairs, barely glancing at the eighteenth-and-nineteenth-century sterling that had been in his family for generations. By law, those items might be considered marital property, but for her they were not. She only wanted to document what Gordon had acquired during their marriage—not his ancestral heirlooms.

She wanted to take one other item away from here tonight. She had already taken almost everything dear to her when she and Gabrielle moved to the boat. The only other thing she wanted to get tonight was her dad's old Rolex trench watch—the one he bought in a Belfast pawn shop while in the RAF during World War Two as a present for *his* dad, then got back twenty-three years later when his dad died. When Virginia married Gordon, Scotty gave it to him.

Now that she was divorcing Gordon, she wanted her dad's watch back.

Heirlooms were supposed to stay in the family. As for this house with all its memories—as soon as the divorce was final and the house was in her name, she would not be able to get a real estate agent fast enough.

In Gordon's first floor game room, amongst the liquor bottles, backgammon boards, pool cues, and sets of darts, she searched for the watch. She even went back upstairs and grimly hunted through Gordon's—formerly hers and Gordon's—bedroom, but the watch was nowhere to be found. Gordon must be wearing it.

*****

Gordon paced impatiently on the wide, uneven planks of the old wooden floor as another crack of thunder split the loud, staccato beating of rain on the tin roof. Seconds later, when lightning flashed through the cobweb-lined windowpanes, he caught a glimpse of ancient marine engine heads, rusted shafts of various lengths, and piles of eroded propellers.

Plunged into near-darkness once more, Gordon thought he heard the door creak. He whirled around, then yelped in pain when his ankle banged against something hard and sharp. Backing up, he knocked over a stack of rusted cans.

Gordon was becoming more irritated by the second. He looked at the luminous dial on his new watch, which he would not have had to buy had he not foolishly taken off his beloved antique watch that night in her apartment.

She should have been here fifteen minutes ago. And why did she insist on returning his watch here this evening, in the marina's old abandoned engine repair shop? Why not at her apartment or my house?

The sharp smell of old gasoline assaulted his nostrils. It must have spilled out of one of those cans he knocked over. He would probably step in it, if he had not already.

The smell of old gasoline was growing stronger. *Damned old yachts and their damned old gasoline engines—all that venting just to start them up.*

Gordon shook his head. Virginia had wanted to keep the two modern diesels in their old Chris-Craft, but he insisted on replacing that dependable pair with a couple of vintage gasoline engines. He should have listened to her. He wished he was on the boat with Virginia now instead of waiting here for the wretched heifer who finally caused Virginia to leave him.

He looked at his watch again. *Where is she?*

Limping through the darkening gloom, he crossed the warped and creaking floor toward the door. He stopped and sniffed. *I must have knocked over an awful lot of that gasoline.* He sniffed again—there was something else in the musty, humid air—something familiar and overly sweet.

She was already here—he would recognize that cloying gardenia scent anywhere. She must have slipped in while he stumbled around in the near darkness.

That's it, thought Gordon. *I'll tell the police she has my watch and how much it is worth. I'll let them deal with her.*

Reaching the door, he found the knob and turned it. Nothing happened.

He gave the door a push. It did not budge. Pushing harder, he lost traction and nearly fell.

What is that on the floor, sand? It wasn't there when I came in. It almost smells like...like black powder, but that isn't possible.

Bracing one hand against the door, he grabbed the rusted doorknob and twisted it violently back and forth until it turned uselessly in his hand.

Feeling knots of panic clench in his stomach, he backed up a step and rammed his shoulder hard against the door. It didn't budge.

Gordon's last thought before the air around him exploded in a blast of heat and light was that he wished he had never fooled around with her.

*****

With a feeling of dread, Virginia put her harmonica away. Shifting down to third, she approached Waccamaw Marina. After escaping the house and grounds undetected, she played a few bars on her harmonica to calm herself down on the short drive back. Now all hell was breaking loose here at *home.* The almost-cool, post-thunderstorm air was smoky and acrid. Through the smoke she could see the flashing lights of two fire trucks, an ambulance, and how many sheriff's department cars? Three? Four? *What is going on?*

Leaning forward, she strained futilely to see the dock where she kept *Chaucer* berthed.

Maybe I can drive around the—Virginia gasped. *Oh, no.* Parked by the tree line was Gordon's Volvo. He must have left his car back here and walked to the dock, so she would not see him. *Did he find out I was in the house taking pictures?*

Please not the boat, Virginia breathed, *please not* Chaucer. And Gabrielle! Did Gordon hate her so much that he set fire to the boat, knowing Gabrielle was aboard, locked inside?

A tall deputy was emerging from the smoke, walking toward Virginia's car. He shook his head adamantly at her and motioned for her to stop.

Rolling down her window, Virginia slowed and stuck her head out.

"I live here, and I need to get my cat off my boat!" She drew her head back in when the tall deputy reached her car and leaned down to the window. "My cat is aboard, and I'm afraid my estranged husband—" hesitating, she took a breath, nodding toward Gordon's car. "I'm afraid he might have might have done something to the b—"

"*That*'s your estranged husband's car?" The tall deputy interrupted, his eyes widening, then narrowing.

"Yes," Virginia wriggled in her seat. She was not getting anywhere with this deputy.

"Please, I need to see if my boat and my cat—"

"Ma'am," the tall deputy interrupted again, "all the boats are fine. The fire was in an old shed next the marine railway." He hesitated, glancing in the direction of the shed. "Is your husband Gordon Seabrook?"

"Yes," Virginia answered. How did they know Gordon's name? "Have you arrested him for something?"

"No." The tall deputy looked grim. "Can you step out of your car, please?"

"Yes. I'll park where I won't be blocking—"

"Leave your car there, ma'am."

Virginia switched off the Porsche's engine, set the hand brake, and got out.

"Step over here, please." The tall deputy walked with her to a patrol car. Opening the back door, he looked down at her. "Please get in."

Virginia stared at him in disbelief.

"Now." His voice was commanding. Gesturing to the car's interior with his hand, he nodded toward the back seat.

Virginia sat down sideways on the edge of the seat, with her feet on the ground.

"Wait here." Never taking his eyes off Virginia, the tall deputy walked over to a shorter deputy.

Virginia strained, to no avail, to hear what they were saying over the noise of the fire truck's idling engine and the radios of the rescue and sheriff's department vehicles.

The two deputies walked back to her. "Ma'am," the shorter one said, touching his fingertips to the front of his hat.

"Sir." Virginia swallowed uncomfortably. Gordon must have reported that she was in his house. She knew he would be furious if he found out she was taking photographs for the divorce, photos of items he did not want listed as marital property, but she had not been breaking the law, had she? It was her house too.

The deputies made brief eye contact with one another. The taller one, scowling slightly, folded his arms, and the shorter one crouched down on one knee on front of Virginia.

She fought hard not to let escape a hysterical giggle—the shorter deputy looked as though he was about to propose. Realizing she was trembling, she clutched her hands together in her lap and cleared her throat.

"Ma'am, where were you right before you drove down here to the marina?" the shorter deputy asked. His pointed gaze was both serious and friendly.

Where should I begin? Unsure where to look, Virginia stared unblinkingly at him. She swallowed. Was her direct gaze showing him she was telling the truth or making him believe she was lying?

"I was at my house, the house I shared with Gordon. But I don't live there anymore, and I was taking pictures."

"What's that address, ma'am?" The shorter deputy asked. "Here in Murrells Inlet?"

Virginia nodded. "It's One Seabrook Drive. It's at the end of the road, the only house."

The taller deputy looked down at her. "You don't live there anymore? Who lives there now?"

"Gordon Seabrook...he's technically still my husband, but we're separated...in the process of our divorce."

The deputies exchanged brief looks.

The shorter deputy stood and nodded toward Gordon's Volvo. "Car's registered to a Gordon Seabrook, One Seabrook Drive." He looked down at Virginia. "That the house address?"

Virginia nodded.

The taller deputy eyed her dubiously. "Anybody see you there?"

"No." Virginia bit her lip. "But I have pictures on my digital camera, with the time and date." Reaching into her windbreaker pocket, she removed her camera.

The shorter deputy took the yellow camera from her. He and the taller deputy began pressing buttons. They pored over the photographs, murmuring and nodding.

Finally the shorter deputy crouched down, eye level with Virginia again, and handed the camera back to her. "Thank you, ma'am."

Virginia swallowed. "Can you tell me what happened here?"

"As best we can tell," the shorter deputy began, "an unused shed by the old marine railway caught on fire or explo—"

Virginia gave a cry and raised her hand to her mouth.

Turning, the shorter deputy rose.

Emerging from the dissipating smoke were two emergency medical technicians laboriously pushing a sheet-draped gurney up the grassy embankment that sloped down to the river.

Leaping up, Virginia ran between the startled deputies. She sprinted across the gravel parking lot, only to slip on the wet grass when she reached the embankment. Nearly falling, she tried to regain her balance but skidded down the slope and fell hard against the gurney, turning it and its burden over onto the grass before the surprised EMTs could react.

The body that lay on the grass beside the overturned gurney was barely recognizable, but Virginia knew without a doubt who it was—Gordon.

*****

February 28

Shivering slightly in the weak winter sunlight, hands clasped behind her back, Virginia kept her head bowed, peering across the river toward the bay through her nearly sheer black veil. Fastened firmly to her black bonnet with a nine-inch-long black hatpin, the long veil fluttered below her black-gloved fingertips in the stiff, chill breeze. She was thankful for her silk long johns and flannel petticoat keeping her toasty and warm under her six-bone hoop. Her meticulously pin-tucked, black cotton-sateen mourning dress— bought in Gettysburg with Gordon—would never have been enough to keep out the damp, salty chill blowing across the bay from the Atlantic this morning.

Her slight shiver, however, was not from the cold breeze, but from something else.

Here she was, swathed from head to toe in black, portraying a Civil War widow in full Victorian mourning, and she had not even gone to Gordon's funeral nearly six months ago. After the questioning from the deputies and Sheriff Bone about her activities on the evening of Gordon's death, after her repeated answering of their identical queries about the missing black powder, the impending divorce and her separation from Gordon, she had decided not to stand beside his grave under the steely-eyed, accusing stare of his older sister.

Virginia looked down at the magnolia-leaf wreath she held, then down to the grey planks of the Harbor Promenade, at least twelve square feet of which were covered by her hoop.

She had not attended Gordon's visitation, either—the "*sitting up,*" Miss Eugenia called it—despite planning it *and* paying for it.

It was nearly time for her to cast the wreath upon the waters. Virginia turned her full attention back to the Commander of the Georgetown Sons of the War Between the States.

"—and thanking you for the safe rescue of nearly all on board, we ask that you bless the soul of the seaman who was the lone, long-ago casualty in the sinking of the paddle-wheel steamer *Harvest Moon.* In Thy name we ask, Amen."

"Amen." Raising her head amidst the chorus of amens from the spectators and Sons and Daughters of the War Between the States gathered on the Harbor Promenade, Virginia glanced at Miss Eugenia Allston, warmly dressed against the chill in a robust purple-and-lavender wool paisley suit, and caught her barely perceptible wink. Despite her mixed feelings over portraying the mourning widow of a nearly century-and-half-old death after declining to mourn her own estranged husband last September, she was grateful to Miss Eugenia, at whose behest she was here, for cajoling her into dressing out for this event.

Miss Eugenia, after well over a half a century of helping plan memorial services with the Georgetown Daughters of the War Between the States, maintained that this, the annual commemoration of February 28, 1865's hastily reconnoitered and highly successful explosion and sinking of the only Federal flagship sunk during the Civil War, was her favorite.

At Miss Eugenia's nod, Virginia carefully tossed the wreath across the boardwalk railing.

Pleased with the grace of her delivery, Virginia watched the wreath arc briefly across the grey February sky and land in the river with barely a splash.

Drawn by the swift outgoing tide, the wreath floated swiftly down the river toward the bay and the ocean, past anchored-out vessels straining at their moorings, before sinking into the briskly white-capping river, just as the commander was introducing the guest speaker.

Just short of the wreath's sinking spot, a sport fisher, flying a red flag with a diagonal white stripe, eased into the visitor's boat slip in front of Buzzard's Roost Pub & Restaurant.

They forgot to lower their dive flag, Virginia thought, watching a woman clad in a full wetsuit hop from the sport fisher's starboard gunwale to the floating dock and tie the line she was holding to the nearest cleat. *Brrrrr,* Virginia thought, noting the woman's dark, damp hair.

The wetsuit-clad pilot, shaking out his damp shoulder-length blond mane, looked toward the ceremony on the Harbor Promenade. Pulling a shiny brass telescope from below the steering console, he trained it on the spectators, then on the Sons and Daughters, focusing on Virginia.

He's looking through that telescope at me, thought Virginia, *or is it my imagination?* She shifted her feet self-consciously, the leather soles of her black lace-up ankle boots tapping the wood beneath them. *Am I just being paranoid,* she wondered, *or is that man in the wetsuit truly staring at me through that telescope?*

There was one way to find out. Glancing around to be sure the speaker had the undivided attention of everyone nearby, she raised one gloved hand a few inches, wiggling her fingers at the telescope-wielding wetsuit-clad pilot.

Not taking the telescope from his eye, he immediately removed one hand from the cylinder and wiggled his fingers in reply.

Stifling a giggle, Virginia turned her attention back to the speaker, willing herself not to look away again. *Thank you, Lord,* she breathed silently. *That was the first time I've almost laughed since last summer.*

Minutes later, when she looked back, the sport fisher was straining against her lines, her deck and topsides devoid of anyone.

Chapter Two

Labor Day weekend

Virginia pulled firmly on the starboard stern line until Chaucer came to, then climbed from the aft deck up onto the catwalk that ran alongside her boat slip. Stepping onto the dock, she brushed a long curl of auburn-gold hair away from her face while scrutinizing the mirror-smooth finish of her old Chris-Craft's wide, curved, mahogany transom glistening in the early morning sun.

When Virginia first saw *Chaucer* two years ago, the transom was dull brown from years of built-up varnish. Now, so glossy with coats of new varnish that it reflected the river, the transom still remained void of a name.

Not for long, though. This afternoon, the commercial artist whose boat-lettering Virginia saw a year ago was coming here to the marina to give her an estimate on gold-leafing the boat's name onto the transom.

She had seen his work twenty-five miles downriver at Georgetown's annual Wooden Boat Festival. That was last October, just over a month after Gordon's death, and her octogenarian friend and customer, Miss Eugenia, insisting Virginia needed to get out more, had driven up from Georgetown, collected Virginia, and taken her to the festival. The outing had worked wonders on Virginia's wounded psyche.

Pleased with the artistry in the names and hail port titles of vessels one artist lettered, she picked up one of his business cards. His back to the admiring throngs, he was busy painting, seemingly oblivious to the crowds and to the swaying of the dinghy in which he sat, hand-lettering the transom of a glistening old Matthews cruiser. *Remy Ravenel Signs*, his card read.

Virginia had felt as if the ground tilted for just a second. *Remy Ravenel*. He was the handsome art major she had begun dating near the end of her senior year at Coastal Carolina University.

Unconsciously she had put her fingertip to her lips, remembering his kisses, his Nordic good looks, his ice-blue eyes, his devil-may-care grin, the way his already blonde sun-bleached hair looked silkier than a girl's hanging down his back in its loose ponytail, the Saturdays they spent windsurfing, their all-night study sessions during exam week, their plans for taking scuba lessons that summer—and then she met Gordon. She had not seen Remy since graduation. Until now. The ponytail was gone, she realized, smiling at the memory of it, and at the memory of the happy-go-lucky girl she once was.

Watching Remy painting a name on the gleaming old wood was an epiphany. The boat she lived aboard and cherished for so long was now hers alone, and she could have its name—the name that she had picked and Gordon had scoffed at—emblazoned in classic gold leaf letters across the gentle curve of the transom. Her home port of Murrells Inlet would be hand-painted below.

Despite the initial mild shock at the estimated cost he gave her when she called him last fall, inquiries amongst other boat owners and her friends at the marina led Virginia to one conclusion—despite the expense, Remy Ravenel was the only person to letter her boat. The name, the *coupe de grace* of her painstaking restoration of this vintage vessel, should be traditionally gold-leafed and hand-shaded on the transom by a professional painter, and Remy Ravenel was considered the best. She hoped it would not be difficult to work with him, considering his now-illustrious reputation and her abrupt dismissal of him years ago.

She was cautioned that since his work was in constant demand, and since most of it stemmed from Georgetown, perhaps she would do better to wait until she took her vessel down to Georgetown for bottom painting and repairs. The quaint, bustling seaport had several marine railways for hauling boats out of the water, and Virginia had an appointment at the oldest of these on Saturday.

Virginia shivered, her thoughts turning to the long-unused boat railway abandoned on the weed-choked canal behind the marina here—and the adjacent ruins of the old engine repair shop where Gordon burned to death a year ago. She was sure neither the fiery explosion nor Gordon's death was accidental—and Sheriff Bone, for a while at least, seemed sure she was the culprit.

Despite the time and date on the photographs she had taken two-and-a-half miles away during the time of Gordon's death, and the two deputies' corroboration that she had driven up right before Gordon's body was brought out of the ruined shed, she was referred to—though not by name—in both the Myrtle Beach and the Georgetown newspapers as 'a person of interest.'

While Sheriff Bone only called her in for questioning twice, he never closed the investigation, either. She was the closest thing he had to a person of interest, what with the missing black powder, the gun room pictures on her camera, and the little derringer on her person that night. Until whoever was responsible for Gordon's death was found, she knew she was still considered the wife who got away with murder.

She forced her thoughts back to the present and away from Gordon's death.

Now, with *Chaucer*'s Georgetown hauling-out just days away, she had an appointment with Remy Ravenel. His estimate was within her grasp, and her Chris-Craft's stern would at last bear a name. *All old boats, if they could talk, have stories to tell,* reasoned Virginia, *so what better name for my old yacht than that of Geoffrey Chaucer, one of the greatest storytellers of all time?*

Her *Chaucer*, however, had yet to reveal any stories. Through the hull number, Virginia traced the vessel from construction in 1948 at the Chris-Craft factory in Algonac, Michigan to the 1949 Chicago Boat Show, where the original owner made purchase. The first owner's name, as well as the boat's whereabouts from then until just a few years ago, when the previous owner purchased her in Maryland, were a mystery.

Virginia's only clue to the boat's early owners and previous moniker was the barely recognizable outline of *"Ch"* she recently uncovered on the transom under dozens of weathered layers of decades-old varnish. Faint and shadowy, the large letters were undoubtedly the beginning of a name. *Could the original owner have named her Chaucer? Or Charmer, or Cherish?* The seven letters fit perfectly, according to the size of the *Ch* Virginia found.

Virginia and Gordon were never able to agree on a name for the boat. They had not agreed on much at all during that last year, mainly due to Gordon's lies and her discovery of his rampant unfaithfulness. Now, with Gordon gone over a year, she was finally able—sometimes—to remember him without focusing on their painful breakup and his death in the fire.

Maybe now, with a proper name gracing her boat's transom, people would stop referring to her home as 'Gordon's boat.'

Virginia looked up when she heard the gate at the foot of the old dock creak open.

Despite its loud, wrenching shriek, neither she nor any of her dock neighbors wanted to oil the creaky sound away. Too tall to step over and too rickety to climb, the gate's creak always alerted them, even from inside a boat, if someone came onto the dock.

Right now it was not Remy Ravenel coming through the gate— someone was leaving.

Virginia saw only the back of a gray-haired man wearing a light brown, tailored linen sport coat and carrying a brown fedora hat. She watched as he left the gate and headed off the dock, putting the hat on his head and positioning it as he walked. He had a slight limp and favored his right leg. *Where did he come from?* The man did not look at all familiar—certainly not tall, blonde Remy Ravenel.

She had only seen Remy once in recent years—last fall at the Wooden Boat Festival—but this definitely was not him. No, this man was someone else, and he had to have been on this dock for at least thirty minutes, as the gate had not creaked in the last half hour or so.

She looked at his retreating back and the parking lot beyond. None of her boat neighbors' cars or trucks were there—the marina was normally very quiet this early in the morning, even in the summer. She looked down the other end of the dock to see if an outboard was tied up, but none was visible. What business had this man on this dock?

This is a private dock. Is he working, or spending time on someone's boat in their absence? Or snooping?

Sighing, she pulled the boat toward the dock once more and stepped across the transom and down onto the aft deck. She had been far too jumpy since Gordon's death—the man was most likely just a sightseer who liked boats. Would she ever cease to feel uncomfortable when strangers came onto the dock?

The gate creaked again, and she turned to see if it was the same man. It was not.

Walking down the dock now was a tall, strikingly handsome man with shiny, gilt hair.

Despite the heat he was wearing a long-sleeved shirt. *Raw silk, or maybe linen,* Virginia thought.

And—he was carrying a sketch pad.

That is Remy, she thought. It had been nearly a year since she had seen him from afar, but this lean-muscled, Nordic-looking blonde was definitely him.

At Virginia's boat slip, he stopped, reached down, and held out his hand to her.

At close range, Virginia saw that his shirt was made of thin, lightweight, oatmeal-colored linen. There was a cigarette pack in the breast pocket.

"Virginia Ross," he said, his eyes twinkling. "Remy Ravenel."

"Yes." As if she could have ever forgotten. Reaching up across the water to meet his proffered hand, Virginia felt warmth rising to her face. She could barely look at Remy, much less meet his eyes. Up close, Remy Ravenel seemed even more handsome, with hints of silver shimmering in his blonde mustache and hair.

Now, he looks like Rutger Hauer in Lady Hawk, she thought.

Remy looked out over *Chaucer*'s starboard side. "She has such character—all this gorgeous wood! No wonder you want her name in gold leaf."

Virginia peered sidelong at Remy while he was busy eyeing *Chaucer.* His hair had grown considerably since last fall, and was caught back in a long, smooth, silky ponytail ending just below his shoulder blades.

"I nearly didn't recognize you," she said. "At the Wooden Boat Festival last year, your hair was shorter."

"I cut it years ago, he said, "and wore it short forever. But this year, I grew it out for pirate reenacting."

"Pirate reenacting!" Virginia grinned. The years melted away. Remy had definitely not lost his adventurous spirit. "You look like a pirate."

"I lettered the name on the pirate tour boat in Georgetown, you know, that two-masted schooner, the *Merry Mistral*, and they shanghaied me, so to speak. It's a great part-time job. You know how I love boats and being on the water."

Virginia nodded. "I know." Of course she knew. How could she have been nervous about seeing him again? "What do you do in your reenacting?"

"I narrate the history of Georgetown, embellishing the pirate parts. And," he grinned, "I swashbuckle a lot."

Virginia grinned, too. He would be good at that. "I'm a reenac-tor, myself," she said. "Civil War."

"Really? That's next on my list. The season's mostly over now, 'til next spring, and most pirate reenactors are crossovers—pirate and Rev War, or pirate and Civil War. What do you do? Soldier or civilian?"

"Both. I started off as cavalry, but the last thing I did was mourning, full mourning, at the *Harvest Moon* memorial service this past February."

"I saw that!" Remy exclaimed. He tilted his head. "You were the one who threw the wreath, the lady with the little forty-caliber derringer on your belt."

"You must have awfully good eyesight to have recognized that as a forty derringer," she said. Could Remy have been the fellow in the wetsuit with the brass telescope?

"I was using my new pirate spyglass," he said, his face coloring slightly.

Virginia looked down at her Sperrys, trying not to smile. So that *was* him, and he recognized her, even with bonnet, veil, and hair braided and bunned beneath.

He walked a few feet down the dock, scrutinizing the fine curved line of the port side and bow.

"Hardly an angle on her," he observed, "she's so streamlined. You said on the phone she was built in the forties?"

"1948." Virginia was pleased he referred to *Chaucer* as "she" so comfortably. She always enjoyed hearing people use the feminine pronoun when speaking of a boat.

"What is she like inside?" Raising one eyebrow, Remy turned to Virginia.

She looked full into his gaze and caught her breath. His eyes were not ice blue, they were *green,* ice-green, the palest, most luminous shade of green eyes she had ever seen. How could she have forgotten?

"I bet there's lots of gorgeous old wood in there," Remy smiled.

"There is," Virginia replied, "and it's all mahogany and oak, all forty feet of her."

"I don't come into this marina much, but I know I've seen this boat. She has more character and more age on her than any craft here, and I've always wondered what she looks like inside."

"Well of course," Virginia said, "come aboard." Normally she was extremely wary of anyone she did not know well boarding her boat, but she was glad Remy wanted to see her home.

As he pulled the stern line to step aboard, she saw the edge of his right sleeve rise to reveal a brown leather watchband.

"I remember you are left-handed," she said, "and wear your watch on your right hand."

"Yes," he said, letting go of the line as he stepped down onto the aft deck. Pushing the edge of his sleeve up, he looked at the face of his watch. "I hope I wasn't late getting here. This is a fine old watch, but sometimes I don't wind it often enough."

"I love old watches," Virginia smiled. "I manage an antiques shop."

"Oh, really? Which one?"

"Fox's Lair Antiques. It is just up the road." She nodded her head east in the direction of the shop. "Now for a tour of my humble abode."

"After you." Remy gestured her forward.

Humble is right, thought Virginia. She knew that people occasionally felt sorry for her because she lived aboard an old boat that she worked on constantly. They didn't realize she loved living aboard and restoring her vintage yacht, and cherished every beautiful plank.

She felt a pang of discomfort with Remy following her down the two steps leading from the aft deck into the master cabin, her bedroom. The placement of the master cabin was the only part of the boat that really bothered her. When entering *Chaucer* from the aft deck, which was the only way to enter without considerable bending, she had to step directly down into the master cabin. Only after walking through her bedroom, and ascending two steps, would she enter the saloon. This was a fine setup for everyday living, but it made her uncomfortable to lead a male guest through her cozy bedroom, which was dominated by a spacious and comfortable-looking built-in double berth, in order to reach the rest of the boat. In most craft of *Chaucer*'s size, the master stateroom was still aft but below a bridge entry above, so guests would never need to walk through sleeping quarters to reach other parts of the boat.

She led Remy quickly through her bedroom, pausing only to say, "This is my cabin," point to a brass-handled door angled in the rear corner, and add, "and in there is the aft head." Smiling, she fought back a mental picture of Remy fast asleep in her bed.

Stepping up into the saloon, she turned to watch Remy's reaction as he ascended from the coziness of her cabin into the opulence of the saloon. Rays of morning sunlight shone through thirteen beveled windows, illuminating the saloon's deep red mahogany and rich golden oak interior. She was not disappointed in Remy's response.

"This is the perfect setting for you," he smiled, gazing around, touching the sepia-hued antique cotton lace tablecloth on the saloon's large mahogany map table. Gesturing down toward the polished floor made of alternating light oak and dark mahogany planks, he added, with an admiring laugh, "It matches your hair."

"Down here's the galley," Virginia said, her face growing warm with Remy's words as she headed down the steps.

Remy followed her, ducking slightly so as not to hit his head on the wide lip of molding edging the ceiling of the galley.

"Ah—something's got me—" he began, quickly slipping off the coated rubber band that held his ponytail, unaware that the sunlit, gilt hair on his descending head piqued the attention of Gabrielle, Virginia's Siamese cat.

Gabrielle had been crouching under the slope of the saloon's forward windows, motionless but for the twitch of her tail, waiting for the visitor's descent into the galley.

Virginia suppressed a laugh and tried to explain, "Gabrielle's got you," while the big playful Siamese continued to bat at the crown of Remy's head, frustrated as pawfuls of his just- released shiny flaxen locks slid between her paws.

"I thought my hair was snagged on a nail or something," Remy said, raising his hand over the ledge to offer it to the Siamese. "What a beautiful cat."

"I think so," Virginia grinned, watching her pet grab Remy's hand with both paws and begin chewing with careless abandon on the skin between his thumb and forefinger. "I forgot to warn you. Stop that, Gabrielle."

"It's okay," Remy laughed, not moving his hand. "I love cats. And I know to keep my hand *really* still when they start switching their tails like that, or lacerations are sure to follow."

Still wisely not moving from Gabrielle's grasp, he stood on the steps, looking down into the galley. "Have you had breakfast yet?"

Virginia shook her head. He loved cats! "Not yet. Have you?"

Remy shook his head. "Why don't we go out for breakfast, and I'll do a sketch of your boat name. We can plan your lettering over some eggs."

"Sounds good—but how about breakfast here in my galley?"

"Dandy." Remy looked at the Siamese, still grasping his hand, and pantomimed a grimace. "I'll start working on your sketch, soon as I get loose from Gabrielle."

"Good luck!" Laughing, Virginia reached into her galley's mini-refrigerator and brought out a box of brown eggs, a red bell pepper, Vermont cheddar cheese, and Portobello mushrooms.

Crouching down, she opened a cabinet for her frying pan.

"Hey. Someone's watching your boat." Remy, his hand disengaged from Gabrielle's grasp, was leaning over the galley sink, peering out of the oval starboard porthole.

Virginia stood up and looked over Remy's shoulder. She loved the galley portholes. Their slanted position in the forward portion of the upper hull's curve allowed her to see out, though no one could see in. She was particularly fond of the one through which Remy was peering intently because she could see out across the water to the river bank and the marina road entrance beyond. *Remy smells wonderful,* she realized as he moved closer to get a better look. *Like new-mown hay.*

"A fellow is over on the bank looking over here at your boat," he said.

"Lots of tourists and sightseers come down and look at the boats," Virginia replied, a chill creeping over her. Could it be the same man she saw leaving the dock a little while ago? She hated for Remy to see how paranoid she was. She reached into a drawer for her spatula. "I'm used to it. It's probably just a sightseer."

"Maybe so," said Remy, straightening up and quickly re-ponytailing his hair, "but that fellow just a second ago was sightseeing through binoculars aimed at *this* boat. He put the binoculars down to write on a pad. And," Remy turned to Virginia, "I saw him limping off the dock in a big rush as I drove up. Don't you think that's a bit strange?"

Chapter Three

Virginia peered out of the porthole again.

Sure enough, there was the man she had seen leaving the dock just before Remy arrived.

He turned, put on his fedora, and limped toward the marina store and the public docks out on the river. His uneven gait did little to slow him down. A moment after he disappeared around the corner of the store, the sound of an engine roared forth, then began to fade into the distance.

"Sounds like he's headed upriver," Remy said as Virginia dialed the marina office.

"Kathy," she said, trying to keep her voice steady, "a strange man was over here on our dock earlier this morning. I then noticed him standing on the riverbank looking at my boat with binoculars and writing on a pad. He just left from the main dock in an outboard, I think, headed upriver." She hesitated. "He was favoring his right leg."

Virginia pressed the speaker button so Remy could hear, too. Breath held, she waited.

"Oh, *him*. Derek and I saw him—that was Mr. Malcolm," Kathy said. "He flies down from North Carolina every now and then to look at the boats and take pictures."

"Is Malcolm his first name or his last name?"

"I'm not sure. He's been coming off and on for years, tying his float plane to the dock. Loves those old wooden yachts. That was his plane you heard."

"I've never seen him before today."

"He hasn't been here in a long time," Kathy said. "You know we try to keep an eye out for anybody unfamiliar. Mike and Derek will ask for an ID in a heartbeat, if they're the least bit suspicious, or don't know somebody."

"Yes, I'm glad. Thanks, Kathy. Talk to you later." Virginia hung up, relieved.

"I bet you get all kinds of people with all kinds of crazy agendas coming down here to the marina," Remy said.

"We do," agreed Virginia. "For example, one Sunday afternoon about a year and a half ago, a woman I had never seen before sat on the riverbank outside my boat for an hour—with me inside working—and sketched it. She was wearing a long white dress and had a wreath of white gardenia flowers in her hair. Before she left, she came over onto the dock. She showed me the sketch—which was pretty good, though her perspective was off—and asked me lots of questions about living here aboard, and about the boat itself. I asked if she might send me a copy of the sketch and she said in a very snooty voice, 'No, I think only the owner should have that privilege.' I wish I'd asked her name. She certainly asked *me* enough questions."

"I thought that you are the owner," said Remy.

"I am now," Virginia replied. "At the time, the owner was technically Gordon, who was my husband. Obviously she knew him." Involuntarily, she shivered.

Remy folded his arms and leaned up against the galley bulkhead. "That man with the binoculars, that really shook you up, didn't it?" He tilted his head to sympathetically to one side.

"A little," she admitted. She took a deep breath. *Should I tell Remy about Gordon?* She hated for him to think she was paranoid.

Before she could decide, Remy spoke.

"I better get started on that sketch of your boat lettering," he smiled, opening his sketch pad.

"Good." Virginia breathed out, relieved. She would tell him later—maybe. "I'll start breakfast. Now where did I set that olive oil?"

Twenty minutes later she placed two cups of coffee, two small glasses of ice-cold orange juice, and two pewter plates, each bearing half of a perfect omelet, on the galley table. She reached behind the wooden dish rack for the paper napkins then, on second thought, opened drawer and brought out cloth napkins. This was, after all a business breakfast.

Remy picked up his silver fork and raised one eyebrow, grinning. "The good silver for breakfast? I must be important."

Virginia grinned back. "I manage an antique shop, remember? I love old things. When I moved here, with limited space, I gave away my modern stainless set and kept my old silver."

Remy picked up his knife. "What, no fish knives? With old silver, I was sure you'd have ornate fish knives."

"I do. We're not eating fish."

"*Touché.*" Remy grinned and took a bite. "Mmmmm—this is de*licious.* Now," he turned his sketch pad around and pushed it gently across the table, "here."

Lying between them on the red checkered cotton tablecloth was Remy's sketch pad, open to his just-completed lettering proposal for *Chaucer*'s stern.

"You didn't make any comments while I was sketching," Remy said, "although you kept peeking. Any changes?"

"It's perfect," Virginia murmured, not raising her eyes from the sketch. "It's exactly what I described in words, but my description was intangible—'antique, but not too old, and late forties but not too post-war.' You saw *Chaucer* and then knew how her name ought to look. You even matched the faded *Ch* script I found under the old varnish."

Remy smiled. "That's my job." He looked around. "Where is the salt? I mean, this omelet is perfect—I just need a little salt."

"There." Sketch pad in one hand, glass of orange juice in the other, Virginia nodded toward the shelf that ran alongside the galley table under the portside portholes.

Remy reached up for the pewter salt and pepper shakers. His sleeve slid back, once again revealing his wristwatch.

Virginia drew a sharp breath. Just a few inches from her face, Remy's old watch was a ringer for Gordon's—but Gordon's, of course, had melted when Gordon died. The sheriff's department included it when they gave her his effects. Virginia kept the lump of melted metal right here in the galley, between the pewter salt and pepper shakers, to help her face what had happened.

"What?" Remy looked at her in alarm, hand in mid-air, salt shaker still.

"Oh, it's your watch," Virginia said. "You don't see those very often. It's an early Rolex isn't it?"

"Yes," Remy answered, "from around nineteen twelve, when the wrist watch was a fairly new innovation. You're the first person to ever recognize mine, and I've had it nearly a year. Rolex wasn't yet putting their name on their watch faces then. The watchmaker I took it to—in the vain hope of getting it to keep perfect time—told me the history."

"I know. It's perfect," said Virginia, touching the watch face with a fingertip. "My dad had one similar to it, but he gave his to someone as a present." *And it melted on that someone's wrist,* she added silently.

"What's this?" Remy replaced the salt shaker and picked up the lump of melted metal. He turned it over and over before placing it back in the shelf. "Interesting."

"Ah—it's melted metal." Virginia nearly choked. *I should have gotten up and handed him the salt myself. I'm not going to be able to avoid telling him what happened if this keeps up.* She looked back at the sketch, desperate to change the subject. "This is—this is wonderful. I still can't believe how you matched the old *Ch*. It's barely noticeable. "

"It was enough to go on," Remy nodded, setting the lump of metal back in its spot. "Did you find anything else that had part of her old name?"

"No, but I'm still looking," Virginia said. "I would love to uncover more about *Chaucer*'s past. The man Gordon bought her from bought her in Maryland, from a man whose father she'd belonged to for years—decades. *He*—the father—thought maybe *his* father bought her down here, from this area."

Remy raised his eyebrows. "No paper trail?"

"No title," Virginia shook her head, "no registration, no documentation. Nothing. Through her hull number—which is engraved on a plaque near the engine, you know—I found where she was built around the end of 1948 and taken new to a Chicago boat show in 1949, then—the trail ends." Virginia shrugged. "When Gordon bought her, he had to have a new title made."

Remy put his plate in the galley sink and reached toward his shirt pocket.

"That was a wonderful omelet."

"Thank you." Virginia glanced at his shirt pocket and wondered if he would light a cigarette. *He never used to smoke,* she thought, *and I did. I wonder when he started?*

Remy sat back down and took a deep swallow of coffee. "I take it you're no longer married?"

Virginia shook her head. "No. I'm not."

"My divorce," Remy continued, looking at the light circle of skin on his left-hand ring finger, "was final just recently."

"I'm sorry," said Virginia.

"It was horrible," he shuddered. "She was unfaithful, and left me for another man."

Remy leaned back in his chair and drank more coffee while Virginia studied the sketch again, silently. "You're divorced too, then?" he prodded.

Virginia shook her head, choosing her words carefully. She dreaded bringing up any inference to Gordon's horrible death—and the resulting implications that she might have been responsible.

"I filed for divorce after I found out why Gordon liked for me to spend so much time at the marina. He had another life I didn't know anything about."

Chapter Four

R emy leaned forward, one eyebrow raised. "He did? How so?"
"Gordon lied to me for years, about lots of women," Virginia said, wondering if she should be telling Remy such personal information. He might even prefer not to hear it.

"I bet he was very sly."

Virginia nodded, relieved. Remy understood, apparently from his own experience with an unfaithful spouse. "He was a talented, creative liar. With his real estate business he could pass off any," she hesitated, "any *lady friend* as a client. If I was suspicious of a personal-sounding call, he'd tell me one of his customers needed someone to talk to."

Remy nodded. "I'm sure. Did something happen to confirm your suspicions?"

"*Yes.* One Thursday, my friend Belinda was driving down from Myrtle Beach to meet me for lunch. She woke up sick with the virus that was going around and called me at work to cancel. Not having brought lunch to the store with me, I went home at noon."

Remy nodded his head sympathetically. "I can guess what's coming. Your friend and—"

"No," she shook her head, "not Belinda." She drew a deep breath. "Gordon told me he didn't feel well, but he planned to be in Myrtle Beach working. When I saw his truck in the driveway, I figured he must have caught the virus too, and came back home. I headed upstairs to the bedroom, quietly in case he was asleep."

Remy blinked. "Gordon didn't have any virus."

"He probably did. Half the county had it." Virginia felt her nostrils involuntarily flare.

After all this time, just thinking about it made her fume. She blinked. "Gordon was lying on the bed talking on the phone. The air conditioner, the big window unit, was running in our room, so he didn't hear me come up the stairs, or know I was at the door."

Virginia looked at her hands on the table. The memory had her clenching them into tense fists. She relaxed her fingers and took a breath.

"Gordon was saying, 'Baby, I'd be there now if I wasn't so sick.' Well, when he saw me at the door he jumped, then he got hold of his composure and smiled like butter could melt in his mouth. He said into the phone, 'I'll have to call you later,' then hung up and proceeded to tell me all about his new client he'd been on the phone with."

Remy nodded. "I bet he told you she was just a friend."

"Yes, and that she was a widow and needed a lot of encouragement." Virginia took another, deeper, breath, narrowing her eyes. "I knew there had to be more to it."

"The next Friday I was leaving for an antiques-buying trip. I asked Gordon to meet me for Friday lunch, since we would be apart all weekend. When I headed back to work, the private investigator I'd hired was right behind Gordon."

"You hired a private investigator?" Remy looked alarmed.

"I surely did," Virginia nodded. "and I had lunch with Gordon so the private investigator wouldn't have to hunt him down. He tailed him for the rest of the day. That evening he videoed Gordon arriving at *our* home with that woman, driving her to hide her car up the road, bringing her back to our house, and taking her to fetch her car the next morning." She tossed her hair. "The light was on in our bedroom *all night.*"

"Whew," Remy shifted uncomfortably in his chair. "It must have been hard watching that video later." He hesitated. "And you're *sure* it wasn't your friend Belinda?"

"*Yes.* I never thought it was. But I never watched the video, either. The private investigator spoke with me on the phone half a dozen times during his stakeout, describing the situation and the woman to me. I didn't recognize her from his description; she was apparently someone I'd never met. Besides the video I couldn't bear to watch, the private investigator gave me a written transcript, which I couldn't bear to read. I moved to the boat, took the video to my attorney and began divorce proceedings. I was tired of waiting for one of Gordon's girlfriends to get sick of his lies and shoot him. But Gordon seemed scared straight, and he shed huge tears and promised he'd never see her or any other woman 'friend' again—"

"And you moved back."

"I'm afraid so."

"And he started seeing her again," Remy nodded sagely.

Yes," said Virginia, primly pursing her lips, "within a week. And my having moved back under the same roof as him made the video inadmissible as evidence of adultery."

"I bet you were fit to be tied," Remy grinned, "and he was harder than ever to catch."

"Yes. So I put a voice-activated tape recorder in his truck." She smiled. "It was activated by road noises and music, as well as voices, but I caught enough conversation to know their plans."

"Whew," Remy repeated, flushing slightly. "*You* should be a private investigator."

Virginia smiled. "Believe me, I've thought about it. Of course Gordon put the boat up for sale as soon as I moved back aboard the next day. But—a wooden boat of that size and age can be very hard to sell, much less get a decent price for, especially if she hasn't been surveyed."

"You've never had a marine survey done on her?" Remy's eyes grew large.

"Not yet." Virginia paused. "A few weeks after Gordon's death, his attorney contacted me with the news that the boat was mine."

"Gordon's *death?*" Remy looked shocked. "When you spoke of him in the past tense, well, I speak of my ex-wife that way too. How did he—" Remy hesitated. "How did he die?"

"He died—in a fire," Virginia said haltingly, "here—in the marina." She drew a deep breath. Telling the story *never* got easier. "It was just after dark, during a huge thunderstorm. For some reason he went into the old engine repair shed down beside the railway, where they used to haul out the larger boats. Apparently there was old fuel in there and it caught on fire and exploded, and Gordon wasn't able to get out."

"How did it start?" Remy's green eyes were wide. "A cigarette?" He fingered his cigarette pack.

"Gordon didn't smoke," she said. "Maybe lightning struck the shed and made a flash fire that exploded old half-empty gas cans in there. With all the heavy rain and thunder that night, no one at the marina heard anything, or even knew Gordon was there. The fire was so bad that the shed burned to the ground in spite of all the rain, so it was difficult to determine how it started."

"Poor guy." Remy shook his head. "And you—it must have awful for you."

"It was, and not just his death, or how he died either. Sheriff Bone *himself* questioned me about it, *after* the deputies did. He questioned everyone in the marina, but then he had me go down to Georgetown for more questioning."

"You were the widow, who benefited from his death. I bet that generated some pointed questions from the sheriff."

"Oh, it did. Especially after he found out about my receiving the boat. And I couldn't really blame Sheriff Bone—I lived right there in the marina on Gordon's boat and, like you said, benefited from his death. Plus, there was no reason for Gordon to be in that old shed. Hardly anyone used it, since the railway had gotten too bad to haul boats out on. In fact, Gordon and I were some of the last ones to use it. Right after he bought the boat, we hauled her out on that railway to scrape and paint the hull. The old shed looked abandoned, even then. We went inside and looked around."

"What was in there?" Remy asked.

"Rusty boat junk—and the floor was half rotted. That was part of my interrogation, asking me questions about the shed, which I hadn't been inside in nearly two years. No one ever went in it; it ought to have been condemned. Sheriff Bone asked me over and over why Gordon was in the shed that night, and why he was at the marina. I didn't know. I still don't know. The questions were phrased a different way each time."

"Did you take a lie detector test?" Remy asked.

"No," Virginia smiled, "but Sheriff Bone obviously thought I set that fire. I didn't have anyone to corroborate where I was, just the time and date on my camera to prove I was elsewhere—and even that can be faked."

"Where were you? Surely someone saw you."

Virginia shook her head. "I was alone at our house photographing marital assets for the divorce. Gordon still lived there, but I was living here aboard the boat. I made sure no one saw me go to the house. I didn't want Gordon to catch me taking pictures."

"I remember reading about the fire and Gordon's death in the paper," Remy said, "although I didn't remember Gordon's name. And the articles never mentioned anyone else in relation to the incident. At least you were spared that."

"Yes—I was spared the divorce too. I'm a *widow* instead of a divorcee, but that's just a technicality." She hesitated. Remy did not seem like the kind of man who would have an unfaithful wife, so she questioned him. "You said your wife was unfaithful, as well?"

Remy grimaced. "Yes. She's already married to him, too. "

"Oh," Virginia replied, ready to change the subject now. She was sharing far too much of her recent personal saga with a man who was practically a stranger now, after all these years.

Stop being so hard on yourself, she thought. It had been so long since she talked about this with anyone. Was it any wonder she would open up to the handsome and personable Remy Ravenel, whose work on her boat she had been anticipating for months, whose dreams she used to know?

Feeling her cheeks grow warm—and thankful in the knowledge that she never turned red when embarrassed—she looked out the starboard porthole at the river, then back at Remy. "I'm excited about taking *Chaucer* to Georgetown. She hasn't been out of Waccamaw Marina since Gordon bought her, so this will be her first trip in years."

"You've never taken her out of the marina? Not even down the river a little way or over to Sandy Island?" Remy raised his left eyebrow. "Gordon never wanted to take her out?"

"Gordon was more interested in the boat's identity as a marine antique and an office to impress his clients. He searched out a pair of Hercules engines identical to the ones in her 1948 factory specifications and had them installed because they were authentic. He didn't care that they wouldn't even turn over."

"And now they run well enough to take you twenty-five miles downriver and through the edge of the bay into Georgetown?"

Virginia smiled. "Yes, I believe they do." She frowned. "These old engines are newly rebuilt, though, and I dread getting them in the salt water."

"Georgetown is a seaport, but it's not exactly salt water, you know." Remy tapped his lighter on the table but did not pick up his cigarette pack. "The town, the port of Georgetown, is on the peninsula where the Sampit River, the Black River, and the Intracoastal Waterway/ Waccamaw River, that you live on here, meet Winyah Bay and become brackish—not completely salty. Winyah Bay meets the ocean a few miles later, after you pass between North and South Islands. It's a river-and-bay-to-ocean peninsula seaport city, just like Charleston, and just as old too, only smaller."

"Staying aboard up on the railway in Georgetown for a week is going to be a big change from here," Virginia laughed. "I love going to Georgetown, but I've never been there via water, or stayed overnight."

"You're staying aboard? Up on the railway? Only diehard boat people do that."

"Scotty—my dad—is staying with me. It'll be an adventure."

Remy smiled. "You'll love it there. And it *will* be an adventure, believe me. It's only twenty-five miles downriver, but sometimes I could *swear* Georgetown is another land."

Chapter Five

"How do you mean, you could swear Georgetown is another land?" Putting her elbows on the table, Virginia folded her arms, leaning forward.

Remy narrowed his eyes. "You know how it's like a curtain is dropping when you leave the modern, glittery, resort-ness of Myrtle Beach and cross the county line into the—" he paused, searching for the right word, "—the *ancient*ness of Murrells Inlet, of Georgetown County, and old places on the waterfront like, say, Oliver's Lodge?"

Virginia nodded. "It *is* like a curtain drops, or like Alice falling down the rabbit hole, and all you hear is halyards clinking against sailboat masts and palmetto fronds rustling."

"Exactly," Remy leaned back, folding his arms. "Then, when you come further south and cross the river bridges into the port of Georgetown, that curtain drops *all* the way—the mist is rising from the river and the bay and the old rice fields, the damp, salty wind is blowing the moss hanging from the huge, gnarled live-oak trees, and you *are* in another world, so to speak."

He leaned forward once more. "How about dinner tonight at Oliver's Lodge?"

*****

At eight twenty-five, Virginia reluctantly put her harmonica away, geared down, and turned off Business Highway 17 onto the bumpy, unpaved road leading to Oliver's Lodge. Of all the restaurants on the inlet, this was the oldest—and the only one she had never been to with Gordon.

Remy wanted to pick her up at the marina, but she politely demurred, agreeing to meet him here instead. This way, she reasoned with herself, it was not a date. She was still reeling over the way she had bared her soul—well, maybe not her soul, but a great big chunk of her personal life—to him this morning.

The road is only an eighth of a mile long, but if it was any longer, she thought, *potential diners who have never been here might be reluctant to venture in, so overgrown are the gardenia bushes and scrub palmettos crowding the edges of the road.*

At the end of the road, surrounded by ancient, moss-draped live oaks, stood the tall, three-story Oliver's Lodge, resplendent with long-unpainted, silver-weathered wooden facades.

Pure Southern Gothic revival splendor, and heavy on the Gothic, thought Virginia.

The wind-ruffled waters of the inlet winked with points of light reflected from the moonless, starry sky and from the hundreds of tiny lights strung twinkling in the lodge's oaks.

Virginia parked easily. The early dinner crowd was gone, but where was Remy?

Climbing deftly from the low roadster, she spied him standing beside a blue Range Rover, smoking a cigarette and gazing out over the inlet. She walked over to him.

"Hey, stranger," he grinned, and leaned over to put out his cigarette on the hard, sandy ground.

"Evening." *Oh,* thought Virginia, *I hope he doesn't leave that there.*

Remy stood back up, deftly field-stripping the butt of his cigarette. He dropped the leftover shreds of paper on the ground and put the filter in his shirt pocket.

Nice, thought Virginia, nodding approvingly, putting on her lightweight sweater.

Remy raised one eyebrow. "I guess you quit?"

Virginia laughed, nodding. "About a year after we graduated. Now I pick up so many filters every spring during Beach and River Sweep that I don't dare add to it."

"Shall we?" Remy offered his arm.

"We shall." Virginia smiled, linking her arm with his.

At the top of the sagging steps, they stepped onto the wide, weathered veranda, turned right, and headed for the entrance.

Inside, from behind double French doors, the hostess saw them, smiled, and held up one finger. "Just a minute," she mouthed.

Virginia and Remy sat on the ancient joggling board that ran nearly half the length of the veranda.

"Whoa, this is the first truly old one I've ever seen," Virginia exclaimed, gently bouncing on the wide, eighteen-foot-long plank held balanced between two rocker-footed headboards. "The reproductions are wonderful, but this one has that certain *je ne sais quoi* that only a well-used antique can."

"Probably been here since this place was built," Remy said, "back before the Civil War. Or maybe from the early part of the century, when it was a bed, board, and fishing charter house." He paused. "You said you've never been here before?"

"I've driven past here so many times. Gordon and I lived just down the road, on Seabrook Drive, but we never came here."

"You're kidding!"

"Gordon didn't like seafood." She smiled. "But *I* do."

Remy touched her hand. "I've eaten here way more times than I can count. You'll love it."

"What do you recommend? Oysters are my favorite, but what's their specialty?"

"It's all great—I always hear the other diners praising everything, but I'm partial to the Oliver's Alaskan King Crab Leg Plate. And—you'll love this—there are old wooden powerboat photographs all over the dining room walls." His cell phone began to buzz, low and muffled, in his pants pocket.

"I'll be right back," Virginia said. "Where is the ladies' room?"

"Soon as you go into the dining room, straight up the stairs to your left," he said, reaching for his pocket.

Virginia went through the French doors, into the dining room and headed up the stairs, glad have a few moments away from Remy. All he did was merely touch her bare skin, but where he touched, her skin felt scalded. This was not good. She did not want to feel any more drawn to him than she already did, at least not yet.

The stairs are unusually steep, she thought. *They obviously pre-date county building codes.*

Though dimly lit, the stairway was hung with dozens of old black-and-white framed photographs of charter boats, as well as pleasure craft, some with this very lodge in the background.

Virginia climbed slowly, enjoying the framed nautical history.

At the head of the stairway, an old tin sign with a painted arrow pointing down the hall read, 'Bathrooms, This Way.'

At the end of the long, narrow hall, she turned the glass door-knob below the 'Ladies' sign, opening the heavy door into a high-ceilinged, faded yellow, beadboard-walled bathroom, complete with a huge, ancient, claw-foot bathtub.

No wonder that old tin sign said 'bathrooms.' An actual antique tub, she thought, eying the blistered spots where rust popped out of the enamel covering the big claw feet.

Hanging above the tub was another old black-and-white photograph, this one of a pleasure boat, a gorgeous old Chris-Craft cabin cruiser. It was a ringer for *Chaucer.*

Virginia caught her breath. It looked *exactly* like *Chaucer*—and there were people aboard too. *Where was this taken? There are buildings in the background, and wharves.* She leaned over the huge tub for a closer look.

I wish I could see this better, she thought.

Thighs pressed against the high rim of the tub, she reached over to tilt the photograph just as the lights went out, plunging Virginia into near-darkness.

The power outage must be only inside the restaurant, she thought, thankful for the faint, distant streetlight glow coming from the parking area behind the lodge. Surely the power would be restored quickly. *I'll wait,* she thought, *and then look at the picture.*

She heard raised voices below in the dining room—or maybe the kitchen? She caught her breath—*what if there is a fire?*

Edging her way out of the bathroom and into the windowless, black hall, she carefully felt her way along the picture-laden wall until she reached the stairs. Gripping the railing, she felt her way down several of the steep steps then saw, to her great relief, a lantern glow at first one table, then another, then another.

Easily she walked down the rest of the stairs, crossed the dining room, and met Remy on the veranda, still sitting on the joggling board.

"I was just about to come after you," he said. "The hostess came out here and said she would have a table for us as soon as the power comes back on."

No sooner had Remy spoken than the lights came up, and seconds later, the hostess stepped onto the veranda, shaking her head sheepishly.

"Your table is ready," she smiled. "You were in the best place possible for that power outage," she added to Remy, eying the joggling board. "And you," she smiled at Virginia, "probably didn't even realize it, in our lamp-lit ladies lounge."

"I was in the bathroom upstairs," Virginia laughed.

"Oh you poor dear," the hostess clicked her tongue, "I'm sorry. Just the staff uses that one now. Our nice new ladies' facility is downstairs. But some of our long-time customers who haven't been here lately don't know it." She looked pointedly at Remy.

"Like me." He hung his head mock-sheepishly. "Last time I was here, it really was upstairs, Virginia, I promise, ladies and men—separate, I mean, but both upstairs."

"Last month we opened the new one," the hostess said. "Sorry about that," she apologized again, putting her hand on Virginia's arm. "One of the girls thought she heard someone up there and went up with a lantern to make sure no one was, ah, marooned, but then the power came back on."

*****

Over an hour later, sated with she crab soup, spinach salad, and lightly fried oysters, Virginia stepped onto the veranda with Remy.

"Thank you for a wonderful evening," she said. *Truly wonderful,* she thought, *especially if you compare it to Labor Day weekend a year ago.*

"Now, you call me when that boat is situated up on the railway in Georgetown," he said, "and if you need anything, any help, call me day or night. Promise me. Moving that big old wooden boat down to the bay after she's been sitting there for—"

"I promise, I promise," Virginia laughed. "And I can barely wait 'til next week! As if I wasn't looking forward to it already, all these old wooden boat photographs have got me ready to get started on—" She stopped.

The picture in the upstairs bathroom! She had meant to go back up and finish studying the old photograph of the boat so similar to *Chaucer,* the one over the bathtub—the one she was beginning to study when the power went out.

"I forgot something—I'll be right back!" Virginia hurried back into the restaurant.

Oliver's Lodge was closing for the evening—already closed, actually, and she and Remy were the last customers—but she needed to see that picture again. The likelihood that it was a photograph of *Chaucer* was very small, but even so, she wanted to scrutinize it for her restoration.

"Only a moment," she called over her shoulder to the surprised hostess.

Anticipating the steepness of the stairs now, as opposed to her initial surprise, Virginia sprinted up to the second floor, trotted down the hall, and whirled into the bathroom.

The yellow-painted beadboard wall behind the bathtub was bare. A rectangle of deeper, un-faded yellow seemed to glare in the spot where the photograph had hung.

Virginia blinked. It seemed impossible, but the photograph of the Chris-Craft that was a ringer for *Chaucer* was gone.

Chapter Six

Labor Day

Two days later, *Chaucer* rested seven feet up in the air at the water's edge on the marine railway beside Cathou's Fish House in Georgetown. The curvature of her hull, nestled securely in the railway's wooden cradle, was held in place by huge wooden chocks.

Awake before dawn, Virginia slipped on jeans and an old flannel shirt, made coffee, and took it up to the bridge. The surreal heat of last week had been replaced with weather rare for the South Carolina low country in early September—cool, breezy and dry, with brilliant topaz-blue skies.

Aft of *Chaucer*, Virginia saw reds and oranges just beginning to show across the bay on the eastern horizon. *Red sky at morning? Please not rain,* she thought. She looked over the captain's wheel, down across *Chaucer*'s red mahogany forward deck.

A movement on the ground just beyond the curvature of *Chaucer*'s hull caught her eye. Who could be below the boat? Would Lester, hired to work on a pressure leak in the part of the bow stem below the waterline, be here this early? He had told her on the phone eight o'clock, and it was not even seven yet.

By the time she got down from the bridge to the aft deck and then down the ladder to the ground, whoever it was had gone.

Virginia saw smoke coming from the stovepipe chimney over the fish house. Maybe Mr. Cathou had seen the person under her boat.

She climbed up onto the wharf and headed into the fish house, stopping to pet Mr. Cathou's huge Maine Coon cat, Rocky. Gabrielle had gone home with Virginia's parents after the sail down from Murrells Inlet yesterday. Virginia, not used to Gabrielle's absence, found Rocky's presence comforting.

"Mornin,' missy." Mr. Cathou, ninety if he was a day, grinned from his straight wooden chair before the pot-belly stove. "Come set a spell, and warm your bones, before your workday begins." He gestured to the assortment of rocking chairs and lawn chairs around the stove, which sat in the middle of the wide-planked floor.

"Mornin'. Thank you, I believe I will." Virginia sat down on the edge of a rocking chair, watching a pair of mallards waddle around Rocky and across the weathered planks to eat duck feed from a pan beside the old, tall ceramic water fountain.

She smiled and nodded at two men, obviously Mr. Cathou's contemporaries, sitting in chairs on either side of him. They both were smoking pipes.

Virginia felt a pang of sad memory. She loved the smell of a pipe. Gordon smoked one, and she had not been around pipe smoke since she moved to the boat before his death.

"Mr. Cathou, did any of you see someone on the railway under my boat just now? I wanted to speak to them before they left."

The three men looked at one another. "That real estate girl was down here this morning," Mr. Cathou nodded, "after me about this place, as usual. But she don't go 'round the boats."

"Humph!" The man on Mr. Cathou's right snorted loudly. "She'd have condominiums right *here*."

"Over my dead body," Mr. Cathou growled. "And not even then!"

The other man, silent until now, pulled the pipe out of his mouth. Holding it between his thumb and forefinger, he gestured toward *Chaucer*, whose stern was visible outside the big open barn-like doors of the fish house.

"I remember a yacht like that, brand new she was, sank just outside the jetties. Damned shame." He shook his head. "Damned shame."

"Sank? Scuttled, more like," the other man growled. "But she were built different than this, at least when she came here first."

"The one the bloke died aboard?" The first man leaned forward.

Virginia swallowed. "Died aboard?"

"Stop it you two old goats," Mr. Cathou growled, "you're scaring the young lady.

"She was nay scuttled—I saw her with me own eyes, hauled—" Mr. Cathou pushed on the arms of his rocking chair and stood. "I said *stop*. A lot of boats come and go through this port, and some come to grief." He looked at Virginia. "But not many. You'll find Georgetown a safe port."

"Did any of you see someone directly under my boat just now?" Virginia looked at the three men. "I wondered if it might be Lester Rhodes— he's going to work on a pressure leak in the bow stem."

"Oh he wouldn't be here 'til seven thirty or so," Mr. Cathou said. "But I did see that other girl, the one that goes around with that sign painter. The girl with blonde hair like him."

"Hmmph. Her. One of the ones caused his wife to divorce him," the second man added sagely.

"Now Edrell, there's no need for to be spreadin' gossip," Mr. Cathou said. "He caused his own divorce."

Virginia raised her eyebrows. The painter? Were they talking about Remy?

"When's Scotty coming back?" Mr. Cathou asked. "I mean, your daddy?"

"This evening," Virginia replied, smiling.

"Thought he was staying for the duration," Mr. Cathou said, "him and your mama both, and that cat, after you all sailed in together."

Virginia shook her head. "My mom took my cat back with her yesterday evening, and Scotty went too."

"Well, don't wait too long to scrape that hull," Mr. Cathou cautioned.

*****

Heading on foot for breakfast at the Thomas Café, two blocks up Front Street—and upriver, too, for the Sampit River ran parallel to the street—Virginia stopped in front of the *Georgetown Times* office and printing press.

"'The oldest newspaper in South Carolina,'" she read aloud from the legend under their sign. *A good breakfast read,* she thought. It would be nice to know what was going on in Georgetown, since she would be here for a few days. And of course, since Remy lived here.

She dropped two quarters in the paper rack in front of the entrance and pulled down the door. She reached inside then stopped. A chill passed over her and she swallowed to keep bile from rising in her throat. Slowly she picked up the top paper from the freshly printed stack.

A Year Later, Labor Day Death Remains a Mystery, read the headline above the photograph of a handsomely grinning Gordon receiving a real estate sales award.

Drawing back with the paper, Virginia barely noticed the rack door slam shut. *Authorities continue to seek the arsonist responsible for the tragic explosion and resulting fire that killed Murrells Inlet businessman*

Gordon Seabrook, she read silently. *While no person of interest has been named, Seabrook's estranged wife was questioned—*

Her fingers trembling only a little, she folded the paper and put it in her purse. She would read this later. At least they had not mentioned her name. And thankfully, she had her list of boat tasks to work on over breakfast. This article would only give her indigestion.

Before reaching the Thomas Café, she saw Remy walk out of a doorway a block and a half down the street, climb into his blue Range Rover, and drive away. *He's out early,* she thought.

Walking into the nearly full, but not crowded, Thomas Café, she was greeted by the aroma of eggs, bacon, and grits, the low clatter of plates, and the hum of breakfast conversation.

Sliding into an available green wooden booth, her eyes lit on the newspaper left by an earlier breakfaster.

It was the new *Georgetown Times,* with Gordon's face still smiling—or smirking—up at her.

Resolutely she placed the newspaper on a nearby empty table and sat back down, her nostrils flaring. It was going to be a long day.

*****

After breakfast it began raining heavily, and Lester, the marine carpenter, stopped by to tell Virginia he would begin work the next day, which was forecast to be clear. There would be no work on the hull today.

Eager to work on *Chaucer* during this boat-dedicated time off from her job, Virginia decided to strip the varnish off the mahogany steering console in the bridge. This task was not at the top of her need-to-do list, but was a job she had long anticipated. Resolutely, she set to work.

*****

After nearly two hours, Virginia gritted her teeth.

On one small section of the steering console, the multi-layered varnish was not coming off. After soaking the console with gel paint remover several times, each time after which she scraped more melted varnish off, she was left with a lumpy section that would not even out. The many coats of undoubtedly decades-old varnish layered on the console, protected by the bridge's canvas Bimini top, were dense and solid, unlike the deck and transom varnish that was brittle with years of sun exposure. Even so, she was able to strip the entire console but for the one uneven, lumpy section.

Finally, realizing the lumpy area was some sort of metal protuberance, she went below, returning with an ice pick. Digging out the indentations, her scraping revealed copper. The raised part began showing, and to her delight, she uncovered a little copper cat with an ear-to-ear grin on its face.

A Cheshire cat? Virginia wondered, studying the tiny grinning face. *Yes,* she thought, *a copper Cheshire cat.*

*****

Virginia had just finished showering at the facilities of the Backlanding Marina next door and was climbing back aboard *Chaucer* when a folded newspaper lying on the aft deck caught her eye.

Picking it up, she felt a twinge of dread. Slowly unfolding the paper, she saw it was another copy of the new issue of the *Georgetown Times* she still had folded up in her purse.

Who would put this here? Maybe, she thought, *somebody just decided to share an extra newspaper.* Biting her lip, she re-read the same headline she read this morning. *I may as well go ahead and read the rest of it,* she thought.

Opening up the paper to see the rest of the article, which continued on page two, she stepped back as a piece of bright red construction paper fell out onto the aft deck.

Individual letters, apparently cut from magazines and newspapers, were pasted to it. With misgivings swirling cold and clammy in her stomach, she reached down to pick it up.

It's going to say I'm a murderer, she thought, angry tears springing up in her eyes.

Virginia gasped, her unshed tears vanishing. The letters spelled out a jagged message: '*ViRgiNiA You'Re nEXt*'.

Chapter Seven

Scotty studied the macabre message. "So they could lift no fingerprints from it?"

Virginia shook her head.

By the time Scotty had arrived, the police were gone, having promised to schedule extra patrols in the Fish House and marina cul-de-sac.

"The law," Scotty said scornfully, "can no more find who did this than they can find out what happened to poor Gordon."

Virginia rolled her eyes, fear and surprise having given way to angry frustration. *Poor Gordon, indeed. His selfish actions no doubt brought his death on himself,* she thought, and now poor Virginia was being held accountable in the press, and, according to this crude missive, 'next' in someone else's mind.

Her dad's scorn, she knew, was not for the police but for the sick individual who created the crude message, and for whomever was responsible for Gordon's demise and Virginia's being blamed.

Not one to dwell in pessimism, Scotty cut his eyes toward Virginia. "Now what did you say is the name of the lad who's lettering the name on the vessel?"

"Rrrremy Rrrrrravenel." Virginia had to grin, deliberately rolling the *R*'s. Remy's name rolled off her tongue so easily and sweetly.

"Rrrremy?" Scotty tested out the name. "His mum and dad must've named him after their favorite brandy, eh?"

"I don't know," Virginia said, laughing. "You'll have many chances to ask him."

What would Scotty think of Remy, Virginia wondered. She had not mentioned, much less introduced her dad to, any man since long before she and Gordon were married. As for her own feelings, she was drawn to Remy, yet knew she needed to draw back from him, to keep her distance.

Regardless of personal strings, she needed to get in touch with him for business. Taking her cell phone out of her pocket, she found his name and rang his number. Suddenly shy, Virginia was almost speechless, taking a deep breath when his answering machine beeped.

"Remy, this is Virginia Ross. My dad and I are finally settled on the railway in Georgetown, and *Chaucer*'s transom is ready for you to letter anytime during the next five days. Thanks."

Five minutes later, she was rendered nearly speechless at the sight of Remy driving up and climbing out of his blue Range Rover, grinning.

"Hey, you must be Scotty. I'm Remy Ravenel," he said, shaking Scotty's hand. "How about you both hop in my truck and let's go have supper buffet?"

"Love to," Scotty immediately responded. "We're starved. And, it's good to meet you, young man."

"How did you get here so fast?" Virginia asked.

"You know I live on Pawleys Island, between Murrells Inlet and Georgetown," Remy explained, "but most of my work is here in Georgetown. I had just finished lettering the starboard side of a commercial shrimp trawling boat when your call came."

"Ah," Virginia said.

"Come on," Remy gestured. "I'm starving too."

Later, when Scotty told Virginia good night, he added, "That Remy's a nice fellow."

*****

Late that night, Virginia lay awake in the galley, comfortably bedded down on the cozy platform bunk that easily converted from the dining table booth. She could hear Scotty deeply breathing, almost, but not quite, snoring, fast asleep in the double berth in her cabin at the other end of the boat. Though she was comfortable, Virginia could not sleep. *Who could have left that horrible message inside that newspaper?*

Scotty did not seem to be alarmed by it, but, she reasoned, he, being Scottish, always followed the adage 'keep calm and carry on.' If he was alarmed he would not show it, mainly to keep her from worrying.

When sleep finally came, Virginia slept fitfully, awaking abruptly from a dream in which she could hear footsteps under the boat. *Or was it a dream? Is someone down there?*

Raising up in the bunk, she peered out of the galley porthole nearest her head, then out of the other portside galley porthole. Sliding down from the bunk, she padded across the cool mahogany-and-oak galley floor to peer out of the starboard portholes.

The only vehicles in the parking lot were her Porsche and Scotty's Jeep. Uneasily, she lay back down. When she awoke, it was almost sunrise.

*****

The mist was still burning off the water an hour later when Remy drove up, handsome in the same paint-splattered cotton shirt and khakis as last night. As though it was the most natural thing in the world, he smiled, handing her two Styrofoam cups of coffee and a paper bag containing egg and sausage biscuits. Then, grinning, he announced he was off to letter the transom and port side of the shrimp trawler he had started on yesterday.

Coming down the ladder set against *Chaucer*'s hull, Scotty sat down on the dock beside Virginia, legs dangling over the water, to enjoy Remy's offering.

"That Remy," Scotty said, nodding sagely between bites, "like I said, is a nice fellow."

*****

Work on *Chaucer*'s hull was going smoothly, and Remy dropped by between his lettering jobs, leaving Virginia little time to brood over the newspaper article and the macabre personal message she received.

Virginia and Scotty, pressure washing the buildup of river slime off the hull, were grateful that *Chaucer*'s home port, though only a few miles from the ocean, was far enough inland that they did not have to worry about barnacles.

While Lester, the marine carpenter, began probing the bow stem pressure leak, Virginia and Scotty began inspecting the hull for every indentation revealing an exposed screw head. Any exposed screw head in the hull was a potential place for water to seep in once *Chaucer* was back in the water.

Each time they came to an area covered by one of the great wooden chocks holding the boat steady in the cradle on the railway, they carefully moved the heavy chock out from the hull, then concentrated on the area they had uncovered. Sliding the chock back into place afterwards, they tested its integrity, making sure to fit it snugly up against the hull in the exact same place from which they had moved it. Any deviation from the chock's placement could cause the high-and-dry boat to slide or even fall over on the railway, with disastrous results.

Every inch of *Chaucer*'s below-waterline appointments, Virginia and Scotty were realizing, needed their attentions.

In the two years since Virginia and Gordon hauled *Chaucer* out at Waccamaw Marina, electrolysis had been eating away the edges of her port propeller.

"This is what happens," stated Scotty, "when a boat is not hauled out of the water yearly. We'll get new zincs and order a new brass propeller for the port shaft."

Scotty, finding that the starboard stuffing box leaked steadily when the shaft's propeller revolved, realized this was due to a bend in the shaft. The shaft, he said, would have to be taken out and straightened. Coupled with the added waiting for the arrival of the ordered propeller, as well as more time needed for Lester repairing the pressure leak, *Chaucer* could not be put back in the water for at least another week. Her time on the rail would be closer to two weeks than the five days they had planned.

Although nearly ill at the thought of the added expense, Virginia was secretly glad she would have to stay in Georgetown a little longer.

Phoning Mr. Kimbel, the owner of the Fox's Lair, she held her breath. To her relief, he agreed for her to take another week off, hinting broadly that she might scout antiques while in what he considered heirloom heaven.

"Maybe," Mr. Kimbel suggested, "you'll see more of Miss Eugenia. I hear she has enough old family relics in her big old pre-Revolutionary house in the Georgetown Historic District, to fill four or five shops. She just brings us a tiny portion at a time."

Several times a year, usually unexpectedly, Miss Eugenia cleaned out her house and drove up from Georgetown in her red diesel dually pickup truck, bringing one-of-a-kind family heirlooms to sell on consignment at Fox's Lair. Miss Eugenia *always* wore purple.

Virginia loved managing the store for Mr. Kimbel, but her time spent on the Georgetown waterfront near Front Street's shops, right on the river in the heart of Georgetown's National Register Historic District with its quaint shops, reawakened a dream Virginia had long cherished—to open her own antiques shop, specializing in maritime antiques. Plus, being there would mean Miss Eugenia could easily drop in for a cup of tea—and Remy could stop by, too.

Virginia was glad to be spending time with him in Scotty's company. She was not ready to spend more time alone with Remy, not yet anyway. It would be so easy to fall back into her pre-Gordon relationship with him, and she was not sure she wanted to do that.

At the close of *Chaucer*'s fourth day on the Georgetown waterfront railway, Remy was making no start on lettering her stern. He was, however, coming to the railway every day, usually several times a day, to inspect progress on the hull and visit Virginia and Scotty. Each evening the three of them went out to eat. During dinner Thursday night, Remy asked Virginia and Scotty to come to dinner at his house on Pawleys Island the next evening.

"Where do you live on Pawleys?" Virginia asked.

"About midway down the island," Remy said, "in an old, old house."

"So you live not only in the Town of Pawleys Island, but on the island itself," Virginia said.

"Right," Remy laughed. "And I'm one of the few who actually live there all year. My house is occupied by me year 'round, and not rented out, not ever."

"What can we bring?" Virginia smiled. *I wonder if he can cook,* she thought.

"Just yourselves," Remy grinned. "Oh, and by the way," he added, his grin fading, "come 'round to the back door—no one ever comes to the front."

Chapter Eight

The scent of fresh steaming oysters greeted Virginia and Scotty Friday night as, looking all around, they climbed a full story of wide lamp-lit wooden steps up to the front porch of Remy's weathered, steeply gabled, fish-scale-shingle-sided home. Up on the top story, light shone from behind colored leaded-glass windows below worn gingerbread trim.

"Where are Hansel and Gretel?" Scotty quipped.

"I don't know," Virginia shrugged, smiling, "but they'd feel at home, wouldn't they?"

Sniffing the salty breeze, she felt her stomach growl. A delicious aroma was wafting out from behind the house. Reaching up to lift the door knocker she stopped, her hand in mid-air.

The ancient little copper door knocker, weathered to a dark patina, was made in the shape of a grinning cat. The rapper was the cat's clasped paws. Head tilted to one side and paws clasped at the waist, the cat's wide, beatific grin made Virginia smile too as she tapped the rapper against the cat's torso. Looking closely, she saw, in tiny letters just below where the rapper tapped the torso, the legend 'Cheshire Cat.'

"Is he home?" Scotty asked after a few minutes.

"Oh no!" Virginia clapped her hand over her mouth, remembering. "He said to come to the back door—no one uses the front." She turned to head down the steps.

Suddenly the front door opened and Remy appeared, clad in tan cotton Levi's and a dark brown Henley shirt.

"Hey, welcome," he said warmly, a grin rivaling the Cheshire cat's lighting his face. "I was out back checking the oysters." He shook Scotty's hand then kissed Virginia lightly on the lips.

"I like your Cheshire cat door knocker," she said.

"Cheshire cat?" Remy raised his eyebrows. "Oh, that. Thanks. I never paid much attention to it."

"It really caught my eye," Virginia said, "because I found a Cheshire cat, a little copper one, embedded in the boat's bridge."

"In the bridge? How—quaint."

Remy led them inside, where the front door opened into a low-ceilinged hearth room dominated by the most striking fireplace Virginia had ever seen. Made of huge, pale brick with over an inch of mortar between each, the fireplace was more curves than angles. From the high brick arc rising rainbow-like over the great single rough timber that formed the mantle, to the walk-in interior above the half-circle of generous hearth, Remy's fireplace was a work of art.

Inhaling the pungent scent of sea island cedar burning deep within the fireplace, Virginia noticed his cigarette pack lying on the mantelpiece. *Why,* she wondered, *is there no lingering hint of cigarette smoke?* After all, most smokers smoke in their own homes.

"I never smoke indoors." Folding his arms across his chest, Remy and leaned his head to one side, surveying Virginia with a look of pleased contentment on his face. "With all this old heart-of-pine black cedar, it's risky enough just using the fireplace."

"This fine hearth," remarked Scotty, "reminds me of some of the highland lodges where I went on holiday as a young man."

"Thank you, sir, I made it myself with these old brick I dug up at a ruined rice mill near here."

"You built it?" Scotty was surprised. "this fireplace looks to be old enough to have warmed William Wallace himself."

Virginia smiled, looking up at the weathered, exposed beams that crossed the ceiling. It was obvious her dad liked Remy. "Dad's a full Scot, so I'm half. Can't you tell?" she grinned playfully, touching one of her auburn-gold curls.

"My heritage is German, Cherokee and French," Remy offered. As if reading her thoughts, he added, "The German is on both sides, so that is my dominant heritage. I haven't been able to trace anything of my Cherokee grandmother, except that she was full-blooded and married to my German great-grandfather. My French ancestor, Remy Ravenel, was a Huguenot refugee who came over here in 1692 and settled in Charleston. He was my seventh great-grandfather."

"Is that the Huguenot cross?" Virginia asked, her eyes drawn to the small blue-and-white enameled pendant suspended from a leather thong and resting in the blond hair just below Remy's collar bone.

"Yes." Remy replied, laying forefinger on the blue fleur-de-lis, dove, and cross medallion. "I'm not one to wear jewelry, but I rarely take this one off." Clearing his throat, he gestured toward half a dozen steps curving down to his right. "Why don't you come into the kitchen while I melt butter for the oysters?"

Virginia and Scotty followed Remy down the narrow, half-flight of stairs to his kitchen, which was dominated by another, smaller hearth.

"This is the house's original antebellum kitchen, halfway between the ground floor and the first floor," Remy said, reaching above his head to lift a cup-sized cast-iron cauldron from its place on an ancient wooden ladder hung horizontally as a pot rack.

"This kitchen," he explained, "was accessed from the rest of the house by an outdoor stairway until the late 1940s. Then whoever owned the house at the time wanted a little more in the way of creature comforts and enclosed the stairs. After that you could still exit the kitchen onto the beach, but you didn't have to come outside the house and brave the frigid Atlantic winds just to get into the kitchen to cook breakfast."

"Your house is gorgeous," Virginia said, looking around her, "with lots of surprises."

"The biggest surprise," Remy laughed, "was when I moved in here. Most of the houses here on the island belong to families who use them only a few weeks out of the year. Those places are kept up pretty well and rent for quite a bit. This house had been *only* a rental ever since it was patched up after Hurricane Hazel in, can you believe, 1954. It needed more renovation than I realized."

"*Major* renovation, no doubt," nodded Scotty. "You've done a good job, lad."

"Not unlike Virginia's been doing with *Chaucer*," Remy smiled warmly at her. Taking a stick of butter from his sleek black refrigerator, he removed the wrapping and placed the butter in the small cauldron. Picking up a fireplace poker, he hung the cauldron over the hearth fire.

"Better than a microwave," he grinned.

Virginia realized she was staring at him. He was even more handsome than he was in college—almost too handsome. And he enjoyed cooking, another plus.

"I must be excused," she said, looking pointedly across the kitchen to where another half dozen wooden stair steps curved up and out of sight. "Is it up there?"

Remy gestured up in the direction she was looking. "Up there, third door to the right."

The candle-lit bathroom, Virginia discovered, was bleached cedar-walled, high ceilinged, and dominated by the largest claw-foot tub she had ever seen. She was delighted to see a light layer of rust coming through the white enamel on one of the claw feet, marking this tub as an authentically aged relic, rather than a reproduction.

Bare of a shower curtain, the tub had droplets of water in the bottom along with a wet washcloth. *Remy is obviously a man who enjoys a nice relaxing soak,* she thought. Gordon always took showers and said baths were unmanly. How refreshing that Remy was comfortable enough in his manhood to enjoy a bath—unless, of course, he was only cleaning the tub.

Leaning over, she ran a fingertip across the inside edge of the tub. *Hmmnn,* she thought, *no cleansing powder residue*—Remy had not been cleaning the tub.

Closing the bathroom door, Virginia could not resist the temptation to critically appraise her appearance in the old gilt-framed full-length mirror on the back of the door. In the candlelight, her long curling waves shone, matching the tiger-eye earrings she wore. Her lithe legs and slender hips were encased in slim-cut Levi's, while her soft, buttery suede chocolate double-breasted shirt, made with a button-on bib like men wore in the Civil War, highlighted her upper body. The cinnamon leather belt riding a fraction below her small waist matched her ankle-length suede boots.

Nearly satisfied with her appearance, she resisted the urge to touch up her hair, which would most likely be windblown in a few minutes anyway.

Washing her hands, she heard the phone begin to ring out in the hall. As she dried her hands on one of the luxuriously thick dark blue towels that hung behind the door, a click sounded after the third ring and the low timbre of Remy's recorded voice came on, suggesting the caller leave a message after the tone. She slowly opened the bathroom door, stepping out as the tone sounded and a sultry female voice floated across the dimly lit hallway.

"Remy? You there?" Then there was a click. *Who was that?*

Embarrassed, Virginia swallowed, heading down the stairs. The phone began ringing again. Virginia paused, her hand on the smooth unvarnished curve of the banister. As before, the third ring was followed by Remy's recorded message inviting the caller to leave a message. Virginia held her breath.

"Remy," the same female voice said, its sultriness more gravelly this time. "Pick up the phone." *Click.*

Mortified by the knowledge that Remy and her father not only heard the messages from the kitchen but knew she had to have heard them as well, Virginia could feel her face growing warm. She would feel more comfortable running naked through the grocery store than facing them right now. If she went back to the bathroom and stayed for a while, that would be almost as bad. She could feel her ears burn as she continued down the short, narrow staircase.

There is no reason to feel so self-conscious, Virginia chided herself. She did not listen to the message intentionally. It was none of her business. If it was so private, the caller ought to have called Remy's cell phone—and maybe she did.

Relief washed over Virginia when, entering the kitchen, she saw that Remy and her father were not there. A yellow sticky note placed on the big old rough-hewn trestle table bore the hastily penciled message, *Gone out back to check on the oysters—come join us. Remy.*

Running her hand over the wide oaken planks of the tabletop, she hesitated, then, biting her lip, picked up the note. Why was she so curious about the phone message? Oh, no, was she jealous? Suspicious? Why? She was holding back from getting involved with Remy, so why were all these emotions creeping up?

Lighten up, Virginia, she told herself. *It was probably his mother or his sister—or his former wife. Just enjoy the evening.*

Squaring her shoulders, she smiled to herself, and with a toss of her wavy mane, went out to join her father and Remy for roasted oysters as the phone began ringing again.

Chapter Nine

With *Chaucer* projected to stay on the rail for a several more days, Scotty decided to go home for the rest of the weekend. He left Saturday afternoon, assuring Virginia he would be back to resume work early Monday morning.

Virginia knew her father was missing her mother and wanted to get back home, but she also suspected him of wanting to give his daughter time alone with Remy.

After a flounder dinner that evening at Buzzard's Roost outside on the second story deck overlooking the Harbor Promenade and the river below, Virginia and Remy went downstairs, to listen to the blues band. As they were leaving they could hear the soulful, wailing guitar intro rift of *Angel From Montgomery* as they walked along the Harbor Promenade.

"I love that song," Virginia said.

"Me too," Remy said. "But I love hearing it now more than I ever did before."

Night was falling, and the masthead lights of the sailboats anchored in the river were pinpoints of brightness against the dark cypress-and-pine density of uninhabited Goat Island across the river. The cool night breeze lifted Virginia's hair and caressed her neck, and when Remy reached for her hand, she didn't find a reason to reach into her pocket instead.

"You know, honey," Remy remarked, "each one of these shops, or restaurants, or bars, is long and narrow. Each one opens here onto the river and Harbor Promenade, on this side, and opens front-side onto Front Street. And each has its own boat slip, to rent or to use. Most have apartments on the second floor, unless, like Buzzard's Roost, the second story is part of the business."

"Some have third floor apartments." Virginia looked up to a lighted screened porch high above the bookstore.

"I'd love to have my shop down here, where most of my work is," Remy said, "but right now I'm happy with my shop below my house at Pawleys."

"These boat slips are handy behind the shops," Virginia said. "I would love to work with *Chaucer* just thirty feet away. Do you have a boat?"

"A sport fisher," Remy answered. "I keep her in Murrells Inlet, but not on the river like you do. Mine's at a salt water marina on the creek, just a couple of minutes from the ocean. Where we had dinner last weekend—Oliver's Lodge? My boat's just south of there."

Now they were walking past the candle shop. Closed for the evening, it was dark but for the candle-like illuminations of carefully placed flicker flame bulbs.

A movement in the lighted window above caught Virginia's eye. She caught a glimpse of long dark hair before the light went out. "Someone must live in that apartment," she said, but Remy was looking toward the water.

"See that sailboat," he said, pointing to a two-masted sixty-footer in the slip behind the candle shop. "It belongs to the couple that own the candle shop—they live aboard too."

"Mmhmmnnn..." Virginia trailed off, deep in thought. None of the Front Street antiques shops were on this side of the street, on the water. If she could open her own antiques shop here, and dock *Chaucer* behind it—

"Virginia." Remy broke into her thoughts. He yawned. "this has been a great evening, but I'm beat. I'm about ready to head home and go to sleep. You've had a long day too, I bet."

"We got started pretty early this morning too," Virginia admitted. "We got a lot done before Dad drove back."

"After a good night's sleep, how about riding across the bay to the lighthouse for a picnic tomorrow?" Remy asked.

"After church?" Virginia raised her eyebrows hopefully.

"After church." Remy confirmed. "That will give me time to get the picnic together and the boat ready."

*****

After driving Virginia back to *Chaucer*, Remy waited at the marina, headlights trained on *Chaucer*, until Virginia reached the top of the ladder and climbed aboard. Virginia blew him a kiss, then he flashed his headlights and left.

He is *such a nice fellow, just like Dad said*, she smiled to herself, unlocking the aft door. *And handsome, charming, attentive, and has his own successful business, and lives on the beach. Any single woman in her right mind would be thrilled with his attentions.*

Entering, she sighed and locked the door behind her. She leaned her back against the door for a moment, arms folded, then walked forward to look into the big round beveled mirror beside her berth. She looked hard at her reflection. *I am thrilled with his attentions, aren't I? So what is bothering me?*

Shaking her head at her reflection, she said aloud, "Get over yourself. He's too good to be true, that's all. Stop picking everything apart and enjoy. "

*****

Rising early, Virginia slipped on her favorite black sheath, pearl necklace and grey suede pumps and went to the eight o'clock Sunday morning service at the circa-seventeen-forty-five colonial Prince George Winyah Episcopal Church.

Out in front beside the church's circa-eighteen-fifty carriage block, she saw Miss Eugenia. Resplendent in a dress of elegant purple georgette, the stout and stately elderly woman wore a veiled lavender pillbox hat and carried a matching handbag.

"Miss Eugenia?" Virginia had never seen her attired so formally, not even at the *Harvest Moon* memorial service in February. Miss Eugenia, Virginia decided, probably had nothing in her wardrobe that was not some shade of purple.

"Virginia!" Miss Eugenia peered through her veil's wide-gauge netting. "What a treat. Aren't you a vision? Like a young Audrey Hepburn! I'm getting up another load of antiques to bring to Fox's Lair this week or next."

Chatting happily, they ended up sharing the boxed pew Miss Eugenia's family had, she informed Virginia, sat in since before the Revolutionary War.

After church, but before leaving for the South Island landing to meet Remy for their North Inlet trip, Virginia went to the boat to change clothes. Leaving, she looked once more at the big, beautiful gold-leaf name *Chaucer* Remy had lettered on the boat's transom on Friday. Pleased, she cast her gaze couple of feet below to where, as a surprise gift, Remy horizontally circled the hull with a three-inch-high painted bootstripe, or waterline gauge, a few inches above *Chaucer*'s natural waterline.

"So Virginia will know if her boat's taking on water," Remy had joked to Scotty, winking at Virginia. "I'll paint over it if you don't like it," he had added anxiously.

"No lad, it's a good precaution, and looks well with her lines," Scotty had replied.

"I agree," Virginia had nodded.

"Good," Remy had smiled, then became somberly serious. "Not to knock the integrity of *Chaucer*'s hull, but wooden hulls are notoriously leaky."

Chapter Ten

Over a polished stem glassed half filled with sweet muscadine wine, Virginia and Remy surveyed the calm Sunday afternoon waters of the pristine estuary of North Inlet as Remy pointed out the creeks winding through the marsh grass.

Glass in hand, standing on the sandy shore of DeBordieu point, Remy nodded across the wide inlet to each creek and where it led.

"DeBordieu Creek, it leads up into DeBordieu Plantation. Town Creek and Jones Creek, they wind all through the marsh part of North Island—we followed them here after crossing Winyah Bay," he explained.

Still shivering from the brisk, chilling ride across the bay and then winding fast through miles of salt marsh, Virginia thankfully savored the warming sun on her face. She sipped her wine, curiously following Remy's pointing hand with her eyes, surveying the magical scene before her.

"Honey, you've really never been here before?" Remy was surprised.

Virginia shook her head. "Never."

"Well, I'm honored to be the one to show you North Inlet for the first time," Remy said. "Coming out to North Inlet is a long-standing Georgetown tradition. Where we are sitting now, DeBordieu point, is the southernmost promontory of one of the oldest resorts on the East Coast. Long before the Civil War, Georgetown County rice planters built summer homes out here to escape the heat and the summer fevers."

With the high dunes of DeBordieu point at their backs to break the damp Atlantic breeze and the early afternoon September sun warming the sand where they sat, Virginia and Remy savored the unseasonable late summer coolness of the remote sea inlet.

"See that narrow channel at the end of this point we're on? That passage, the North Island cut, joins North Inlet with the Atlantic," Remy said, nodding to the left. "Across the channel is North Island, where the Marquis de Lafayette landed during the Revolutionary

War. We'll have our next picnic there, on the other side of the island by the lighthouse. Lots of summer homes stood there in the
early eighteen hundreds, but they're all gone now, swept away by
a hurricane. No one lives on the island now."

"An island that size is totally uninhabited?" Virginia was surprised.

"Well there's the old North Island lighthouse, but it's automated
and unmanned now. Rice planters had a whole summer village over
there, but the hurricane of 1822 swept most of them away. *One* two-
story cottage," he paused, lowering his voice, "was swept out to sea
with people still inside and lamps still burning at the windows."

"Sounds about as bad as Pawleys Island fared during Hurricane
Hugo of 1989," Virginia commented, "though I don't believe anyone
was still on Pawleys when the storm hit."

"As far as anybody knows," Remy added ominously, reaching
into the old woven picnic basket he had brought. "I heard Hurricane Hazel, of 1954, was worse." He reached into a box of chicken.

"Mmmmm—crispy fried chicken and sweet red wine," Virginia
sighed, watching Remy lift out warm to-go boxes.

"And coleslaw, biscuits, and mashed potatoes with gravy," Remy
added, unfurling a blue checkered cotton table cloth to reveal two
silver forks and two Blue Willow plates. He grinned broadly, picking up a biscuit. "Let's eat."

He took a bite of the biscuit and laid it down. Reaching into the
basket once more, he carefully drew out another bottle of wine.

"I love this red wine," Virginia smiled, "It is so sweet." She
looked at Remy. "I'm glad it's not dry and tart."

"I usually drink tequila or lager," Remy nodded, winding the
corkscrew down into the cork and pulling it from the bottleneck.
"I brought this for you." He held out the bottle, smiling.

"Thank you." Virginia held out her not-yet-quite-empty glass,
suppressing a grin. Remy might have brought it for her, but he was
drinking most of it. No doubt his lips would loosen and let fall some
interesting tidbits of information about his recent past, namely
concerning his social life and women. She wanted to be sure he
did not have any of Gordon's wandering tendencies before she even
thought about getting more involved with him.

Virginia took a sip. "Wine, sweet red wine, is just about the only
alcohol I drink, besides cognac. I love a good cognac."

"I'll remember that," Remy grinned.

Half an hour later Virginia and Remy reclined in the sand, basking in the warmth sun amidst the ruins of their delicious meal and marveling aloud how antebellum belles and their beaus must have picnicked on this same spot over a century and a half ago.

Refilling their glasses, Remy became solemn.

"Honey, you know I'm having serious thoughts about you. I believe you're having the same kind of thoughts about me, and I don't want anything you hear to change your opinion."

Virginia held her breath. Hear? What was there to hear? That Remy littered or shoplifted? Or that he was a serial killer? Or worse, a serial adulterer like Gordon?

"I was seeing a woman, casually dating her, up until last week."

Relieved, Virginia suppressed a smile. Remy sounded like he was confessing to a dire crime.

"Since then," Remy continued, "I've told her I won't be seeing her anymore."

"Remy—" Virginia was nearly speechless. This was the kind of statement Gordon would have only made in extreme sarcasm. But Remy was serious.

"I told her that I reconnected with someone I dated in college, someone I'm becoming serious about again," Remy continued, "and she wished me well."

"Ha! I'll just bet she did," laughed Virginia.

Remy colored slightly, and Virginia regretted her flip reply. She had become so good at using protective banter to counter Gordon's caustic remarks that it was hard to relax her guard, even after all this time.

"Actually," Remy said, "I wasn't serious about her, and she wasn't serious about me either," he grinned mischievously, "or else I might have been lynched."

"It takes at least two perpetrators to lynch someone," Virginia said.

"Well then it would have been a lynching because there were two of them," Remy grinned, "and if both of them were serious about me, they would have killed me when I told them that I'm in love with you."

"Remy!" Virginia interrupted, a smile softening her face. "You're truly serious, aren't you? I mean about me, not the two women."

"Truly serious. About you. And it was one woman, not two. And she was, ah, somewhat older."

"A couple of years older than you?"

"More than that."

Virginia raised her eyebrows. "A cougar, eh?"

Remy's face colored deeply, and he cleared his throat.

He is actually blushing, thought Virginia.

Remy took both her hands in his and looked deeply into her eyes. She stared back. His green eyes were guileless, she was sure—he was as honest and good and kind as he appeared.

"Virginia," he said, "I tried to stay busy. Getting divorced was sad and awkward, even though the marriage was over. I'm not proud of the fact that I kept company with her just to get me through the divorce. That wasn't fair to her, and I knew at the time it wasn't."

"She assumed you were serious about her?" Virginia was skeptical.

"No. She was very understanding of what I was going through. I took advantage of her good nature and owe her a debt of gratitude."

"You have quite an effect on people, Remy Ravenel."

"I know Gordon lied to you and broke your trust, then died before you could come to terms with the breakup. You got being hurt and angry confused with mourning, and you haven't trusted many people since. But you can trust me."

It was Virginia's turn to color. She was ashamed to have been tricked by Gordon but felt guilty about being angry with him. While it seemed wrong to be angry with someone who was dead, it was hard to feel remorse about his death when he had treated her so callously toward the end of their relationship.

"I also know you didn't kill Gordon. A lot of people have black powder."

Virginia nearly choked on her wine. What would make Remy say that? She had never even told him about black powder being one of the accelerants that caused the explosion, or about the black powder missing from Gordon's gunroom, or how the deputies searching her car found her little derringer that she had just taken from the black powder drawer, or how they saw the gun room pictures on her camera and wanted to charge her with murder right then and there but lacked enough evidence. None of that was even in the newspaper, either.

"Black powder was never mentioned in the newspaper," she managed, swallowing.

Remy blinked. "Oh honey, it was in one of the comments after the article online, then the comment was deleted by the newspaper. You know how that goes."

For a second, the dark cloud of suspicion that seemed to hover over her during those first few horrible weeks after Gordon's death threatened to return. Then like magic, the cloud dissipated as the full import of Remy's words hit her. Remy was the first person to ever tell her he knew she didn't kill Gordon—Remy, who spoke frankly and truthfully.

"It's just not in your nature to harm anyone," Remy continued. "Anyone who'd ever dream you were responsible for Gordon's death is a true jackass."

"You are a very perceptive man, Remy Ravenel," she said, clenching the stem of her glass to keep it from trembling.

Raising her face to Remy's kiss and looking again into his green eyes, she knew, as sure as she was sitting here, that she could trust Remy Ravenel. He was not only too good to be true, he was perfect.

Chapter Eleven

After midnight on her last night in Georgetown, Virginia drove back to *Chaucer* with lighthearted abandon following Friday night dinner at Remy's house.

It is hard to believe I have been in Georgetown for two weeks, she thought. *And even harder to believe I've only been seeing Remy for that long.*

Driving back into town, past the wrought iron gates and quaint gardens of the colonial and antebellum houses in the seaport Historic District, she felt right at home. Despite the awful cut-and-paste message slipped inside that newspaper she was anonymously given, being here, away from her home marina, kept thoughts of Gordon's horrible death in that old marina shed at bay.

I wish I lived here, Virginia thought.

As much as she hated to leave Georgetown and go back upriver, she looked forward to the morning, when after these past two weeks on the railway, *Chaucer* would float once again.

She and Scotty rolled the final coat of blue bottom paint on the hull early this afternoon. They were scheduled to ease her back into the water and put out for Murrells Inlet in the morning. Virginia's mother and Gabrielle would sail with them. Virginia could hardly wait. She was also eager to get back to Murrells Inlet and put her galley back to normal—with electricity—so she could prepare one of her culinary specialties for Remy—stuffed, roasted Cornish hens.

Pulling into the big parking lot shared by Cathou's Fish House and the Backlanding Marina, Virginia parked as close to *Chaucer* as possible, between the railway and the land end of the Fish House. At the sound of another engine across the parking lot, her eyes immediately sought her rear view mirror.

A hundred or so yards behind her, a car was at the stop sign, about to leave the parking lot and turn onto Front Street. As the car's slightly crooked rear windshield brake light went out and the car turned to the left, something about the brake light reminded Virginia of—she shook her head, waiting until the car was out of sight—reminded her of what?

Keys in hand, she looked carefully around her before locking the car door and heading for the dock. The marina and fish house were deserted. Her dad, she knew, was up inside the boat, no doubt fast asleep.

She quietly climbed the ladder, slid open the rear door, entered, closed it, tiptoed through the main cabin past her sleeping father, reached the galley and changed out of her jeans and long-sleeved t-shirt into her favorite flannel nightshirt. She was soon snuggled in the galley bunk.

She was nearly asleep when a jarring, grating movement of the entire boat shook her instantly awake. She knew immediately what had happened and might happen again any moment.

Chaucer, perched high above the river's edge, had slid on the rails.

"Dad!" She called out to waken him, certain he had been asleep. Suddenly she felt sheepish, unsettled by a creak or groan of the hull. *Chaucer* was stable, high and dry. There should be no creaks, groans, or jarring grating motions—yet just now there was.

"The boat moved on the railway," she called out.

"No, she was just settling in the chocks."

"All right," Virginia called back uneasily, certain her father did not want to alarm her.

She knew he would wait until he thought she was asleep, then slip outside alone and make sure *Chaucer* was secure on the rails. She also knew what was foremost in his mind—after two weeks on the rails, the boat should be settled. She put her t-shirt back on and was fastening the last button of her jeans when the jarring, grating motion—this time longer in duration—occurred again.

She hurried aft to the main cabin, where her father was already dressed and cautiously opening the aft cabin door.

"I thought I might go down and make sure the chocks were secure," he said, heading onto the aft deck. Turning back, he mildly added, "and don't jump around so."

"I won't," Virginia replied, grateful he left unspoken the fact that boats had been known to fall off chocks and marine railways with disastrous results.

She followed her father out onto the aft deck. Climbing gingerly over the port side, she began to descend the ladder with a great deal more care than usual, as did her father.

"Did you bring a flashlight?" Virginia asked.

"I was about to ask you the same thing," Scotty answered. "Let's not risk climbing back up there 'til we know she's stable. We can see to examine the chocks on the port side."

All four port chocks, supporting the half of the boat lit by the street light that illuminated the Fish House dock, were securely curved into *Chaucer*'s hull, they soon discovered.

The starboard side of *Chaucer*, however, was in almost total darkness. Enough light shone beneath the hull from the port side for them to make their way between the huge wooden beams crossing the iron rail. At each beam they stopped and reached up into the darkness, making sure the chock that sat on the beam was tucked snuggly into the curvature of the boat's hull.

"I don't really expect to find anything amiss with the way *Chaucer* is chocked," Scotty said. "After all, we spent all day today working on the bow without moving any of them. And Lester has had no reason to move them, either."

"Every chock was secure late yesterday afternoon when we finished working on her," Virginia said.

"Well now that we've given ourselves a pep talk," Scotty said, "we might as well start checking this dark starboard side."

In deep shadow, Virginia checked the two forward chocks while Scotty checked the aft two.

"So far so good!" she called, feeling the first chock snugged tightly under the hold. She was reaching for the second chock when Scotty spoke.

"*These* aft chocks," he said, "are far from secure."

"What?" Virginia made her way across the railway timbers.

"Can you believe that?" Scotty said, aghast.

Virginia gulped. In the semi-darkness, she could see that one chock was pulled several inches out and no longer touching the hull. The other chock, the farthest aft, was pulled several feet out.

In shocked silence, Virginia and her father pushed the farthest chock back along the wide cross beam toward the boat, snugging it in place so that it once again hugged the curvature of the hull.

Only after shoving the second chock tightly into place against the hull did Virginia break the silence and voice what they had both left unspoken.

"I *know* we left the chocks secure and in place. *Chaucer* is forty feet long and weighs thousands of pounds—if she had fallen with us aboard..."

"—or fallen *on* us as we worked beneath her hull." Scotty frowned. "Who would have moved the chocks and put us in danger?"

Chapter Twelve

Virginia roused from a deep sleep to the urgent sound of her telephone ringing in the semi-darkness of her cabin. Not her cell phone—it was the ring of her land line, the one that ran from the land down the dock to her slip and inside to her phone aboard *Chaucer.*

It took her a few seconds to realize she and *Chaucer* were back home in their slip at Waccamaw Marina. By her side, Remy snored softly and Gabrielle, waking, leaped to the floor. Peering across the cabin at her alarm clock's luminous dial, Virginia sat up and reached over Remy's sleeping form for the receiver. Three-twenty. It must be a wrong number or something was terribly wrong—no one in their right mind would be calling her at this hour unless there was an emergency.

"Hello?"

"Tell Remy," the unsteady female voice at the other end said, "that I'm watchin' his house like I'm supposed to."

Virginia handed the phone to Remy, who had raised up on one elbow. "It's about your house. Someone from your neighborhood watch group?"

Remy sleepily raised the phone to his ear.

Virginia reached up and turned on the bedside cabin light just in time to see Remy's concerned face grow taut, then furious as he sat straight up in bed. "What the hell are you doing in my house?" he spoke icily into the phone, his tone accusing rather than questioning. "Get out of my house now."

Virginia could not make out any words from the other end of Remy's phone call, but she could hear the female voice on the line rising and falling until Remy interrupted.

"Did you hear me? Get out." Remy's voice was taut with quiet fury.

Virginia could not make out any words, but she could hear the female voice on the other end rushing on again, and rising as if in question.

"No. There is nothing to talk about. Get out of my house now."

Virginia forced herself to lie back down. *Who could be in Remy's house?*

"I'm calling the sheriff's department, and I suggest you be gone when they get there," he said. He hung up the phone and reached for his clothes. When the phone began ringing again, he picked up the receiver and quickly cut off the call.

"Don't answer your phone after I leave," he said to Virginia, punching numbers into the key pad of the receiver. Holding the phone under his chin, he pulled on his trousers. "And *don't* answer your door. If anybody steps on this boat, you call the sheriff's department. Cam—that woman I used to go out with—she broke into my house. She's way too drunk to drive up here, but stay locked up anyway. She—" he broke off. "Yes, hello, I'm in Murrells Inlet, and a drunk woman called me from my home on Pawleys Island. She broke in. Yes—Cam Jamison. Yes. I was asleep at my fiancée's home." He listened, then drew a sharp breath, hesitating. "Yes. Some are loaded. But she never mentioned guns, probably hasn't thought about them." He gave the dispatcher his address while buttoning his shirt.

"Don't worry, I'll be fine," Virginia said, watching him hang up. *Fiancée?* "Are you sure you should go home? From what you just said on the phone, she sounds dangerous."

"She is, believe me, but more to herself than anyone else. I have to go home—I couldn't go back to sleep wondering what damage she's done there."

He leaned over and kissed Virginia, then picked up his watch and strapped it on. "I'll call you in the morning. Go back to sleep, everything's all right, just aggravating as hell."

Virginia rose up to lock up behind him as he slid the aft cabin door open. "Remy, be careful."

Stepping out onto the aft deck, Remy turned and lit a cigarette. He exhaled a plume of smoke into the dark humid air. "I love you," he said, sliding the door shut.

Back in her berth, snuggled alone under the light down comforter, listening to the air conditioner humming comfortingly up in the saloon, Virginia hesitated before reaching up to pull the chain that turned off the bedside light.

She felt *Chaucer* move aft as Remy pulled her to the dock, then rock slightly to starboard as he stepped up onto the catwalk at the aft starboard corner.

I never could feel Gordon stepping off the boat, thought Virginia. *Remy steps off hard.*

She heard Remy's footsteps disappearing down the dock and felt the slight release of *Chaucer* sliding back forward then pulling lightly at her lines.

Her mind churned with questions and the events of the last few minutes. Why would a former girlfriend of Remy's break into his home? Why did she call him here, at Virginia's boat? And how did she even know he was here? *Fiancée.* What would it be like to be married to Remy?

Remy would reach his house soon. Would he get there before the deputies or Sheriff Bone? Remy had answered that there were loaded guns in his house. Virginia knew that, like Gordon had, Remy kept an extensive collection of firearms, all in perfect firing order, even the oldest weapons. What if that girl was drunk enough to shoot Remy? Most of his guns were not locked up, and any one he had been cleaning was usually left right out in the open, maybe even on the kitchen table.

Fighting the urge to call Remy's house and find out what was going on, Virginia turned out the light and closed her eyes. She would surely find out in the morning.

Just when Virginia's thoughts began to drift, a sure sign that sleep was near, a light bright enough to break through the filter of her curtains brought her back. A flash of distant headlights swept through Virginia's cabin, as occasionally occurred when a vehicle turned around in the middle of the marina parking lot. Only this time the lights stopped, their reflection motionless and glaring in the large round mirror over the vanity beside Virginia's berth.

She was out of her bunk, up the saloon steps, across the saloon, and down the galley steps within seconds. All she saw out of the galley porthole was the red glow of a broken tail light rounding the bend at the top of the hill leading out of the marina. At least it was leaving. Where had she seen a broken tail light like that before?

And what was going on right now at Remy's house? Remy had not yet had time to get there. Would he be up all night filing a report at the sheriff's department, if he wasn't shot dead first by that crazy drunk girl?

Remy will be fine, Virginia told herself. *There is nothing I can do right now that would not add to the confusion.*

She went back into her cabin, got in the bed, and pulled up the sheet.

Could this woman in Remy's house tonight be the same woman who left a voice message on Remy's answering machine the first night she and her dad had dinner at his house?

Virginia sat up, picked up the receiver, and dialed Remy's land line.

After one ring, the call was answered. "Remy. Remy, I know it's you. When are——"

Virginia slowly replaced the receiver. It sounded like the same woman, but she could not be sure.

Scritch, scritch.

Virginia started, then relaxed. The sound was only that of Gabrielle digging earnestly in her litter box.

Virginia's phone rang. Virginia bit her lip it as it rang twice more. Taking a deep breath, she picked up the receiver before the next ring. She bit her lip and placed the receiver against her ear.

"Virginia, you're *gone*." A loud click followed.

Slowly, Virginia replaced the receiver. It sounded like the same woman, but was it?

Chapter Thirteen

Morning found Virginia tossing fitfully in her bed, finally heading toward deep sleep despite the incessant ringing of the burglar alarm going off at Remy's house. *But how could that be?* He had told her himself that he did not have a burglar alarm, did not need one on Pawleys Island, and did not even lock his doors half the time.

Eventually Virginia's alarm clock wound down. She used a wind-up model due to the short-lived, but frequent, power outages the marina had experienced for years. When she finally woke and realized what happened, there was no time to call Remy. She had barely enough time to get dressed and make it to the shop in time to open at nine. Besides, she hoped Remy was able to sleep late after what had probably been a nearly sleepless night for him.

Releasing her parking brake and slowly easing her clutch out while backing up the riverside slope where she always parked facing the river, Virginia thought about the headlights shining in her boat last night. She paused after backing out and looked back at *Chaucer*. The headlights had shone from the stopped vehicle at about the same spot she was on now. From across the water you couldn't tell much about *Chaucer*'s interior—unless the curtains were open and someone was using binoculars, like that stranger was doing the day Remy first came there.

Virginia shook her head.

I'm getting paranoid again after last night, she chided herself, wishing she knew details.

Driving away from the river, she rolled down her window. The morning air was still humid, with a slight cool breeze off the river; cooler than her car's air conditioner would make the vehicle interior. The air-cooled engine of Virginia's 1976 Porsche supported a barely functioning air conditioning system unique to vehicles without a water-cooled engine. But the lack frigid air was worth it; she adored her old roadster.

She lifted her hair off her neck to catch one more river breeze as she rumbled out of the marina parking lot and onto Waccamaw Road, the winding two-and-a-half-mile-long live-oak-canopied road leading up to Ocean Highway 17. A cool breeze was easy to catch here on the river and over by the ocean, but the antique store she managed was located right between those two waters on Murrells Inlet's section of the Waccamaw Neck, the hottest, most humid stretch of land in the Carolinas.

The unseasonably cool weather front of the last two weeks, a blessing for the time she had spent on the marine railway, was just a memory now. By midday, the heat would be surreal with shimmery lines rising off the highway. She pulled up in front of Fox's Lair Antiques with ten minutes to spare.

As usual, she was cheered by the old brass fox-face door knocker on the weathered, rough-planked front door of the store. Then, her heart skipping a beat, she was reminded of the Cheshire cat knocker on Remy's front door. What on earth had finally happened there last night?

Was that woman—Cam—in jail now?

As Virginia turned her key in the lock of the heavy door, she heard the unmistakable rattling rumble of a diesel engine. Smiling to herself, she did not even have to turn around to know who was about to pull up in front of the store.

Seconds later, she heard tires crunch on the gravel, the diesel shut off, and a creaky door open. This was one of the reasons Virginia made sure to always have Fox's Lair Antiques open at nine sharp or earlier. Tourists meandered in and out in the late morning and through the afternoon, but locals like Miss Eugenia depended on her being open at nine sharp. Sometimes Miss Eugenia arrived even before that.

Pushing the big door open and leaving it, Virginia walked over to the big red dually pick-up truck as Miss Eugenia, adorned in three shades of flowing purple, slid off of the worn leather seat, climbed down the door sill, and stepped cautiously onto the gravel.

"What have you brought for us today, Miss Eugenia?"

"Some relics my dear, some relics, but it was most too hot to drive them up here, even with my air conditioner on full blast." Miss Eugenia took off her lavender straw hat and fanned her face.

"Are those, ah, relics in the back?" Virginia gestured toward the truck's high-sided bed.

"No, honey lamb, they're right here in the back seat."

Miss Eugenia reached up and opened the driver's side back door of the truck's crew cab.

"Looky here." She stepped back.

Virginia peered into the truck and gasped as she saw the top of a head. Last night still had her jumpy.

There on the seat of the truck lay a ship's figurehead. Another lay on the floor. Peering in, she saw that each was a nearly life-size wooden representation of a woman from just below the waist on up. Speechless, she gingerly placed her fingertips on the worn, cracked wood of the figurehead on the seat.

"That one's original," said Miss Eugenia proudly. "It's from one of those Civil War blockade runners, a paddle-wheeling steamship. Made to look like one of the ship owner's daughters since the ship was named after her."

"What was the ship's name—the daughter's name?" managed Virginia.

"George Trenholm, a good friend of my grandmama's grand-daddy, was the ship owner—he had lots of ships and several daughters. Grandmama told me he gave her granddaddy this figurehead, but I'm not sure of the name of his daughter or the ship. I'll have to try and remember. You know Georgetown is full of history, and relics like this."

Virginia looked down at the figurehead on the truck floor. A stately blue-eyed blonde in a sky-blue gown stared fixedly, one gloved hand shading her eyes. "And this one?"

"Not original, but still a relic," stated Miss Eugenia. "A replica relic."

Virginia tilted her head to one side, taking in the opera-length gloves encasing the replica figurehead's arms and the short capped sleeves, low-cut bodice, and drop-waist of her painted wooden dress. "Replica regency," she murmured.

"A good reproduction," Miss Eugenia added.

Although pristinely cool and crisp in air-conditioner preserved purple silk and linen, Miss Eugenia had begun sprouting beads of perspiration at her hairline as soon as her skin came into contact with the rapidly heating early morning humidity. Now a rivulet was trickling down the side of her forehead, sending her searching her purse for one of the cotton hankies she favored.

"Let's get you out of the sun, Miss Eugenia," said Virginia. "I just left the river, where there was a cool breeze. This is too hot to stand out in."

"Dear child," she mopped her face, "I believe you are finally going to need to open an antique shop on Front Street in Georgetown, and I know of just the place. It's busy, on the Harbor Promenade part of the river, on the boardwalk, and it catches a breeze off the bay all the time."

Virginia held her breath. She loved Fox's Lair Antiques and was proud to manage it, but she was longing for her own shop. Not just any antique shop, but one that specialized in maritime antiques, and antiques that could have been in antebellum seaside homes and sea captain's homes. She had gotten the idea of an antique shop in Georgetown during the Wooden Boat Festival last year, and walking on Front Street with Remy when *Chaucer* was on the railway last week had made her think about it again. And now this one was available. She bit her lip.

"That candle shop near the town clock," Miss Eugenia continued. "You know, the shop with the nice scent and the cedar shavings on the floor? They're moving, and they need someone to take over their lease—maybe even with an option to buy."

Virginia dared not hope. With its front door opening onto quaint, busy Front Street, and its back door opening onto Georgetown Harbor and the fabulous half-mile Sampit River Harbor Promenade, the candle shop would be a prime location for a maritime antique shop.

"Are you certain? The candle shop seemed to be doing well last week." The shop, right in the heart of Front Street, had its own boat slip on the Harbor Promenade, Virginia remembered. Maybe she could—

"The candle shop owners are moving the shop and their boat to Charleston. You know they live aboard that big sailboat behind the shop? The owner of the building is eager to get someone else in the building *and* the boat slip right away."

"Oh Miss Eugenia, you know I want to do this but now it's so sudden—it's been my dream for a long time but—"

Virginia turned as a British-racing-green Range Rover—same model Remy's, she thought, only green—pulled into the space next to Miss Eugenia's. With a swish of long, wavy sienna-and-gold hair, the driver smiled warmly at the women as she got out and headed toward the door of Fox's Lair Antiques.

"I'll tell the owner of the candle shop—his mother is my next-door-neighbor—that you'll be at the shop this evening, six o'clock. I'd be there myself, but I have a Daughters of the War Between the States field trip to the Relic Room at the State House in Columbia and likely won't be back yet," Miss Eugenia said, turning to begin laboriously climbing up into the seat of her truck. "Thank you, my dear," she breathed as Virginia gave her a hand up. "I'll just hold onto these treasures a bit longer—you may need them for inventory in your new shop!"

Facing east as Miss Eugenia backed up onto the frontage road, Virginia shaded her eyes from the morning sun. She knew Miss Eugenia meant well, but this was so sudden.

Miss Eugenia rolled her window down before she drove away and leaned out.

"There's a big copper slipper-shaped bathing tub back here, too," she gestured with her thumb toward her truck bed. "I'll save it for your new shop!"

"I'll try to be there before—" Virginia called, but Miss Eugenia was already roaring away, "—before six," she finished, laughing to herself as she caught a glimpse of the copper slipper bathing tub glinting in the sun. Whimsical and mercurial, Miss Eugenia was also a shrewd business woman—two ship's figure heads and a rare copper bathing tub in the window of a new antique shop were bound to draw lots of customers.

She headed into Fox's Lair in the wake of her newly arrived customer. The woman, dressed in rough-textured cinnamon-colored raw silk blouse and trousers, looked slightly sun-kissed and very well-exercised. With an elegant toss of her long tresses, she extended her hand and smiled. "Are you Virginia, Remy Ravenel's fiancée?"

Fiancée? Fiancée? Virginia gulped. Oh no, was this another ex-girlfriend? Surely not Cam from last night—she'd still have a hangover.

"No! I'm not, I mean, yes, I'm Virginia." Flustered, Virginia smiled, extending her hand. "How do you do?"

"Very well, and pleased to meet you. I'm Renee Ravenel-Ryan, Remy's former wife."

Uh-oh, thought Virginia. "I'm pleased to meet you, too," she said, returning the woman's firm but gentle handshake.

How very formal, Virginia thought, until the woman put her hand on Virginia's arm and locked Virginia's gaze with her large, expressive brown eyes.

"Honey," said Renee gently, "I've come to warn you the way I wish someone had warned me."

Oh no, Virginia thought again. *First, his former girlfriend going ballistic last night, and now his ex-wife going from formal to cozy in seconds and then warning me about him.*

"It's not what you think." Renee brushed a long lock of silky hair away from her cheek. Tilting her head prettily to one side, she regarded Virginia soberly. "I just hate to see him hurt you."

Virginia raised her eyebrows and nodded expectantly. She would listen, but wasn't this the unfaithful wife who left Remy for another man?

"Remy," said Renee carefully, "is a cheater. More than a cheater... he can't *stop* cheating. I used to believe if I waited long enough, one of his girlfriends would eventually kill him." She sighed. "But," she paused, narrowing her eyes slightly, "I finally had to divorce him."

Virginia swallowed. That was exactly what she had thought about Gordon! But Remy had assured her his wife was unfaithful to him and left him for another man. *Oh no, oh no. No, no.* This was strange. Very strange. "Thank you," she managed.

"He called the other day to tell me he'd gotten serious about you," Renee continued. "Actually, he talked to my husband and told *him*. They get along well. And me? I've found true happiness," she smiled, putting her hand gently on Virginia's arm once more. Her smile warmed the corners of her eyes, then she shook her head. "But that could never have happened with someone like Remy. People like him never change. I hate to use a cliché, but you know, a leopard won't *ever* change his spots." Renee smiled again, and with a little wave of her fingers, was out the door.

Watching Renee's Range Rover head south onto the highway, Virginia tapped her forefinger thoughtfully against her chin. *Remy and Renee*, she thought *Remy and Renee Ravenel. How precious.*

She looked up as the nineteenth-century moon-phase grandfather clock standing against the wall beside the front door chimed once for nine-thirty. It had been an eventful morning already, and the store had only been open half an hour.

Remy had not been divorced long, and his ex was already married? And issuing warnings about Remy? *Hmmnnn.* The similarities were too coincidental for Virginia's liking.

Reaching into the roll-top desk beside the cash register, she took out a pair of gloves and the container of silver polish. She had a lot to do before her twelve-thirty lunch with her friend

Belinda. Pulling on the gloves, Virginia had to smile. *Wait until I tell Belinda*, she thought.

Dr. Belinda Bunnelle, a clinical psychologist with a busy counseling office in Myrtle Beach, was one of Virginia's closest friends. She had moved her practice from Charlotte, North Carolina two years ago. Now, in addition to her regular practice, she stayed busy writing a syndicated self-help column based with the Myrtle Beach newspaper and hosted a weekly local radio show during which listeners called in their problems. She was going to have a fit when she heard about Virginia's experiences last night and this morning.

Chapter Fourteen

Just before noon Virginia answered the phone on the seventh ring. "Fox's Lair Antiques."

"Hey, honey." Remy sounded relaxed.

"Remy—" she shifted the phone to her shoulder as she finished polishing the last crevice of tarnish from a Victorian sterling tea ball, "are you all right?"

"Oh yes. You must be busy—took you a while to answer the phone."

"A lot has happened in the past twelve hours," Virginia replied, "and I'm just catching up. Thank goodness you're all right. Did she harm anything?"

"Cam? She just harmed her dignity, that's all. Everything's fine now."

Virginia could hardly believe her ears. "Last night you felt it was urgent to get her out of your house—I was afraid she'd shoot you or something. Does the sheriff's department think everything's fine now?"

"Those two deputies were glad she was okay," Remy said. "When they opened the front door, they saw my Henry hanging on the hall tree first thing."

"Right where you keep it," said Virginia, picturing his Civil War-era repeating rifle resting in its brass hooks on the antique hall tree.

"And the second thing they saw was my Army Colt on the kitchen table."

"Where you'd left it after you finished cleaning it," Virginia surmised.

"Right. And they didn't know how many other guns were in the house. They weren't even sure Cam was still there. The liquor cabinet was wrecked—every bottle was open. Some of them were empty, others spilled on the rug. The CD player was wide open, CD cases all over the rug...the place was a big mess."

Virginia winced, picturing the gorgeous oriental carpet near the CD player.

"They found her upstairs, passed out across my bed. But when they first saw her—"

"They thought she had shot herself. On your bed."

"Right. When I arrived, they were helping her up, having just discovered she was alive."

"Has anyone bailed her out?"

"She left here a couple of hours ago. She's okay, and very, very embarrassed. She said to tell you she was sorry for ruining our night."

Virginia could scarcely believe her ears. "You didn't have her arrested? *She's been at your house all night?* And half the morning? *After what she did?*"

"Well, she couldn't drive herself, and there was no one to come and get her—"

"Remy, how could you even sleep with such a *deranged person* in your house? I would have been *beside* myself with worry if I had known—there was nowhere else she could have been taken until she was sober enough to drive?"

"Well, nowhere here on the island. Most of the houses close by are weekly rentals this time of year and—" he stopped. "Honey," he asked incredulously, "you're not angry are you? I mean, she's just a friend."

"*Just a friend?*"

"Yes. While I was going through such a hard time with my divorce, she was an understanding friend, just a friend, and she," he lowered his voice, "took things a bit too seriously. Last night happened because she was a little upset that you and I are so suddenly nearly engaged—"

"Nearly *engaged?*" Virginia sucked in her breath. "Remy, I don't understand what you mean by that. And your wife—"

"Virginia, honey, I have been so swept away by you—you can have dinner over here tonight, can't you?" A door shut in the background.

"Remy? What was that noise?"

"What? Oh, the wind blew the door shut."

"What does she look like? In case she comes up here."

"Cam—oh she's small, has blonde hair—but honey, don't worry about her, she meant no harm—I know last night must have freaked you out. Let's relax tonight."

"This has been such a day—I have to be in Georgetown this evening after work. Remember how I mentioned I was interested in opening my own antique store? To specialize in nautical antiques?"

"Yeeeesssss…." Remy drew a breath. "*Seriously*? In Georgetown?"

"Yes! I'm going to look at the store this evening—it's where that candle shop is near the town clock."

"Virginia, that's a perfect location—it has a boat slip too."

"I know."

Remy was quiet for a few seconds. "How did you hear about this?"

"Miss Eugenia Allston, from Georgetown. She's been bringing antiques up here to Fox's Lair for years."

"Oh, I know who you mean. I've never actually met her, but I know who you're talking about. She's quite a character." Remy paused. "Well, let's have dinner afterwards in Georgetown. At the River Room?"

"I'd love to. Meet me at the candle shop, about six?"

"Six it is. I love you."

"I love you, too. 'Bye."

"Oh, Virginia, wait. Did you find my watch by the bed?"

"No, I remember you strapping it on while you were standing there telling me goodbye."

"Oh." Remy sounded disappointed. "I thought I remembered putting it on, too, but my leaving was so sudden, and I can't find it anywhere."

"I'll keep an eye out for it," Virginia promised. "See you this evening. Oh—I nearly forgot—your—Renee stopped by." Virginia held her breath.

"*Renee!*" Remy said her name as though pronouncing a food that gave him indigestion. He sighed. "Well, I guess it was inevitable. Don't listen to anything she says. She has a silver tongue. And she's a professional storyteller, you know. See you tonight."

Hanging up the phone, Virginia felt she might burst with excitement. She could be on the cusp of opening her own store! And she and Remy were together —but she was certainly not about to marry again, not any time soon, despite what he might be telling people. She would definitely have to do some serious thinking about that, at a later time. *I wonder why he thinks it is okay to be telling people that? We haven't even discussed such a possibility!*

Still, Virginia reasoned, *Remy is a treasure, and anyone our age naturally has baggage. I certainly have my share—a dead husband who might have been murdered, and a cloud of suspicion hanging over my head.* She gnawed her lower lip. *But why would Remy's former wife feel the need to warn her?*

*****

"Virginia." Belinda laid her spinach-and-chicken quesadilla down on her plate, shaking her head in disbelief. "It's a good thing we're having lunch today. This is some serious stuff. I don't know whether to encourage you to hang in there because Remy sounds like such a prize or to urge you to cut your losses because this man could be a classic womanizer." She delicately blew upwards at an errant strand of blonde hair. "That helmet doesn't do much for my hair, but I wouldn't even take my bike to the end of my driveway without it."

Dr. Belinda Bunnelle, as femininely elegant as she was strong, rode her Harley-Davidson nearly everywhere she went—in good weather. She was a stickler for safety.

"Belinda, he's not a womanizer," Virginia protested, heaping sour cream on her own plain spinach quesadilla. "He's just too sympathetic in regards to his crazy ex-girlfriend."

"And now he's referring to you as his fiancée! Honestly, girl, I don't know whether to start shopping for a bridesmaid's dress or planning an intervention!"

Virginia looked furtively at the nearby tables in El Casa Grande to make sure no one was being entertained by this conversation. "I must say I was a little taken aback when Remy's ex-wife quoted him referring to me his fiancée."

Belinda made a face. "A little taken aback? You mean a little shocked, don't you?"

"Yes, but in a good way." Virginia grinned.

"A good way as in warm fuzzies, hearts, and rainbows? Or a good way as in ready-to-commit-after-a-couple-of-weeks? If it's the latter, that's not good. And him so newly divorced!"

"I told you how carefully he explained his divorce—"

"Remember the way Gordon was always explaining things?" Belinda asked. "And he didn't even have a painful divorce to blame his behavior on—the jackass had never even been married before. How about that time you were stuck on the ski lift with Gordon, and he entertained himself by confessing to you about the girl he spent the night with and took out on a date in your car while you were visiting your folks for Thanksgiving? Then after you got upset, he told you he was joking. And *then* you married him!"

"He wasn't joking," Virginia replied. "He just didn't want me to push him out of the lift two hundred feet off the ground. *But*, Remy is *not* Gordon."

"Well," replied Belinda, returning to her quesadilla, "maybe Remy doesn't have that sadistic streak that Gordon called a 'sense of humor,' but he seems to be carrying around a lot of the past—a recent ex-girlfriend, an ex-wife who actually came and warned you about him—" she stopped to nibble a dangling bit of spinach.

"Oh, Belinda," Virginia sighed, "if anyone's carrying around too much of the past, it's me. Sometimes I get so angry just thinking about Gordon's little sordid affairs—especially the last one—and how gullible I was not to see they were happening. Then I remember he's dead, and I feel guilty about being angry. And, I feel naïve for not seeing how unfaithful he was for so long. " She surveyed her quesadilla. "I can't pick this up with all this sour cream." She busied herself with her knife and fork, cutting off a bite-sized morsel.

"You didn't *want* to see how unfaithful Gordon was," Belinda said gently. "You didn't want to know because you didn't want to be hurt and angry and end things with him."

"And then when I *did* see how unfaithful he was, I was actually hoping one of his girlfriends would get fed up with his lying ways and off him, so I could be a widow and not have to get divorced. I certainly didn't want to stay married to him, but I really didn't want to be a divorcée."

"Maybe that's what happened," Belinda suggested. "Remember the florist, I mean *floral designer*, who did the plants and flower arrangements for his office—and landscaping—what was her name— Pamela? Camille? I thought she sounded a little unstable."

"Cameron. But she tried to hurt herself, not Gordon, when he broke up with her."

"Anyone who will hurt themselves will hurt someone else, given the right circumstances."

"I don't know. All I know is if I hadn't been divorcing him, he might be alive now."

Virginia's fork trembled the tiniest bit as she finally lifted the bite to her mouth.

Belinda gave Virginia a pointedly unsympathetic look. "Stop wasting your sympathy on Gordon. If he'd been faithful to you, you'd still be together and he would have been with you that night instead of rummaging around in that god-forsaken old shed."

"No one ever did figure out what he was doing there," Virginia said moodily, swirling the ice in her sweet tea with her straw. "There was a reason. There had to have been. Gordon always had a mental agenda—nothing he did was without purpose."

"Hey, I'm sorry," Belinda sighed. "I didn't mean to get on the subject of Gordon—and you know I'm saying this as a friend, but it's the same advice I'd give one of my patients. You know that women tend to be attracted to the same kind of man over and over again, and this 'rapid' Remy—"

"—is like no one else in the world." *Rapid Remy, indeed.* Smiling, Virginia held up her tea glass in a mock toast. "Remy is my reward for all I went through with Gordon." She leaned back in her chair.

Raising her eyebrows, Belinda folded her arms. "He is, huh?"

"I know things are moving awfully fast with Remy, but—" she hesitated, "I knew him before, though not for very long. He and I dated near the end of my senior year at Coastal."

Belinda frowned. "I thought you met Gordon near the end of your senior year at Coastal."

"I did." Virginia smiled one-sidedly, her voice wistful. "That's when I stopped seeing Remy, when I met Gordon. I dated Gordon for nearly eight years. And he was in graduate school there before we married. Then everything was great for five years, until he got his first girlfriend—"

"—that you *knew* of," interrupted Belinda.

"—that I knew of," amended Virginia.

"And this has what to do with Rapid Remy?"

Virginia smiled. If she responded to the "Rapid Remy" nickname, Belinda would always call him that. "After thirteen years," she said carefully, "Gordon turned out to be a terrible husband. Eight years is a long time to date someone to make sure he's the one, and then he's not. So maybe a," she cleared her throat, "*rapid* involvement is not such a bad thing, eh?"

"Point taken," Belinda nodded. "Still, I hear you trying to convince yourself. You *do* have doubts and questions about him—Remy—right now. Why?"

Virginia was silent for a moment, nibbling thoughtfully on a tortilla chip. Finally, she spoke. "I just can't seem to appreciate him. Something is holding me back, and I don't know what it is."

"There's nothing wrong with holding back. After all, you haven't been together very long. It's wise to hold back."

"Every time I begin relaxing with him, I start feeling watchful. And jumpy. That can't be normal, can it?"

"After what you went through with Gordon, yes." Belinda tilted her head. "Virginia, enjoy. Just be careful. Don't forget that his trust quotient is measured in deeds, not words. And remember this—"

Sliding to the edge of her chair, Virginia leaned forward. Any time Belinda said, 'remember this—' she was about to impart a pearl of wisdom worth memorizing word for word.

"Don't listen to what he says." Belinda pointed her fork at Virginia. *Watch what he does.*

Chapter Fifteen

A cooling breeze was blowing in from the Atlantic across Winyah Bay and the Sampit River when Virginia rolled down her car window on Georgetown's Front Street. The light wind lifted her hair off her neck.

I can't wait to open a shop here, she thought. *I hope.*

A mental picture of the awful cryptic message falling out of the newspaper flashed, unbidden, across her mind. *Could someone here in Georgetown know who was responsible for Gordon's death? And why,* she thought, *did the message say I'm next?*

Stop it, she told herself. *Next you'll have the sky darkening and buzzards circling.*

Curtains billowed out from between the open shutters and casements of the windows in the story above the candle shop. *I wonder who lives up there,* she thought—*will that be vacant too? And the boat slip behind the shop—I wonder how soon I can move* Chaucer *there.* She smiled at her childlike optimism. It might be a good idea to see if she could afford the store rental first.

Remy's blue Range Rover was already there parked in front of the candle shop. She smiled again, shaking her head. His ex-wife's vehicle was identical, but for the color.

Virginia pulled into the space next to his, shifted into neutral, and set the parking brake, just to make sure it was in working order. Usually she sufficed with leaving the transmission in gear.

Seconds later she stood at the open door of what she hoped would soon be Cheshire Cat Maritime Antiques—she hadn't been able to get Remy's copper Cheshire cat door knocker out of her thoughts. For now, it was still a candle shop, with fragrant cedar shavings on the hardwood floor, but the display windows were empty and packing boxes lined the walls.

She saw Remy silhouetted against the open back door, his lithe, Levi-clad frame backlit by the late afternoon sun reflecting off the Sampit River. The breeze ruffled his golden hair, and across the river, the tops of the pines and cedars on Goat Island. Virginia was struck by the juxtaposition of Remy compared to the small, mousy young man with whom he was animatedly conversing.

They both turned when Virginia walked in.

Remy winked at the man and stepped forward to take Virginia's hand and kiss her on the cheek. "And here she is. Andy, this is my fiancée, Virginia. Virginia, Andy," Remy smiled.

"Andy and his wife are moving their candle shop and sailboat to Charleston, as Miss Eugenia probably told you."

Virginia pursed her lips and then smiled. *Fiancée—again!* She must speak to Remy in private about that immediately. He had not even asked her! Even if he had, it was too soon anyway.

"You're a lifesaver, Virginia, if you lease this shop," said Andy, shaking her hand. "After renting it for three years, we bought it last month, then a fantastic location below Charleston opened up, a waterfront store like this with dockage nearby. We're keeping our house here in Georgetown, next door to Miss Eugenia," he added. "She's a wonderful next door neighbor, and our house has been in my mother's family since the mid-1700s, just like Miss Eugenia's. Come on," he gestured toward the front of the store, "I'll show you a couple of quirks in the lighting system you need to know how to tweak. Save you a lot of electrician bills. Sometimes this wiring is ornery."

"I'll be out here having a smoke," called Remy, heading out the back door onto the river walk as Virginia followed Andy toward the front of the store.

After showing Virginia the switchbox and its oddities, Andy peeked around the corner and down the length of the store. Remy was on the back deck, his back to them, cigarette in one hand, hips against the railing, facing the river and Goat Island. His head was tilted back and a perfect ring of smoke rose above him into the air.

"A complete hedonist, that one," Andy said quietly, smiling and shaking his head. "How long have you known him?"

"We dated in college, but," Virginia admitted, "up until recently, we hadn't spent any time together since."

"Well, keep your eyes open. People change. Don't get me wrong, he's a nice guy." Andy said, heading toward the back of the store. "Just be aware."

Virginia's eyes widened with surprise, then she nodded knowingly back at Andy—not beware but *be aware*. He meant well, bless his heart. Men like him were always a little envious of men like Remy.

*****

Half an hour later, Virginia and Remy left the shop. Virginia had a handshake deal with Andy for a year's rental of the building and boat slip. She had forgotten to ask Andy about the upstairs renter but surely she would run into the renter soon. Andy's comment about Remy had thrown her for a second—until she realized Andy was just a little jealous of Remy. Still, she would definitely keep her eyes open.

Dinner, including an entrée of mouthwatering grilled salmon and lightly fried oysters, flew by. Over shared desserts of chocolate mud pie and crème Brule, she excitedly planned period window displays and told Remy about the ship's figureheads Miss Eugenia had for the shop. As they walked out of the River Room, past the tall, life-like pirate guarding the door, Remy put his arm around her shoulders.

"How about some vintage mannequins?"

"*Vintage* mannequins?" Virginia tilted her head to one side, looking up at Remy. "I'd love some, but they're pretty rare. Most of the wax ones from the twenties melted in storage attics or hot display windows, and the earlier papier-mâché ones disintegrated if they got wet."

"These are early fiberglass ones, probably from the 1930s." Remy replied. "If you have any vintage nautical clothing from that period, they'd be perfect. And they'd be better than modern mannequins for showing historic clothing, like your Civil War reenactment clothing, for example, to compliment your ship's figureheads or other antiques."

"I'd love to look at them," Virginia said, as they rounded the corner onto Front Street. "Where did you see them?"

"Right up there," Remy smiled and pointed, dipping his head and looking up.

Virginia looked up at the second story of the building on the end of the block. Clustered at each end of the building's three windows were several motionless forms staring out over the darkened street.

"How eerie!" Involuntarily, she shivered.

"Yes, but up close they look pretty friendly. And they really are antiques. None of them need wigs—they have stylized molded hair, like ship's figureheads. They do need some work—but auto body filler should do the trick—if you're interested."

"I am—but I don't even know if they're for sale and—"

"They're for sale," Remy smiled.

"But how did—"

"I checked," Remy grinned. "Three hundred dollars for the lot of them. A dozen or so."

At Virginia's surprised look he went on. "I've been busy since you told me this afternoon about wanting your own store here. Mr. Vogel is having his old department store building," Remy nodded toward the mannequins, "made into river-front resort condos on the second floor and specialty shops on the ground level. He's selling those mannequins as soon as he can. But they do need some work."

"How much work?"

"Most of it you could do with the auto body filler and paint," Remy answered. "Mr. Vogel said the removable parts—arms, hands, some of the legs—are the most damaged but are mostly interchangeable since they were all made by the same company. He said you should be able to get at least three complete mannequins out of the group."

"I would love to get them and repair them," Virginia. "Real antique mannequins, with stylized molded hair—but I don't have the space to put a dozen mannequins."

Remy cocked his head to one side. "I do."

Virginia raised her eyebrows. "But your workshop doesn't have room for—"

"The breezeway beneath my house—it has all the elements you need for the job—cool, sheltered, plenty of ventilation—"

"—your excellent company," Virginia chimed in.

"—and my excellent company," Remy grinned. "How about it? Deal?"

"Deal," Virginia grinned, looking from Remy to the candle shop, her soon-to-be maritime antiques shop. Glancing up as a movement caught her eye, she caught a fleeting glimpse of a face drawing back from the one of the second story apartment windows.

I wonder who lives upstairs, she thought, taking a second look. The only movement now was the cream-colored curtains wafting in the breeze.

Chapter Sixteen

The next morning Virginia gave a month's notice to Mr. Kimbel at Fox's Lair Antiques. Congratulating her and applauding her decision to specialize in maritime antiques, he insisted she did not need to work a notice with him. "Honey, I'm so proud that you'll be down there in Georgetown sending customers my way, I want you to start on your own shop immediately."

"Oh, Mr. Kimbel, I couldn't leave you in a lurch like that," Virginia said.

"*Au contraire*, my dear, it'll do me good to be my only employee for a while. Now you know you must send customers my way, like Herbert does," Mr. Kimbel enthused, clasping his hands engagingly across his chest. "You are my second manager-protégé to go out on your own, and I am so very proud."

Herbert was the previous manager of Fox's Lair. He had left to open a highly successful golfing antiques shop up above Myrtle Beach in Little River.

"I hope my shop will be as successful as Herbert's, and yours," Virginia said, humbled and slightly awed. Mr. Kimbel's endorsement was akin to a prophesy of success.

"Honey, you'd swear you were in nineteenth-century Edinburgh the moment you walk the front door of Herbert's shop," Mr. Kimbel enthused. "When I come visit your store down in Georgetown, I expect to feel as if Humphrey Bogart had just fired up the *African Queen*, or Blackbeard was going to invite me aboard the *Queen Anne's Revenge*, or Johnny Depp was about to set sail on the *Black Pearl*."

"I'll make you proud," Virginia promised.

"Now you take any or all of the nautical antiques from Fox's Lair on consignment to start the inventory of your new store," Mr. Kimbel insisted.

Fox's Lair mainly specialized in fox hunting antiques due to its immediate proximity to the highly equine Waccamaw Plantation, a former rice plantation now known for its equestrian center and avid fox hunters.

"You need all this—this *water* stuff. There's more in the storage room, old fly-fishing gear and such."

*****

That afternoon in the storage room, Virginia nearly whooped for joy, finding a cornucopia of antique nautical treasures: wooden ice-fishing decoys, hand-carved duck decoys, turn-of-the-century hand-tied flies, and wooden-handled dip nets, several brass-based compasses, and a brass sextant for celestial navigation.

Underneath the nets she discovered an antique fishing basket with copper buckles on aged leather straps. *This,* she decided, *would be perfect for Remy.*

Backing out of her parking space at the store that afternoon, the brake light on her dashboard began flashing. Automatically reaching down beside her seat for the emergency hand brake, she discovered it was already down, in the disengaged position, and the vivid red light was still flashing.

Gingerly pulling up, expecting to feel a drag in the car's momentum, she grimaced as nothing happened. Lowering the handle, she worked it up and down to no avail.

Sighing, Virginia headed toward Georgetown and the only garage she trusted to deal with the idiosyncrasies of her beloved car. She had never needed to use the emergency hand brake for stopping, but it was a necessary piece of safety equipment, and she wanted it to be repaired immediately.

While she rarely used the brake for parking on a hill, preferring to leave her car in gear, Remy set the emergency brake when parking anywhere near the slope overlooking the marina.

It was a good thing the light came on, or she would never have known the brake was out.

At the garage, Virginia was informed that the ratcheting mechanism had worn out and was not exacting enough pressure for the brake to hold.

A new brake and handle were ordered and would arrive at the garage in five days.

Gage, the owner, taped black electrical tape over the vividly flashing brake light, so Virginia could drive without distraction.

"Be careful, now," he told her, scowling. "I don't like sending you off without an emergency brake for five days."

"I doubt I'll even need it," Virginia smiled. "I hardly ever use it. But I'll warn my friend who does, in case he drives it."

*****

Thursday morning dawned foggy, damp, and grey, the kind of weather Virginia had loved ever since she moved aboard the boat. On days like this, when boating sounded like the last thing a person would want to do, she relished *Chaucer*'s cheery snugness.

This morning she settled down with a bowl of pumpkin granola and cup of coffee at the mahogany map table in the saloon. She looked out across the steely grey water of the marina.

Sliding her bare feet along the smooth red and gold planks under her captain's chair, Virginia felt peaceful and relaxed, and ready to face future adventures. Mentally, she mapped out the next few days.

Saturday she would move into her new store in Georgetown. Remy was working on her sign. Andy and his wife were moving their candle shop out today and tomorrow, and had assured her she could go ahead and move in, then apply to City Hall for a business license on Monday morning. She would keep *Chaucer* here in Murrells Inlet at the marina until the end of the month. Her dockage was paid through then, and she would hopefully be finished settling into her new shop at that point. She would commute the twenty-five miles to Georgetown each day until she was ready to bring *Chaucer* down.

Last night, Remy had announced his plan to install a CD player and new speakers in Virginia's car as a grand opening present for her new commute. It was only half an hour's drive from the marina down to Georgetown, but Remy had insisted it be thirty minutes with music and state-of-the-art audio.

"You can't play your harmonica all the time you're driving," he grinned, merrily refusing to divulge any details about the sound system. "It's already not a surprise, so I can't tell you anything else."

"Remember," Virginia cautioned, "the emergency brake is out, so be careful. I'll never enjoy my new CD player if you get run over installing it."

"I'll move your car back onto the parking lot then, on flat, level ground. I'm not like you crazy daredevil boat dwellers who have to park their cars on the slippery grass sloping down to the river."

Virginia smiled to herself, remembering Remy clowning around the night before, trying to make light of the fact he was installing a very expensive sound system in her car. She was surprised and delighted when she accidentally spied the boxes in the back seat of his Range Rover. He was installing in her car a sound system identical to the one he had installed in his own vehicle.

If Remy is going to that much trouble for me, she thought, *he ought to have a clean car to work in.*

Since Remy was gone, doing some early morning fishing, Virginia decided to take the Porsche out to wash it and to vacuum and detail the interior.

Taking her second cup of coffee with her, she sat in the driver's seat, drinking it while waiting for the engine of the Porsche to warm up. Warming up was crucial to the old engine in this weather, despite careful maintenance. If not idled long enough on a damp morning, it would cause the engine to skip miserably and stall as she backed up the grassy slope.

The needle on the RPM gauge fell gradually, indicating that the engine was getting warm.

Virginia pressed the accelerator experimentally. Perfect. The engine was purring smoothly. It was time to move.

Depressing the clutch and brake, she maneuvered the wooden-knobbed steel shifter into reverse. Taking her foot off the brake, she let up on the clutch as she depressed the accelerator.

The Porsche seemed to rise a bit, but no backward motion was occurring. Frowning, Virginia tried again. Had she missed reverse? Was the reverse gear wearing out? Easing the shifter into neutral then slowly back into reverse, she tried letting up the clutch once more. She was definitely in reverse—the car was pulling and straining back. It just was not moving.

Trying again, she shook her head, biting her lower lip, concentrating hard.

Each time she returned the shifter to neutral, the car rolled several inches down the incline toward the river as Virginia removed her foot from the clutch to apply the brake.

That emergency brake would surely come in good now, Virginia thought. Shifting into reverse, she turned off the ignition, exasperated. Maybe Remy was right when he said she and her neighbors were crazy daredevils to park on the grass sloping down toward the river. A driver less experienced with straight drive transmission like she had, and a faulty emergency brake, would have been in the river by now.

Virginia stepped out of the car and peered beneath the low-slung chassis. What mechanical disaster was awaiting her under there?

Surprised, she stared for a few seconds. The only thing amiss underneath the Porsche was a pair of concrete blocks, one behind each rear tire.

Slightly angled as the car was toward the dock, Virginia did not see these when she approached the car from the dock ten minutes earlier.

Someone deliberately placed those concrete blocks behind my wheels, she thought—the placement was far too accurate to assume otherwise.

Virginia shivered in the damp air, the ominous implications of what had just occurred filling her mind. Her car had rolled a few inches every time she changed it in and out of gear and braked in between. The rolling was a natural occurrence, even for the most skilled driver, in such a situation, she reasoned, so the car could have, without its emergency brake, rolled into the river had Virginia not kept her wits about her.

The river here was quite deep even at the edge, she knew, having been dredged for the marina. Virginia hated to think about rolling unexpectedly into the deep, fog-shrouded water.

Striding angrily to the rear of the car, she dragged the first heavy block aside.

On flat ground this stunt would have been merely irritating, but here on the steep incline at river's edge it could have ruined her car—or caused her to drown. Virginia banished the thought that one or both of these outcomes may have been the culprit's intention.

Careful not to let the car roll any closer to the river, she depressed the clutch and the brake, cranked the engine, took her foot off the brake and slowly released the clutch while accelerating as she backed up the steep incline.

Breathing a shaky sigh of relief, she heard the crunch of gravel as her tires backed onto the level ground of the gravel road that ran between the incline and the parking lot. In her rear view she saw Derek in the marina pickup truck.

He got out and came to her window. "Hey Virginia," he said, nodding toward the blocks sitting on the grassy slope, "you chock your wheels to park?"

"No. Those blocks were *behind* my tires. Someone put them there for me to back up against."

Derek scowled. "That's sick. That could've put you in the river, and we've got it dredged to seventeen feet there."

"See anyone suspicious, this morning, last night?" Virginia asked hopefully.

Derek shook his head. "Nope, but I'll keep an eye out."

*****

Later, sitting on the vinyl-covered sofa of the customer's lounge at Inlet Car Clean waiting for her car to be finished, she pulled the receipt for the emergency brake out of her purse. *It should have arrived by now,* she thought, but the garage had not called. If, perchance it had arrived, she needed it installed immediately. What if she had panicked? Or if Remy had started the engine and not her? He always used the emergency brake and would probably have rolled off the steep bank into the deep river. He didn't even know the emergency brake was out until last night—she hadn't mentioned it before, since he had not been in the car in the three days since the brake had malfunctioned. Well, this was day four. The new brake would be here tomorrow at the latest and she would make sure it was installed as soon as it arrived.

Virginia left the coolness of the customers' lounge and walked into the muggy heat outside. Taking her cell phone out of her purse, she pressed the garage number as the cool, damp wind off the ocean chilled the backs of her knees.

After listening to her inquiry, the mechanic who answered the phone asked her to hold. In a moment the familiar voice of Gage, the owner who had worked on her car for years, came on the line. He did not sound as friendly as usual.

"We still have the emergency brake," Gage said. "I hadn't de-cided yet whether to send it back or keep it for stock, although for your model and year, it's not an item we get calls for very often."

"Send it back?" Virginia was puzzled. "Since it's here, can you install it this morning, if you can work me in?"

"Virginia, what are you talking about? We don't often order a specialty part for a good customer, pay for it C.O.D., then have the customer call us and say they don't need the part anymore because they've already had the work done by another garage who got the part faster."

"There must have been a mix-up in the message," Virginia said. "My car still needs an emergency brake, and I *never* called to say otherwise. And no one else has worked on this car in years."

"Well, I know I haven't talked to you since the day you came in needing it," Gage admitted, "but I got a message when I came back from my lunch hour yesterday that you had called to cancel your emergency brake because you'd already had one installed some-where else. Right after the brake arrived by truck." The slightly miffed tone returned to his voice. "We could have ordered it to be here the next day if you had asked."

"Oh no, regular shipping was fine," Virginia assured him. "I just had a little incident this morning that made me want the new emergency brake installed as soon as it came in. Since it's here, is there any chance of having it installed this morning?"

"Sure thing. Bring it on in."

*****

Driving back to the marina with her Porsche sleekly detailed in-side and out and its newly installed emergency brake glinting blackly from beside the driver's seat, Virginia pulled out her harmonica and played a few bars, trying to dispel her unpleasant thoughts.

Placing the harmonica on her lap to gear down to fourth, then third, as she turned on to Waccamaw Road, she bit her lip.

Who could have put those cement blocks behind her wheels? She was lucky she did not have to wait another week for her emergency brake. Normally the garage was meticulous about parts ordered. How could they have messed up a message so badly as to think she had called and cancelled her order? Unless someone actually did call and cancel her order, but why would anyone do that?

Chapter Seventeen

Preoccupied with celebrating her new shop, Virginia forgot to even mention to Remy the morning's disturbing events.

As cautious as she was accustomed to being after Gordon's death, she could scarcely believe she was crazily, happily falling in love and forgetting to list reasons not to do so.

Remy stepped aboard *Chaucer* with an armful of roses at six o'clock, two hours before their date. Kissing Virginia soundly on the lips, he grinned. "I have some wiring to do. And don't peek!"

*****

"How did you stay so clean?" she asked, an hour and a half later, after he spent the interim in the marina parking lot, wiring the new CD player and speakers into the old Porsche while Virginia showered and dressed.

"It's just a matter of care and concentration," he pretend-bragged, brushing at imaginary grass stains on the side of his pressed and ironed khakis.

He had reservations for eight-thirty at Murrells Inlet's Japanese steak house, where he and Virginia, after sampling tiny portions of everything on the sushi bar menu, settled down with other dining couples on the floor around one of the massive wooden tables in the main dining room.

As the young Japanese chef worked his magic on the huge grill in the center of their table, deftly chopping vegetable after mouthwatering vegetable along with tender meats and grilling them before the hungry eyes of his audience, Virginia could feel Remy's eyes on her.

Glancing over at him, she felt herself meeting his warm green gaze when he silently mouthed "I love you."

Virginia, smiling in reply, reached over to gently kiss his lips.

Letting out a whoop and a grin, the Japanese chef pointed unabashedly at Remy and Virginia while leading the table in a round of applause.

Remy and Virginia, ending their kiss, and joined in the cheering while the chef skillfully juggled salt and pepper mills, coyly pretending to drop them on the diners.

At the end of their meal, Remy and Virginia were the only ones left at their table, lingering long over coffee. Soon the empty seats were filling as a group of tipsy vacationing male golfers was seated by the hostess for a late dinner. One of their number, after unsuspectingly laying his starched cotton napkin in front of his plate on the great flat grill in the center of the table, grabbed his napkin just as it burst into flames. Panicking, he put out the flames with his glass of water, much to the delight of his already-merry companions, and Remy and Virginia, who were nearly choking on their coffees with suppressed giggles.

Remy shook his head, smiling sagely. "That was a pure slapstick comedy moment, but think if no one was at the napkin when it caught on fire—it could have been disastrous."

"Disaster can strike when no one is looking," Virginia nodded, her laughter subsiding. "Just like at the marina. One night I woke up and was getting a drink of water. The bow railing of the *Helen Z* in the next slip caught my eye through my galley porthole. Her bow railing normally was higher than my porthole, so I'd never see it from there. I looked outside and sure enough, her bow was low—it was even with her stern instead of proud. And the boot stripe marking her waterline was out of sight, underwater. The marina manager spent the rest of the night pumping her out. But if I hadn't glimpsed the bow railing—"

"—that boat would've been on the bottom," Remy nodded, his eyes narrowing.

Chapter Eighteen

Leaving the restaurant arm in arm with Remy, Virginia smiled. *I'm happy,* she thought, *not just pleased, but actually happy. How joyous it is to have the freedom to be this happy, and how different from those dark, bewildering days before and after Gordon died.*

She squared her shoulders. If only I could find out who was responsible for Gordon's death—and that macabre note that said I was next.

"You're mighty quiet," Remy grinned. "What are you thinking about?"

"You," Virginia grinned back.

Walking with him down the dock toward *Chaucer,* she decided not to temper the delicious lightheartedness of the evening by telling him about her morning's brake saga. It was a combination, she decided—a mechanical failure, a prank, and a missed message—that's all it was.

Remy reached for the port aft jump line. Pulling *Chaucer's* stern slowly over toward the dock, he waited for Virginia to turn on the shore water and step aboard.

"Just a sec, you go ahead," Virginia said as the boat came to. Remy stepped aboard, while she pulled out her keys and opened the padlock to her dock box, where she had hidden the fishing creel for Remy. The creel tucked under one arm, she pulled *Chaucer* back over and stepped aboard. She followed Remy into boat.

"There's no water," he said from the galley.

"Oh, wait—I forgot to turn it on." She went back out onto the aft deck, pulled the boat over again, stepped up onto the dock, and bent down to turn on the valve attached near her dock spigot.

Back aboard *Chaucer,* Virginia presented Remy with the antique fishing creel. Raving happily about the old creel's well-tanned and oiled leather straps burnished copper buckles, he insisted the creel would have a place of honor on the mantel above his fireplace.

Virginia was pleased her first gift to Remy was something he liked so much. She poured them each two fingers of cognac in polished glass snifters while Remy went forward and opened the heavy overhead hatch that led up onto the forward deck. She handed him a snifter, followed him up the ladder into the balmy night air and stepped onto the polished mahogany deck.

They sat on the deck silently sipping the cognac and drinking in the breezy, moonlit night that had replaced the morning's muggy dampness. Rain was coming sometime after midnight, according to the weather forecast, but for now, the evening was balmy and dry.

"Cam called me today." Remy studied his cognac, swirling it slowly before taking another swallow. "She asked me to tell you that she wishes us well, and that she is embarrassed about how she behaved."

"She already told you that," Virginia said, "the day after it happened. I think she just wants an excuse to call you."

"You may be right," Remy put his arm around Virginia, "but she is sincere. As a matter of fact, she sent several jobs my way in the last few days—her customers."

"Where does she work, that she hears of jobs to send your way? I meet new customers every day, but it's rare that any of them need their boat lettered or a sign for their business."

"She works at a plant nursery," Remy explained, "that also has a floral design shop and sells cut flowers. Customers come in for landscaping the grounds and putting plants and flower arrangements in the entrances of new businesses, so Cam keeps my cards there and gives them to people who are opening new businesses. *Some* of those people need signs."

"And Cam is short for Cameron? And she has short blond hair?"

Nodding, Remy swallowed. "You know her?"

"Not exactly—she must be the same woman who was one of *Gordon's* mistresses. I didn't realize she was the same person until you said she works at a plant nursery and florist business."

Remy looked crestfallen. "Oh."

Virginia was silent for a moment. "How does she get your cards?"

"Well...she comes by my shop and gets them."

"At your house."

"Of course," Remy said matter-of-factly. "That's where my shop is, isn't it? Anyway, she means no harm to us. She even said you had great hair."

"Remy." Virginia turned within the curve of Remy's arm to face him, then leaned back to look directly in to his face. "Cam has never even met me. How could she know anything about my hair?"

"Virginia, I have no idea. Maybe I told her. Maybe she's seen you around. You do have great hair, you know." He buried his face in her moonlight-gilded mane and inhaled loudly and comically, shaking his head.

Though annoyed, Virginia could not help but smile.

Remy touched the corner of her mouth gently with one finger. "Don't worry about Cam. She just wants to be friends, to talk on the phone sometimes, and it would be pretty cold to tell her no." He hesitated. "A few months before I met her, her fiancé died in an accident. Virginia, I feel sorry for her. That's all."

Virginia regarded Remy. He was sincere, she was sure, and she felt sorry for Cam too. Virginia didn't believe for one minute that Cam wished them well, but that didn't matter. Cam would soon find someone else and stop mooning over Remy.

"Let's go below for some more cognac," she said.

*****

Saturday morning dawned hot with a brand of steamy and muggy that only a South Carolina September morning can offer in the wake of a night of heavy rain.

By the time the sun was rising, Virginia had been up for an hour, her quiet excitement fairly crackling. Today was her first day in her new shop—Cheshire Cat Maritime Antiques.

Leaving late yesterday evening, pleading early morning work in his shop, Remy invited Virginia come to his house to stay the night with him, but she declined, opting to spend the night aboard *Chaucer*, in order to load up the small consignment items from Fox's Lair Antiques she temporarily stored in the boat. Remy was meeting her in Georgetown later this morning, and she wanted to get as much as possible done in the shop early before he arrived.

Compiling a mental list of the day's events while making coffee, feeding Gabrielle, and getting dressed, she was eager to get to the shop.

Although she would not officially open the shop for business until Thursday's Georgetown Chamber of Commerce-endorsed ribbon cutting, she planned to keep the front door open today and tomorrow while she set up.

She had gone ahead and gotten her business license yesterday—*better safe than sorry*, she thought, no matter how blithely candle shop owner Andy had spoken of getting it on Monday—and Remy was installing the hanger for her sign this morning.

Her sign—the *pièce de résistance* of her shop, her Victorian-style wooden hanging sign—was at last finished. Sandblasted into four-inch-thick cedar for a three-dimensional hand-carved effect, the double-sided sign was to swing from a wrought iron arm. Below the name Cheshire Cat was a nineteenth-century grinning Cheshire cat crouched on the words Maritime Antiques. Remy took great pains to make the sign exactly what she wanted and was hoping to hang it today.

Miss Eugenia was meeting her at the store this morning with the ships' figureheads and the slipper-shaped copper bathing tub.

Virginia planned to stock antique Naval firearms, too, and had already been in touch with several dealers. She could presently sell seriously old pirate-style weapons such as the blunderbuss and black powder pistols, which were sold as antiques rather than firearms. With the Federal Firearms License for Curios and Relics she acquired during her tenure at Fox's Lair Antiques, she was able to purchase firearms over fifty years of age, provided she did not resell them commercially. These would be for occasional private sales until she acquired a retail Federal Firearms License in order to buy and sell to the public.

A truckload of maritime antiques was scheduled to arrive sometime this morning, thanks to Mr. Kimbel. He had put her in touch with the soon-to-retire owners of Blockade Runner Antiques, a riverfront maritime antiques store in Savannah.

The Blockade Runner Antiques owners, a husband and wife team, wanted to close their store but keep its name, while staying in business as antiques dealers. Long familiar with seaport Georgetown's tourism and riverfront antiques community, they were delighted to send their entire inventory up to Virginia's new store for consignment.

This way they would have freedom to pursue their true passion of traveling and seeking out maritime antiques while sending their finds to Virginia for consignment sales.

As she carried her consignment inventory, all small items, from Fox's Lair Antiques to her car and loaded it all into the back trunk, front trunk and passenger seat of the Porsche, just thinking of the inventory of maritime antiques she would carry in her new shop made her heart lift.

While Virginia locked the boat to leave, so preoccupied was she with her mental inventory that she was halfway down the dock before she realized she had forgotten to turn off her shore water. She went back to her slip and turned off the valve. The hose leading down into *Chaucer*'s hull shuddered slightly as the water pressure was cut off at the dock.

I cannot believe I nearly left it on, she chided herself. If the hose split or one of its metal couplings or aluminum clamps came loose while she was gone, the perpetual flow of water pouring into Chaucer's bilge would be enough to burn out the bilge pump motor and sink the boat.

Thunder rumbled to the south, toward Georgetown, as she unlocked the door of the Porsche.

I hope it won't be raining when the truck from Savannah arrives to offload, she thought, reaching for her harmonica, then putting it back in the console. This morning she would play her new stereo instead.

*****

The early morning drive to Georgetown was less than half an hour on Ocean Highway 17. Passing through Pawleys Island halfway to Georgetown, Virginia smiled, thinking of Remy, and turned the volume on her new stereo a notch higher.

The mannequins she had bought were still in the breezeway under Remy's house. The first one would soon be ready for the store. Maybe it—she—could be in the front window by the end of this week, drawing attention to Miss Eugenia's copper bathing tub.

Driving over the two bridges spanning the Black, Pee Dee and Waccamaw Rivers at the entrance to Georgetown, Virginia looked out to the left across Winyah Bay at the mouth of the rivers. She could hardly wait until hurricane season was over so she could dock *Chaucer* here.

Water sprayed over her car's hood as she drove through a huge puddle, turning off Ocean Highway 17 onto St. James Street, headed for Front Street and the river. *There must have been a heavy rain here early this morning or last night.*

When Virginia drove onto Front Street, her heart lifted. A breeze was blowing the leaves in the live oak trees, and puddled water sparkled in dips along the street.

The town clock was chiming seven o'clock as Virginia drove by it. She loved how the tower had a clock on each side—the south one faced her store, the west one faced Screven Street, the north one faced Murrells Inlet, and the east one faced the river, the bay, and the Atlantic.

Remy's Range Rover was already there. A tall aluminum A-frame ladder was attached to the roof rack.

Remy is out early this morning, Virginia thought, *to get my new sign up before the business day starts. Such a wonderful man!*

She parked beside his vehicle and got out, holding the stack of flyers she had brought to give to other Front Street merchants introducing her new store and announcing the ribbon cutting.

As she looked in her purse for the store key, a breezy gust swooped the top papers off her stack and onto the high hood of Remy's Range Rover. Virginia put her hand down on the fluttering papers as the wind began to lift them once more.

Through the paper, she felt the cool hood of the Rover. He must have been here quite while for the hood of his truck to be completely cold. Several papers had blown under the edge of his truck. Virginia sighed. Those would be wet and ruined. She crouched down to retrieve them.

The papers were completely dry—as was the pavement underneath Remy's SUV. Remy had been here since before it rained—did it rain here last night the way it did back at the marina?

As she unlocked the door of the shop, Virginia heard footsteps on the stairs leading to the second floor apartment. The street doorway at the bottom of the stairs was right next to her shop door. Good—she would have a chance to meet her upstairs neighbor.

As she turned her knob and removed the key, the sound of the footsteps stopped. When Virginia looked up to see who was opening the door at the foot of the stairs, she gasped in surprise.

Chapter Nineteen

The coffee in Remy's mug sloshed over the rim as he stopped abruptly, startled and surprised, on the bottom stair step. He stepped down onto the sidewalk-level landing.

"Honey! You're out early," he said, smoothing his mustache with one hand.

"Not as early as you," Virginia raised her eyebrows. "You must have been here a good while."

"No," Remy took long drink of coffee, "I just got here a little while ago."

Virginia looked up the stairs Remy had just walked down. Maybe soon she'd get to meet whoever lived in the upstairs apartment. "You have a buddy who lives up there?"

Oh," Remy jerked his thumb over his shoulder, "—the lady that lives up there let me in so I could measure out the window for your sign arm." He glanced back up the stairs. "I may be able to mount it out the window up there, but I might have to still use the ladder." With one last look up the stairs he closed the door. "Are you ready to go into your new store?"

"Sure thing," she said, slowly pushing her door open. She walked inside, looking up at the high sky-blue ceiling where its edges met the ancient brick walls. She turned around to Remy and flung her arms out. "This is a dream come true! My own store!"

"*We're* a dream come true," Remy smiled, tilting her chin up gently before kissing her. "Now let's hang your sign before it gets too hot." He leaned out the door, looked up at the sky, and squinted. "No telling when it might rain again."

Two hours later the sign was hung. Virginia and Remy stood back and admired it.

The Cheshire cat's grin spread mischievously from ear to ear under twinkling eyes.

"Remy, it's perfect!" Virginia said. "It's pure Victoriana. And the cat's grin and eyes seem to twinkle, just a little bit. I love it! How did you put a twinkle in the cat's eyes?"

"A few well-placed flakes of gold leaf," Remy said, his grin almost as wide as that of the Cheshire cat.

The clock in the tower rang nine times.

At the last stroke of nine, Miss Eugenia braked, pulling her red dually up next to Virginia's car. A moment later, purple umbrella in hand, she made her way to the shop door.

"Virginia," Miss Eugenia sighed, after closing the shop door behind her, "My house is only two blocks away but in this heat, it might well be two miles. Your air conditioning feels divine." She set her umbrella down and looked up at Remy. "Is this him?"

"Miss Eugenia, this is Remy Ravenel," smiled Virginia. "Remy, this is Miss Eugenia Allston."

"Enchanted," said Remy, taking Miss Eugenia's hand and bringing it to his lips.

Miss Eugenia rolled her eyes and smiled coyly at Virginia. "Dear girl, he's a keeper. I commend you on your good taste."

"Thank you," Virginia smiled, curtsying. "I *am* right proud of him."

"Think he'll carry these heavy antiques in for us?" Miss Eugenia winked at Virginia.

"I'd be honored," Remy offered.

An hour later, the ships' figureheads were both hung in the shop window above the copper bathing tub, and Remy stepped out the back door onto the Harbor Promenade for a smoke.

"Miss Eugenia, I need some history on this figurehead." Nearly backing into the copper bathing tub, Virginia eyed the nearly life-sized, hand-carved wooden head and torso gracing the wall of Cheshire Cat Maritime Antiques' window. It was hard to believe this beautiful relic, the only remaining part of a ship flying across the waves over a century and a half ago, was here in her shop.

The young woman depicted in the mid-nineteenth century carving gazed straight ahead, a faraway look in her wooden eyes, a slight, Mona Lisa smile gracing her countenance. Unlike many ships' figureheads, including the authentic-looking reproduction on the other side of the shop window, the neckline of this one's carved bodice was modestly high, with no swelling bosom spilling over the top of her dress.

Virginia could hardly believe Miss Eugenia was willing to part with this figurehead. She would have loved to buy it herself and keep it on permanent display in the shop, but at Miss Eugenia's asking price, she hoped only to entrust the figurehead that once graced a Confederate blockade runner to an appreciative owner. In order to do that, however, she needed as much background information as possible.

Miss Eugenia grimaced, adjusting the large purple amethyst screw-back earring clinging to her left earlobe. "It came from a company in California, I think, that specializes in nautical repro—" She stopped, seeing the incredulous expression on Virginia's face. "Oh—you mean the old one."

Virginia rolled her eyes, pantomiming impatience. "Yes. The old one, silly. The one from the blockade runner that belonged to George Trenholm."

"Yes, yes, ahem." Clearing her throat, Miss Eugenia drew herself up to her full five feet and straightened the neckline of her paisley-patterned purple-and-lavender dress. With a small grimace, she stepped up into the closed back window. Looking fondly at the carved features of the figurehead, she reached out and touched the back of her hand to one wooden cheek.

"She graced the bowsprit of the *Emily St. Pierre*," Miss Eugenia said softly. "She's all that's left of her."

"Do you remember her?"

Miss Eugenia gave Virginia an incredulous look.

"I mean—" Virginia floundered, her cheeks flushing. "I mean, Civil War-era folks were still around when you were a child, and some ships from that era are still around even now so—"

"I know what you mean," Miss Eugenia nodded, appeased. "But both Emily St. Pierre the lady, and *Emily St. Pierre* the blockade runner vessel, were long gone before I was born. I remember my Grandmama Virginia talking about them."

"Your grandmother was named Virginia? I hardly ever meet any other Virginias."

"Yes! Child, back in her day, Virginia was a very oft-heard name. Virginia, Geneva, Eugenia—such names are rare today but were very popular back then. Beautiful names." Miss Eugenia looked sad for a few seconds. "But," she raised a forefinger and took a breath, "back to Emily St. Pierre."

"Who was she?"

"She," Miss Eugenia glanced at the figurehead, "was the daughter of George Trenholm, a Charleston man. Trenholm had a shipping business, an import-export firm, down in Charleston. When the War Between the States started, he continued his work, even though Charleston harbor was blockaded by Federal ships. Through careful planning and what we would now call espionage, he was able, on most runs, to bring supplies into Charleston from Britain via Bermuda. And ship cotton to Britain. He had more ships built, fast-sailing ships with steam-powered paddle wheels. One of these he named *Emily St. Pierre*, after his daughter, Emily St. Pierre Trenholm. During the War, Emily married a Confederate scout, last name of Hazzard, and her father bought them a rice plantation here in Georgetown County."

"Why here, when the Trenholms were from Charleston?"

"I'm not sure. Georgetown was—and still is—just like Charleston, geographically and culturally, only smaller. Only difference then was, Georgetown's international seaport wasn't blockaded from the Federals until nearly the middle of the War, while Charleston's was blockaded from the very beginning—the War started there, you know."

Virginia nodded.

"Anyway, he bought all, or nearly all, his children each a Georgetown rice plantation during the War. He was making a living with his blockade running, and he bought these plantations from folks who couldn't afford to run them anymore—did them a favor. And he wanted to leave each of his children a plantation—a farm, really—so they could make a living after the War."

"How do you know all this?" Virginia asked. She wanted to ask, 'And what does all this have to do with this figurehead of the *Emily St. Pierre*?' but she knew better. Miss Eugenia was getting around to that, and when she did, all the little details she was mentioning now would prove to be important, as usual.

"Why, my Grandmama Virginia told me. Remember, George Trenholm was good friends with her grandfather," Miss Eugenia answered.

"Your great-great grandfather?"

"Ah—yes, yes that's right. My great-great grandfather. He lived out on North Island, you know, where the lighthouse is. He had a summer house there, and for the last sixty or seventy years of his life after his wife died—he became a widower so very, very young and never remarried—he lived on North Island. He was one of the few that built his house back after the Hurricane of twenty-two—that's *eighteen*-twenty-two—swept away the whole summer town of rice planters' summer cottages on North Island. He was living there in his house during the War Between the States, when the Confederates had the lighthouse. He never left even when the Federals took over the lighthouse late in the War. And he was there when the War ended, too."

"A dangerous spot sometimes, North Island, eh?" Virginia said.

"Sometimes," Miss Eugenia conceded. "And sometimes just the right spot."

"Emily St. Pierre Trenholm Hazzard's rice plantation, hers and her husband's, I mean," Miss Eugenia took a breath, "was down off South Island Road right next to my great-great grandfather's rice plantation, though his son, my Grandmama Virginia's father, was running it by then. My great-great grandfather and Mr. Trenholm, Emily St. Pierre's father, became fast friends. Mr. Trenholm would come out to South Island and hunt with him. My great-great grandfather donated a cache of very old gold, silver and jewels—buried there by pirates, no doubt—that he had dug up on North Island to the Confederate Treasury, through Mr. Trenholm."

Virginia's mouth fell open. "No."

"Yes." Miss Eugenia grinned, delighted with her story. "You see, George Trenholm, during the last year of the War, became Secretary of the Confederate Treasury. When the War ended, when the capitol at Richmond fell, Mr. Trenholm and other members of the Cabinet spirited the treasury out of Richmond on a southbound train. A lot of it was lost, stolen, thrown into rivers the train crossed, unofficially pensioned out to homebound soldiers—who knows?"

She took a breath. "But some of it went back to the original owners who donated it."

Virginia's eyes grew wide. *I should have* known *Miss Eugenia knew the whereabouts of at least part of the legendary missing Confederate Treasury,* she thought.

"George Trenholm came to see my great-great grandfather on South Island a year and a half after the War was over. Trenholm, who had been imprisoned at a Georgia fort and finally pardoned—though he never asked for pardon since he'd done no wrong—apologized to my great-great grandfather for taking so long, and gave him back the cache of gold, silver, and jewels he'd donated to the Cause. Heaven knows how he'd been able to hang onto it. And—he gave him the figurehead of the *Emily St. Pierre*. The figurehead was all that was left after her captain ran her aground and burned her to the waterline to avoid capture while running the Federal blockade between Charleston and Georgetown."

Virginia swallowed. What a story! "What did your great-great grandfather do with the, ah, treasure?" Miss Eugenia shook her head and smiled. "He re-buried it on North Island."

"So it's still there," breathed Virginia.

"Of course not," Remy said quickly, standing quietly, just in from his smoke. "Hurricanes and tides, erosion—no way."

Miss Eugenia shrugged elegantly. "I'm sure he hid it well. But enough of that." She reached into the copper bathing tub, lifted out an ancient linen bath towel, and laid it across the rim of the tub. "You know, terry cloth towels were not used until the 1890s," she said. "In this tub's day, bathing was an event, not an everyday occurrence."

"I would have filled up this tub and bathed every day," Virginia said.

"Not me," Miss Eugenia wrinkled her nose. "I take showers."

"Me too," Remy agreed. "I never take baths. I like showers."

"I love baths," Virginia said. "My boat has a shower but no tub, so for me, a bath is a luxury. She turned to Remy. "And you do take baths. The first time I ever saw your main bathroom, the one with the big claw foot bathtub, the tub was still wet. And," she turned to Miss Eugenia, "there's no shower head. So I know he took a tub bath."

"I was just cleaning that bathtub because I knew you'd go in there, and I wanted to make a good impression," said Remy. "I take showers in the other bathroom."

"Well, I'm going home to have a nice shower *now*," said Miss Eugenia, picking up her umbrella and walking toward the door. "I'll be back later and see how you're coming along."

Virginia and Remy walked her to the door.

"It's clouding up again," Remy observed.

"The weather changes so rapidly here—I'll probably put a water barometer by the door," Virginia said. "You know, a glass storm ball."

"Like sea captains kept on their ships," Remy added, "to find out when the barometric pressure was dropping and a storm might be brewing."

"I wonder if a storm's brewing now?" Miss Eugenia said as she stepped outside. "The wind has picked up." She raised her eyes to the sky. "Ye gods!"

"What is it?" Remy looked up then grabbed Miss Eugenia's arm as she sagged down. Putting his other arm around her, he helped her back into the store.

"Miss Eugenia! Miss Eugenia!" Virginia fanned Miss Eugenia's face with an envelope as Remy settled her onto the wooden rocking chair near the front door.

"I'm all right, dear," managed Miss Eugenia, fanning her face with her hand. "Your new sign gave me a turn. Remy, can you get me some water?"

Remy headed for the water fountain at the back of the store, and Virginia went to the doorway to close the still-open front door. Was her sign about to fall? She stepped outside first to look up at it.

Grinning merrily, the Cheshire cat moved slightly in the stiffening breeze, the wrought iron arm it swung on creaking almost imperceptibly.

Puzzled, Virginia came back inside. What could have distressed Miss Eugenia?

"It's that, that—that Cheshire cat," Miss Eugenia said, her voice quivering. "I didn't see it when I came in. I didn't see it until—just now." She shivered.

Virginia's brows knitted. "Oh, Miss Eugenia, I'm so sorry—I know the cat is crouching, but it's grinning, not growling, and it's not meant to be frightening."

"No, my dears." She looked at Virginia then took the cup of water Remy proffered.

"Thank you, Remy." She looked back at Virginia. "It's a lovely sign. The cat is charming. It was just a bit of a shock," she fanned her face with her hand, "and took me by surprise, especially amongst the boat antiques, and being here on the waterfront."

Remy, sipping from a cup of water also, crouched down in front of Miss Eugenia, his green eyes filled with concern. "What was a shock, Miss Eugenia?"

Miss Eugenia accepted an ivory fan from Virginia and began to slowly fan her face with it.

"I had a sister, a younger sister," she began, drawing a shaky breath. "Five years before she—" Miss Eugenia hesitated, her voice trembling. "Five years before she left us, her gentleman friend, Maxwell, disappeared off her boat. The boat was named *Cheshire*."

Chapter Twenty

"*Cheshire*!" Virginia exclaimed. *Chaucer, Charmer*—she had never thought of *Cheshire*, C–H–E–S–H–I–R–E...just one letter longer.

"Yes. *Cheshire*." Miss Eugenia took a deep breath and exhaled slowly. "Geneva loved boats. When she turned twenty-one in 1949, she came into her inheritance from her mother—we were half-sisters, we had the same father—and we went straight up to the Chicago Boat Show where she bought herself a big, new Chris-Craft and named it *Cheshire*."

"A Chris-Craft?" Virginia sat down on the floor at Miss Eugenia's feet.

"Yes. A Chris-Craft. That 'friend' of hers, Maxwell, went too. He's the one put it into her head to get that boat."

"Why did she name her boat *Cheshire*?" asked Virginia, wrapping her arms around her knees. She glanced at Remy, who had pulled up a leather hassock.

"Want to sit here, honey?" he asked her.

"No, thanks," Virginia smiled at him, thankful he was here. She looked back nervously up at Miss Eugenia.

"Geneva loved Cheshire cats," Miss Eugenia said, her voice stronger now, "ever since she was little. Her mother's family's house on Pawleys Island had a Cheshire cat picture on the wall, a Cheshire cat statue up in a huge gardenia bush—a small tree, actually—at the bottom of the garden, and other Cheshire cats as well, too many to remember. I spent summers there starting when I was seven, when my father married Geneva's mother." Miss Eugenia smiled.

"That next summer, Geneva was born, right at that house, and she grew up seeing those Cheshire cats."

"Was there a Cheshire cat door knocker on the front door?" Virginia asked, thinking of Remy's house on the island.

"I don't recall anything about the front door or door knockers," Miss Eugenia said, squinching her eyebrows slightly, "but there were Cheshire cats everywhere, to be sure. That's how Geneva got her love of Cheshire cats, but it was him, that Maxwell, who convinced her she ought to have a great big boat."

Virginia glanced at Remy. He was listening raptly, gazing fixedly at Miss Eugenia.

"What happened to Geneva?" Virginia asked, kneeling by Remy and placing her hand on Miss Eugenia's. "You said she, ah, left?"

Remy put his hand to his mouth as he continued to listen.

Miss Eugenia sighed. "She disappeared. She was wrongly blamed for Maxwell's death, and it haunted her until she disappeared." She shook her head and lowered her eyes. "After Maxwell went missing off the boat, Geneva was accused of his murder."

Virginia swallowed. "Of his murder? What happened to him?"

"She was never arrested, mind you, but there was blood on the boat, and Maxwell was gone. And she had been the last person seen with him."

"That's just circumstantial," Virginia said, remembering how she been alone in the house when Gordon died, and no one had seen her. No one had been able to say she had not been at the marina and set the shed on fire with Gordon in it. What was it Remy said? *Rumor and innuendo are sometimes more powerful than the truth.*

"It was right here on the river at the Labor Day Boat races," sighed Miss Eugenia. "So many people saw her with him that day—and heard them arguing that night."

"Boat races? They raced her?" Virginia was surprised. Racing a big Chris-Craft cruiser?

"No—no, they were tied up over here on the Front Street side of the river," Miss Eugenia gestured toward the back of the shop and the river behind it, "watching the races. They had the best view on the river—and folks had a good view of them."

"And it was that night Maxwell—disappeared?"

"That very night," Miss Eugenia nodded. "And it ate at her until she disappeared, five years later, during Hurricane Hazel."

Virginia gulped. Being suspected wrongly of Gordon's fiery death leaped to her mind.

"But—your sister would have known she didn't kill him."

"No." Miss Eugenia looked at Virginia and shook her head. "She didn't know. She drank too much that night and was unconscious. When she woke up, Maxwell was gone, but for his blood on the aft starboard cleat."

"They were sure it was his blood?"

"But who else's?" Miss Eugenia sighed, looking at her hands. "They were alone that night, drinking on that boat. They had a huge argument, loud enough to be heard on other boats. Lots of folks were still down here that night and heard them. You know how sound carries across the water. No one else saw him after that."

Virginia bit her lip. She knew all too well about the power of circumstance and supposition and how Geneva must have felt. "Miss Eugenia, what do *you* think happened?"

"Geneva was like a lamb," Miss Eugenia raised her eyes to meet Virginia's. "She was just like a lamb—frisky, but gentle and hurtful to no one. Feisty, yes. And she could have a sharp tongue on occasion. But she could never *hurt* another human being, let alone someone she cared for. But Sheriff Bone questioned her several times, and they never resolved Maxwell's disappearance. Lots of folks figured Geneva was responsible. That, and Maxwell's death itself, drove her mad. She was already an impetuous, unpredictable soul, probably resulting from her mother being a relation—a cousin. Cousins married all the time back in the old days, and my father was certainly head-over-heels for her, but now, you know, they're saying it's not a good idea for cousins to marry because of how—" Miss Eugenia lowered her voice, "—of how the children might turn out."

"Sheriff *Bone* questioned her?" Virginia was surprised. "Are you sure it was Sheriff Bone, Miss Eugenia?"

"Not the present Sheriff Bone—the first Sheriff Bone. Father of the one now," Miss Eugenia said. Holding the chair's arms, she slowly rose and looked at Virginia, then at Remy. "I must be going, dears. I didn't mean to put a damper on your first day. Your sign and store name are excellent—they just brought back such bad memories. But no more—from this day forward, Cheshire Cat will only refer to your happy and successful shop."

"Are you sure you're all right, Miss Eugenia?" Virginia asked.

Miss Eugenia patted Virginia's hand. "I'll be back tomorrow morning," she said, walking toward the door. She pulled her truck keys out of her purse. There are a good deal more things I want to bring in for your store." She turned back and winked. "This is going to be one of the hottest little antique shops on the East coast."

"Man," Remy shook his head, watching her head for her truck, "that was a shock."

Miss Eugenia had been gone less than a minute when the front door opened.

Virginia and Remy turned to see a tall, slim woman in a crisp red linen summer suit.

I've seen her before, thought Virginia. *But where?*

Her glossy dark shoulder-length bob swinging as she moved, the woman entered. "Hey, Remy," she nodded at him, then turned to Virginia with a warm smile. "I'm Charisse. I've been wanting to meet the new shop owner and see the shop—when the candle people left so fast, with their boat, they told me another person who lives aboard a boat is opening an antique shop here. I am so happy to meet you! I live upstairs," she nodded toward the ceiling. "And I love your store name," she gestured to the new sign. "I'm glad it finally stopped raining, so he could hang it. The way it stormed all night, you wouldn't have thought anyone could put a ladder up outside this morning."

"Thanks for letting Remy use your window upstairs to hang the sign."

"Oh sure, that was fine," Charisse shrugged. "I was glad to help."

"It rained all night?" Virginia asked.

"Yes, drizzling mostly, with thunder and lightning, too. I bet it's something, sleeping on your boat with all that going on."

"It is," agreed Virginia. "Would you like some coffee? I just put on a pot."

"Oh, thanks—but I've had my quota this morning." She glanced at her watch. "I have to be at the office in five minutes anyway."

"Ye gods—" Remy mimicked Miss Eugenia and looked at his watch. "Mine stopped at 7:09." He pinched out the watch stem and began adjusting the hands.

Virginia glanced at Remy's wrist then looked up and smiled at Charisse. "These antiques don't always run on modern time—guess that's why I love the antique business." She looked at Remy's wrist again. "I'm glad you found your watch."

"It was good to meet you, Virginia. Welcome to Front Street—I know we'll be seeing a lot of each other. 'Bye, Remy." Charisse gave a little wave and was gone.

"She found my house for me last year," Remy explained. "I've known her a long time, but I didn't know she lived above this shop until this morning."

Virginia was quiet. She felt her nostrils flare involuntarily, the way they used to when she felt Gordon was lying to her, and walked to the rear of the shop toward the coffee pot, so Remy wouldn't see.

"What's wrong?" Remy followed her "Honey?"

Virginia turned to face him. Tilting her head to one side, she gave him a long look. "Remy, I thought you said you just got here, right before I did this morning," she said. "But some of my papers blew under you truck, and they didn't even get wet—your truck must have been here before it rained."

"Well, I—" Remy began.

"It rained all night here, according to Charisse just now."

"After you left yesterday evening, I drove down here just before sundown to take measurements for the arm for your swinging sign," Remy explained. "My truck," he gestured to his Rover, "wouldn't start when I was ready to leave, so I went to a friend's down the street. After he and I found my truck's ignition glitch," he rolled his eyes, "we went for a beer at the Riverfront." He gestured to the pub on the next block. "I ended up staying the night at his house. I wanted to call you and tell you in case something happened and you needed me, but something was wrong with the phone at the Riverfront and my cell phone was dead, since I didn't have my charger, and when we got back to his house, it was too late to call. I knew you were getting up early."

"You and your friend must have gotten up early too," Virginia said.

"Oh, David-Earl, yes, well he's a commercial fisherman," Remy said, "actually, a musician working as a commercial fisherman. He was up and out of here before dawn. I wanted to surprise you with your sign hanging when you got here. But," he smiled, "you were early."

He folded his arms and looked at Virginia. "But something else is bothering you."

Virginia swallowed. "You heard Miss Eugenia. Her sister Geneva had a Chris-Craft, about the same year as mine, right here in Georgetown."

Remy folded his arms, and cocked his head to one side, smiling. "So?"

"She was suspected in the death, or mysterious disappearance of her, ah, significant other," Virginia bit her lip, "like I was."

Remy put his hands on her shoulders and looked into her eyes. "A coincidence."

"No one ever found out what happened to him, and Geneva was blamed," Virginia said, "just like with Gordon—and me. It's kind of spooky."

"And how can you be sure Miss Eugenia isn't making all of this up?" Remy folded his arms, cocking his head to one side.

Virginia gasped. "She wouldn't. She would never—"

"Maybe not on purpose," Remy said, "but haven't you ever heard her repeat things she said before?"

"Well, of course," Virginia said. "I do that on occasion. Hey, even you do that sometimes. Sure, I've sat through some of her stories twice. But they're always interesting. Even the second time around. And what's more, she only repeats things that are very important."

"Okay, okay, enough already." Remy ducked his head, raising his hands in mock fear.

Virginia rolled her eyes. "Okay—but I'm going to the library to look this up in the old Georgetown newspapers on microfilm—tomorrow."

After Remy left, Virginia realized she would not be looking up anything on microfilm tomorrow—tomorrow was Sunday, and the library was probably closed, and even if it was open, she would not be driving over here to Georgetown again until Monday morning.

At noon, with no one in the store but her, she locked the door, left a 'Be back at one o'clock' note on the front door, and promised herself she would never do this again, not after her grand opening next week. 'Be right back' notes, she knew, were often the harbingers of failed retail stores. She then headed for the Georgetown County Library. Later on, she felt sure Miss Eugenia could be counted on to cover for her, but for the present and near future, she, the owner-proprietor, needed to be there during operating hours.

Virginia parallel-parked on Highmarket Street beside the Prince George Winyah Episcopal Church, the cemetery of which backed right up to the library. Hoping the fact that other cars were parked nearby indicated that the library was still open, she headed for the wooden entrance door.

Pressing the fat thumb-button on the brass handle of the door, she was pleased to find that it opened right up. Walking in, she and looked around, pleased. With ancient, polished wide-planked heart of pine beneath her feet and oriental carpets artfully layered as to look haphazard, she was in, at least floor-wise, the environment she hoped to create in Cheshire Cat Maritime Antiques. Looking at the wall and high, vaulted ceilings, however, she felt as if she was in a Renaissance castle wine cellar filled with books.

Her delight must have shown on her face because the first thing she heard was a pleasant, throaty laugh. She turned and a lady with waist-length dark blonde hair appeared from behind a display of children's books and said, "It's okay—make yourself at home. We don't close until two on Saturdays. How can I help you?"

"Hey, thanks—1949 newspapers? September 1949?"

"Right this way to the local history room—we've got that on microfilm."

Virginia followed as the lady, hair swishing at every turn, led the way through a veritable maze of book racks to a wooden door beside a huge wooden rice-pounding mortar-and-pestle.

The lady turned the brass knob and opened the door into a noticeably cooler room in which an air conditioner window unit droned. She pointed toward the microfilm reading machine at back of the room.

"There she sits. Have you used one before?"

Virginia nodded, eying the microfilm reader. "Reels in those file cabinets?"

"Yes," the lady smiled. "I'm Fiona Sutherland."

"I'm Virginia Ross."

"Oh—you've opened that new antique shop in the old candle shop," Fiona said.

It was Virginia's turn to smile. "News travels fast—please come visit."

"Sure thing—I'm looking forward to it. Now," she nodded toward the microfilm reader, "call me if you need anything."

"Thanks," Virginia smiled again.

Fiona closed the door, leaving Virginia alone.

Virginia looked around, breathing in the antiquated air of the high-ceilinged room. She walked over to the file cabinet and read the labels on the outside of the old metal drawers.

"Census, census, census," she murmured, scanning the drawer fronts. She looked at the next cabinet. "*Georgetown Times* 1735-1800," she read aloud. "*Georgetown Times* 1801-1861, *Georgetown Times* 1866-1889." *They must have halted publication during the War,* she thought. "*Georgetown Times* 1890-1900, *Georgetown Times* 1900-1910, *Georgetown Times* 1911-1920." *The papers are getting longer,* she thought—*prosperous times.*

She scanned the next row of drawers, noting the Depression Years took up painfully little space, as did the years of World War Two. Then she stopped and caught her breath.

"1946-1952," she read. *This is it,* she thought, opening the drawer. Each reel was contained in a white cardboard box.

Virginia scanned the boxes. "January 1949-June 1949, no," she murmured, "August 1949-December 1949—this is it!"

She pulled out the box, opened it, and sat down on the wooden chair in front of the microfilm reader. Carefully, she took the reel of film from the box, placed it on the spindle, rolled a few inches of film off the reel and threaded the end of the film through the first roller, past the reading lens, through the roller on the opposite side of the lens, and onto the securing spindle.

She turned the spindle a couple of times to make sure the film would not slip out, then turned the start knob. Slowly the film rolled, page after sepia-toned page of words and pictures. Virginia stopped.

"Three Cases Polio Reported in Georgetown," she read aloud the front page headline.

She looked at the date—August 30, 1949. The next paper, or the next, would be the issue after Labor Day. Would it chronicle the Labor Day Boat Races—and the mysterious disappearance of Geneva McKenna's gentleman friend?

Slowly she turned the knob, passing pages of grocery store ads advertising quarts of milk and loaves of bread for pennies. There were photographs of automobiles with wide running boards and huge-looking headlights mounted in great rounded front quarter-panel fenders. Just after an article about a graveside ceremony for a Georgetown soldier being reinterred in Elmwood Cemetery five years after his World War II death and original burial on a French hillside, she saw it.

Hundreds Entertained at Sampit River Labor Day Boat Races, the bottom headline on the front page read. *Racers vie for Trophies* was the subtitle. Virginia scanned the article, reading quickly over names of all the racers and their speeds and times. There was no mention of Geneva McKenna or—what was his name? She saw no familiar names, then she remembered—*Maxwell, that was it. Maxwell.* She didn't have his last name, but all the participants here were identified by both first and last names, and there was no Maxwell listed here.

Wait, she thought—*didn't Miss Eugenia say Geneva and Maxwell did not participate, but instead docked on the river, or anchored out in the river, for race day?*

Beside the article was a photograph of several long-bowed, barrel-backed wooden runabouts tearing down the river.

Virginia looked closer. In the foreground, docked parallel to the riverfront, tied to the old pilings that the Harbor Promenade replaced, was a large boat—or to be exact, the bow of a large boat. Virginia smiled. It was wonderful to see old photographs featuring boats from *Chaucer*'s day—and a bow that looked so much like *Chaucer*'s.

This bow stem, straight up and down from the waterline to the bowsprit, had none of the inward angle of earlier and later models. Besides that, the bowsprit was rounded in the manner of cars of that period—no angles or points on the tip of this bow.

She turned the knob until the next page appeared, then the next, and the next; until she came to the end of the newspaper. She tapped her forefinger on the counter of the microfilm reader. There had been nothing about a disappearance.

She checked the date at the top of the paper—this edition came out just the day after Labor Day. This paper would have already been 'put to bed' by the time Maxwell disappeared.

She turned the knob, rolling the reel to the next date, to the front page of the then-bi-weekly newspaper. She scanned the front page. There was no mention of the boat races or of a disappearance. Slowly she turned the knob, scanning until she was on the third page.

There, in the upper corner of the page three, a one-column-wide article, about three inches long, announced, *Man Missing After Boat Races.*

Virginia leaned forward in her chair and read.

Police investigated the disappearance of a man off the yacht Cheshire *after the Sampit River Labor Day Boat Races early Tuesday morning. Maxwell Trapier, of Miami, Florida, disappeared off the motor yacht* Cheshire *in Georgetown harbor early Tuesday morning. Mr. Trapier, staying in Myrtle Beach on business, had been visiting in Georgetown and attended the Sampit River Labor Day Boat Races the day before his disappearance.*

Not a mention of Geneva, Virginia thought. Geneva had been spared that, though according to Miss Eugenia, many presumed she was

****

responsible for Maxwell's demise through foul play, and Sheriff
Bone questioned her more than once.

Just like me, thought Virginia. *Just like me.*

Chapter Twenty-One

Virginia parked her car under the cypress at the end of her dock. Thankful her favorite parking spot in the shade had been vacant, she pulled up on her the new emergency brake and depressed the clutch. She put the Porsche in neutral and pressed the accelerator just to hear the resounding thump of the engine before switching off the ignition.

Spirits high, she had to hold back from hand-springing over the squeaky gate and skipping down the dock.

Her new shop was off to a great start. Her location was better than she dared to hope. The promised delivery van from Blockade Runner Maritime Antiques had arrived that afternoon from Savannah, bearing a cornucopia of antique seafaring delights—captain's chairs, more ships' figureheads, blue-and-white nautical tiles, brass ships' lanterns now green with age, ancient harpoons, skeleton keys, and much, much more. While Virginia had declined to sell anything before she took a full inventory, she closed at the end of the day with a list of deposits on held items.

Miss Eugenia ventured back an hour before closing, professing adoration for the new sign now that the shock of the Cheshire cat had worn off. She offered to bring in her own as well as her long-gone sister Geneva's 1940s ladies' boating attire for the antique mannequins Virginia was refinishing at Remy's house.

Above it all, the brand new Cheshire Cat Maritime Antiques sign, the only new item on the premises, hung merrily, drawing visitors near and welcoming them in with its mischievous grin.

Walking down the dock toward *Chaucer*, Virginia noticed from several slips away that the folding wood-framed screen door over her rear sliding hatch was ajar. She caught her breath, then smiled as she got closer. There in her screen door was shiny green cellophane with creamy white petals exposed—a bouquet! As she got closer, she heard the hum of her bilge pump running just before it came to a stop. Seconds later she heard the splash of water pumping out the starboard side abruptly stop.

Yes, life is good, she thought—*no doubt the flowers are from Remy, for my first day in the store.*

In her haste to pick up the bouquet, she passed her dock water spigot, then stepped back to turn on her shore water. She would need water for the bouquet. Reaching down, she flipped the plastic lever, hearing the tiny whoosh as water flowed into the hose. Standing back up, she noticed, as always, the slight movement of the hose filling with water pressure.

The tide was nearly out, leaving *Chaucer* well below the dock, so Virginia stepped down to the catwalk that ran from the dock a dozen feet along the side of the boat slip next to *Chaucer*'s port side. Grasping the rope hung length-wise above the catwalk, she dropped lightly down onto the aft deck. She pulled back the folding screen that covered the aft cabin door and picked up the bouquet as the intoxicating aroma of the gardenia blossoms rose up to meet her.

Remy was so thoughtful, to surprise her like this. She loved gardenia bushes and rarely passed one without stopping to take a whiff, but she would never have expected them in a bouquet. With their strong, sweet fragrance and easily bruised petals, gardenias seemed an unusual choice for a bouquet. And gardenias were out of season. These had to have come from a florist.

Gardenias, she mused, breathing in the scent as she unlocked the sliding rear hatch, were more often cut, in season, from bushes outside the home and brought inside by those who like their strong fragrance. Or, she frowned, used long ago at funerals. She smiled to herself. Remy had kind of a Gothic streak, with that big old early-eighteenth century house. He probably liked gardenias. Come to think of it, one of the huge bushes outside his house looked like a gardenia.

She would know for certain when it flowered next year.

Gordon had hated gardenias, she remembered, heading for the galley. And Gordon never brought her flowers, not when they were dating, not when they were married, not ever. She opened the cabinet under the sink and pulled out a wide-bottomed vase just as the bilge pump came on. She frowned. The bilge pump had just finished a minute-long pump-out when she arrived—it shouldn't be coming on again for hours. As soon as she put these flowers in some water, she would investigate.

"Hey, Gabrielle." She rubbed Gabrielle's ears.

Gabrielle hissed and spit, lashing out with unsheathed front claws before stalking under the galley table.

"Gosh, kitty," Virginia said. *Gabrielle is in a foul mood,* she thought.

She turned on the water and set the vase in the small aluminum sink under the spigot. A little water sputtered out then—nothing.

Virginia shook her head. She had definitely turned on the shore water. Maybe her hose had sprung a leak. She opened her low galley refrigerator, pulled out a bottle of water, and filled the vase.

Heading back to her cabin with the vase, she frowned again, deeper this time. The pump ought to turn off soon. It ought to have already turned off.

She picked up the bouquet from where she had left it on the bed. Did the bottom of it move ever so slightly? Impossible. She'd had a long and exciting day—maybe too long and too exciting. The bilge pump was still running, too. The sooner she got these flowers in the vase and solved her water problem, the better.

She untwisted the wire holding the dark green cellophane. The cellophane fell to the floor as a small bright flash of wriggling copper darted forth from beneath the bouquet and onto her hands.

Virginia screamed, dropping the bouquet as the copper-hued snake latched onto the palm of her right hand. She gasped and shook her hand, flinging the reptile off.

She grabbed her right hand with her left and stared at her right palm. Tiny drops of blood had already sprung up on the tiny bite. Panic rose in her chest. Didn't young venomous snakes have an even more potent bite than adults?

Get out on the dock, get some help, she thought wildly. There has to be someone around.

Was the marina store closed yet? It was just about time for one of the staff to walk the docks and make final rounds, if they had not done so already. The few other live-aboards here were usually already inside their boats making their dinner about this time, while the non-live-aboards who ventured down to the marina on a weekday had finished with their boats and left.

How long do I have before I lose consciousness, she wondered, heading toward her open rear hatch, swaying as the blue sky over the river outside grew grey and fuzzy.

Sinking to her knees, she reached for the folding screen door just as everything went grey. Then she was falling and only stopped when her hand-sanded, hand-varnished mahogany-and-oak cabin deck boards hit her left cheekbone.

Chapter Twenty-Two

Virginia opened her eyes and blinked. Her left cheek was pressed against the floor. Vile-tasting water had seeped into the corner of her mouth. Water was in her left eye, too.

Pushing herself into a sitting position, she wiped her eye. Looking down, she saw she was sitting in more than an inch of water. The bilge pump was running—she had to turn off the shore water—and the snake! She was snake bit! And where was Gabrielle?

She jumped up, nearly slipping in the water on the slick varnished floor. Hands in front of her, she splashed to the folding screen door, threw it open and stepped up onto the aft deck. How long had she been passed out? She clambered up onto the catwalk, grabbed the rope that ran above it, pulled herself up and stepped onto the dock. With a shaky gasp she turned off the shore water then sank down on the dock to look at her palm.

With the blood washed away from lying in the water, the tiny pricks were barely visible. Her hand was not even swelling yet. *Strange,* she thought. She had never seen a snake bite before, but wasn't it important to take care of it right away? Her bite had gone unattended for what, twenty minutes, half an hour? An hour?

"Virginia!" Captain Mike, the marina manager, was hurrying down the dock toward her.

"Fellow on that sailboat over there on B dock," he panted, pointing across the marina to a sixty-foot motorsailer, "he called on the radio and said your boat's low in the water. I was in the office late or I wouldn't have heard it."

Stopping where Virginia sat on the dock, he stared at *Chaucer*'s waterline. "Have mercy, she's down a foot or more!" He looked down at Virginia, her left side soaking wet, her right side dry. "You fall in the bilge trying to get that pump going?"

"No," said Virginia, wondering where to start. She raised her hand, palm up. "I passed out after a snake bit me—"

"A snake—" Taking hold of her hand, Mike scrutinized the bite.

"—inside the boat," Virginia murmured, casting her eyes toward *Chaucer*.

"Are you sure this is a snake bite?" He shook his head, still looking at the bite. "All I see is a little stick mark—just one, and a scratch. If it's a snake bite, it wasn't from a poisonous snake. There's no swelling. Maybe you passed out from fright."

"It was copper-colored," Virginia said, remembering her glimpse of the reptile. "A copperhead. Someone tied it up in cellophane at the bottom of a flower bouquet and left it in my door. And Gabrielle's in there with it."

"Gabrielle?"

"My cat."

Mike raised his eyebrows and climbed down onto the aft deck. "Your shore water running?"

"I just turned that off," said Virginia.

Mike pulled at her dock hose where it ran into the hull.

The end of the hose came out in his hand, a few drops of water trickling from the jagged end.

"Looks like it was cut through," he said, turning the ragged end of the hose back and forth. "I know you allowed a good deal of slack in the hose for the tides. What they must've done was pulled all the slackness of the hose out of the hull, cut it, then pushed it back through the hull fitting." He shook his head, then stepped down into Virginia's cabin.

"What the—" he jumped back, then moved to the side out of Virginia's range of sight.

She craned her neck to see into the boat as the sounds of scuffling, followed by a loud *whack*, came forth from her cabin.

Mike stepped up onto the aft deck holding up a small snake. "Baby corn snake," he stated, wiping his brow with his other hand. "Not a copperhead."

Virginia gasped and looked at her hand.

"Even if it bit you," he said. "It's not poisonous."

"It was still horrible," she swallowed, "and I still feel sick."

"No doubt," Mike replied. "Now let's see about that leak."

Laying the dead snake up on the catwalk, he headed back down into the boat.

Virginia looked at her hand again. No poisonous snake bite—but someone deliberately enclosed the snake in the cellophane wrapping at the bottom of the bouquet.

Mike came out of Virginia's cabin and stepped up onto the aft deck. "I'm gonna get the big pump," he said. "Your bilge pump is slowly sucking that water out, but we need to get it down faster. If there's a hull leak, and it cuts loose, your boat could heel over right here in the slip."

"I have to get my cat." Virginia began rising.

"No, you stay put. You have had a bad shock. Is this your cat carrier here?" He pointed to Gabrielle's carrier in the corner of the aft deck.

Virginia nodded. "She was in the galley under the table before the snake bit me."

He took the carrier inside the boat and came out a moment later holding the carrier with a glaring, tail-twitching Gabrielle inside. He reached up and set the carrier on the dock beside Virginia and shook his head. "I thought your cat was friendly. She bit the tar outta me."

Forty-five minutes later, *Chaucer* was pumped out, her waterline showing evenly above the surface of the river once more.

As Mike put away the pump, *Chaucer*'s bilge pump came on once again.

Mike shook his head. "Virginia, it's for certain now—you've got water coming in from somewhere else too. Diver's been on B dock cleaning the bottom of Derek's trawler," he said, jerking his shoulder in the direction several slips down. "I stopped by and asked him if he'll give the underside of your hull a look-see."

Virginia gulped. "You know *Chaucer* was just hauled last month. All the fittings were fine; she hasn't been taking on much water at all."

"Well she is now. Her clean hull will make it easy for him to see what's wrong quick," Mike replied. "You might as well go aboard Derek's trawler and try to relax. He's left the air conditioner on, and there's nothing you can do here."

"I'll stay here and see what the diver finds out," Virginia said. "He might need to ask me something." She looked up as the gate creaked.

"Virginia!" Remy was striding down the dock, his face a mask of concern. "Fellow over there at his truck says he's been diving, cleaning a hull and that he's about to go again, this time to search *Chaucer*'s hull for a leak—he said *Chaucer* nearly sank?"

Virginia jumped to her feet. "She took on a foot of water, and a snake bit me, but it wasn't poisonous." She steadied herself against her dock box, lightheaded from standing quickly after sitting so long.

Remy reached her and grasped her shoulders as she sat shakily down on the dock box.

"Virginia, honey, what—" He caught her as she slid down the front of the box.

Chapter Twenty-Three

Virginia sat with Remy in *Chaucer*'s saloon, sipping cognac at the map table and looking down, for perhaps the hundredth time, at the tiny, barely visible marks on her palm. She crossed herself, thankful the snake was not a copperhead. The corn snake had not even gotten a good grip, but the fright of being bitten was still a shock. Any snake bite, as well as boat near-sinking, called for cognac.

Her trembling was subsiding, but the evening's events continued to play over and over in her mind, like excerpts from a disturbing movie.

After a cursory visit—at Remy's insistence and with the dead snake in a jar—to the Waccamaw Hospital Emergency Room, Virginia and Remy remained at the marina with the diver, who found and patched with underwater epoxy the little holes apparently drilled into *Chaucer*'s side. The diver also found deep scratches, gouges, and scrape marks on the hull around the mouth of the starboard shaft stuffing box, but no damage there. Though some of Virginia's clothing in a bottom drawer had gotten wet, *Chaucer* had suffered no real water damage.

The deputy who responded from the sheriff's department arrived before Virginia went to the ER. Following a quick look at *Chaucer*, he dutifully wrote everything down and left.

Virginia leaned back in her rattan chair. Slowly running her finger across the dry, cottony texture of her mother's antique lace tablecloth, she looked across the table at Remy.

"Remy," she said, "you know everything that happened this afternoon was deliberately done by someone and directed toward me."

Remy leaned back in his chair and swirled his cognac in the bottom of the big snifter.

"Seems so. The snake *had* to have been put in the bouquet, and the hose was obviously cut—hacked, really, as though whoever did it didn't have anything sharp enough. And the holes in the hull, the diver said they looked drilled. But the visibility in this dark water is so poor, he *did* say they *could* have been worm holes. And the gouges where the shaft enters the hull—"

"The stuffing box?

"Yeah, the stuffing box—he couldn't be sure they weren't from *Chaucer* passing over a submerged branch—"

"*Chaucer* hasn't been—" Virginia began.

"I know, but honey, I honestly believe the flowers and the snake and cutting the hose were vandalism. Deliberate, but random, *vandalism*. Dangerous pranks. That's what the deputy thought."

Virginia was silent.

"Ruthless, random vandalism, honey, that's all it is. I heard Mike telling that deputy he's going to hire a night security guard as soon as he gets back in the marina office. Now security here at the marina will be tighter."

"But all this happened in broad daylight," Virginia protested. "The marina store and office are open all day, and they're careful, but they can't see all the docks.

Remy shrugged. "It'll still be safe. This was just a freak incident."

"What about Cam? She works in a florist shop."

"Yes, but Cam—uh-uh. Impossible. There's no way she would have done those things." He sat up in his chair. "No way she could have. She hates snakes. She's not an animal person."

"Snakes are reptiles."

"You know what I mean, honey," Remy said. "Creatures. And she couldn't dive under your boat and make holes."

"She could have snorkeled."

"She can't even swim."

"Are you sure she can't swim?"

"I'm sure. She's afraid of deep water."

Virginia solemnly regarded Remy. "The holes were only two feet below the waterline. A person could have been in a life vest and reached down and drilled those holes."

"With what? An electric drill under the water?" Remy shook his head dismissively.

"No, a manual hand drill."

"Nobody uses manual hand drills anymore."

"Some boat people do—I do. And it's not difficult to—"

"Well maybe you did it," Remy raised one eyebrow.

Virginia's eyes widened. She felt her nostrils flare. After all she'd been through this evening! "Me—"

"Honey, I'm just teasing you." Remy took another sip of his cognac.

"—and I suppose I got under there, under the water, and tried to tear into the starboard stuffing box too."

"Virginia," Remy half closed one eye and gestured toward her with the snifter, raising his index finger off the glass to point at her, "I promise, I was just teasing." Sitting up straight in his chair, he set down his snifter, put his elbows on the table, and reached across to take both of Virginia's hands. It's just," he said gently, "this is not the first unexplained event that's happened to you." He hesitated. "I mean, they never did find out what happened to Gordon."

Virginia felt tears pricking the inside of her eyelids.

"And my Walther PPK is missing."

"Your handgun?"

"Yes—the one I keep in my truck. It's been gone for two days."

Virginia felt tears burn in her eyes. "Remy, you never lock your truck—"

"And my Huguenot cross and my watch—I'm sure I left them here."

"Your watch is missing again? Whoever came into the boat and did all that stuff this afternoon must have taken it, and your Huguenot cross." Virginia struggled to keep her voice even. This had been a horrible evening. Remy should be comforting her. Instead, he sounded like Rod Serling narrating an old *Outer Limits* episode. *What is wrong with him?*

Shaking his head, Remy stood up. "I'm just thankful you're all right."

He turned up his snifter, drained it, and set it down gently on the table. "Honey, I hate to go, but when I rushed over here this afternoon, I left several pieces I was painting outside, under the breezeway. And I have to get up early. Come with me, please."

"I shouldn't leave the boat unattended tonight, not after she nearly sank."

"All right, then." Leaning over, Remy kissed the top of Virginia's head. "Good night."

"Good night."

Walking aft through the saloon, he headed down through Virginia's cabin and within seconds was out on the aft deck, up on the dock and heading toward his truck.

Virginia sat sipping her cognac, listening to Remy's footsteps fading down the dock.

She could feel tears gathering behind her eyelids again.

Still at the table, she heard the creak of the dock gates as he left. Hearing his Range Rover crank, she felt a tear of frustration roll down her cheek. Who could have left that bouquet? What *had* happened to Gordon? Was someone else there in the shed with him in those last minutes before the explosion? With the storm, no one had seen or heard a vehicle or anything out of the ordinary.

Sighing, she took another sip of cognac. Her need to find out what truly happened had until now been for her own closure and because the finger of guilt seemed to point wrongly at her. Now she needed to find out for another reason—because maybe whoever killed Gordon was trying to kill *her*, too. Maybe that crude cut-and-paste *'Virginia you're next'* missive that fell out the newspaper was more than just a cruel joke.

An hour later, Virginia was falling into a restless sleep when the phone began ringing.

Instantly awake, she answered. "Hello?"

The sultry female voice on the other end chilled her to the bone. "Virginia, you're gone."

Virginia looked at her caller ID. *Unknown*, it read. Sighing, she reached for the telephone plug, then reconsidered. She laid her telephone receiver on the bed and placed a pillow over it.

No matter how many times the caller tried again, she—whoever she was—would only receive a busy signal. At least whoever it was did not have her cell number.

Chapter Twenty-Four

On Monday morning, Virginia put Gabrielle in her cat box. Sunday had been peaceful; they had not left the boat. Virginia had spoken with Remy briefly on the phone, but decided she wanted to stay in and rest with Gabrielle in the hopes that the cat, and Virginia herself, would both return to normal. When she awoke on Monday, Virginia still felt that after her experience on Saturday, the usually playful, though still slightly grumpy, Siamese should not spend the day alone in the boat. She already had a litter box for Gabrielle at the shop, having planned on her spending some time there.

Despite Saturday's bizarre events, and the phone call, Virginia had been able to rest up Saturday night and Sunday, too tired to stay awake worrying. But Gabrielle, usually affectionate and playful, had snuggled up close to Virginia's face on the pillow all night and growled if disturbed. When Virginia picked her up, she hissed and spit. She remained unpleasant all day Sunday.

On the way out of Murrells Inlet, Virginia stopped at Gasoline Alley, her favorite small grocery store, and picked up cat food and litter.

Passing Pawleys Island's North Causeway entrance, she felt a pang. Should she turn onto the causeway now and stop by to see Remy? She could hardly believe he meant his inference Saturday night about Gordon's death. It must have been the tension of the snake bite and the boat nearly sinking to make him even suggest she might have been involved in what happened to Gordon.

It must have been like this for Miss Eugenia's sister, she thought. *She said it drove Geneva crazy not knowing what happened to Maxwell and never having any closure in the disappearance.*

Virginia bit her bottom lip. If Geneva had found closure, maybe she would still be alive today. At least she would not have not have been driven crazy from wondering, and from others wondering. It would be good for Miss Eugenia, after all these years, to know what finally happened to her vanished sister—and her sister's vanished lover.

And Remy—he must have heard some gossip about her alleged role in Gordon's death for him to make the comment he had made. She knew there was still talk about her marriage to Gordon and his death. Most folks in Murrells Inlet were nice to her face, but she saw the occasional nods, whispers, and meaningful looks. Lots of folks still believed she trapped Gordon in that shed and set fire to it. She was going to have to find out exactly what happened that night, for her own peace of mind as well as to clear her name.

In the meantime, however, Remy should be her champion, never wondering.

As she approached the South Causeway, the island's other entrance, she made up her mind. She would face Remy. If he thought she had anything to do with Gordon's death he could tell her this morning, in the fresh light of day. Hopefully, he would have a reasonable explanation for his insinuations, though she would never ask him for one.

Remy's Range Rover was gone. Seven o'clock in the morning, and he was not home. His newspaper was lying on his front doorstep. It always arrived very early, sometimes before dawn.

Had he left that early? Had he even spent the night here? Or had he left through his kitchen like he usually did, and not thought about the paper?

Virginia sighed. Was she having leftover suspicions because of Gordon's behavior or was Remy giving cause for suspicion himself?

Whatever the case, she was not going to let this be a wasted detour. Parking, she got out, went into the breezeway under Remy's house, and surveyed the mannequins. She had nearly finished sanding the auto body filler repairs on the three she had been working on, and could do the rest of the sanding and the finishing touches on one at a time at the shop.

Selecting the one that needed the least sanding, she removed the hands, then the arms, placing them in the spacious rear trunk of the Porsche. Taking the armless torso—with head—by the shoulders, she twisted gently until the torso came off at the waist. She set this in the trunk. Removing the single-piece lower torso and legs from the stand, she placed these in the trunk, too.

As this left no room for the stand, she headed for the small forward trunk, then got an idea. She took the head and torso section and set this upright in her front seat beside the cat carrier. Except for the stylized molded hair, it looked almost like a person sitting there. Placing the stand in the trunk, she closed the lid then headed off the island, the head and shoulders of her mannequin in the passenger seat, riding even with her own head and shoulders.

When Virginia reached her shop, Remy's Rover was parked there, backed up to the sidewalk in front of her store. He was standing in front of her shop window, putting the finishing touches on a grinning Cheshire cat, identical to the one on her hanging sign. He stood back from the glass and grinned. "Ta da!"

Just like on her hanging sign, the cat on the window crouched within the legend Cheshire Cat Maritime Antiques.

"I usually letter store windows from the inside," he smiled, "but I wanted this to be a surprise, and I didn't have a key."

"Nice," murmured Virginia, looking at the window.

"A gift," smiled Remy. "I know I should charge you, since the hanging sign was a gift, but I'm so, so very, very sorry about what I said the other night. You know I didn't mean it." He stopped to take a sip of coffee then set his coffee mug, pale green and etched with large sea scallop shells, on the window ledge before leaning forward to kiss Virginia on the lips. He looked beyond her to her Porsche, where the mannequin occupied the passenger seat. "Wow. You've got a passenger."

"I stopped by your house and picked her up," Virginia said. "I was hoping to see you, but hey, at least somebody was there."

Remy glanced at his watch. "Time to head out—I've got to letter a boat up in Little River at eleven."

"That's almost in North Carolina," Virginia observed.

"They love me up there, too," Remy grinned. "I better go—got to stop by my house and get some gold leafing stuff out of my shop. I used the bit in my paint kit on your kitty eyes." He pressed the lid down on the two cans of enamel paint he had been using. "Oh, and don't leave your car unlocked at the marina—my Walther PPK is gone, you know." Quickly he cleaned his brushes, not looking up.

Good, he must feel terrible about insinuating that trouble follows me, she thought.

Virginia watched him pick up the enamel paint set he always carried with him and carefully load it into his Rover through the open tailgate.

He took Virginia's face in his hands. "I love you, honey."

"I love you, too."

Remy grinned, saluted, and was gone.

Virginia gulped. She had told him she loved him—without any trepidation. She let herself into the shop as Remy drove away. Propping the door open, she brought Gabrielle in her cat box inside, then carried all the mannequin parts, the cat food and the litter into the rear of the shop, all the while thinking that the door opened and closed much too quietly.

Since she would most likely be in the back working on the mannequin today, she chose a small, ornately carved copper bell and hung it on her door to alert her when customers came in, then opened the door to test the bell. It was perfect, just perfect. Before closing the door, she heard a diesel rumble from down Front Street—Miss Eugenia would likely be here soon. From the inside, she stood back and admired the window with the Cheshire cat and her store name in reverse. Once again, Remy had free-handedly captured the Victorian feel and devil-may-care grin of the Cheshire cat crouching in her shop name.

She jumped as the front door bell jingled, then smiled as Miss Eugenia came though the door, layered amethyst necklaces darker purple against her lighter purple cotton dress.

"Didn't mean to startle you, my dear."

"Oh, I just hung this bell. It's one of the consignment items you brought in yesterday. Having it on the door will surely bring attention to it. I better affix a price to it. On second thought, I might buy it myself."

"Let it be my grand opening gift to you and your shop," said Miss Eugenia. "It was Geneva's bell—she had it on her boat for a while, always changing things on that boat. Ever since we, ah, talked about Geneva yesterday, I've been remembering so many little things about her. Not things I forgot, mind you, but little things I hadn't thought about in years—such as how she loved copper, and Cheshire cats."

"I love copper, too," said Virginia. "And you know I like Cheshire cats." She gestured toward her sign.

"I may have a picture of that same copper bell hanging on Geneva's boat, a stern-sided picture showing the rear door where Geneva had hung it. I had some close-ups of *Cheshire* and also pictures from across the river I took during the Labor Day boat races."

"The day leading up to the night Maxwell disappeared," Virginia said, softly tinkling the bell with her finger.

"Yes," Miss Eugenia said sadly. "Maybe the last day Geneva ever laughed."

"Was 1949 the last year the Labor Day Boat Races were held here?" Virginia asked. "I looked it up in the old newspapers on microfilm—the newspaper gave the races good coverage. But for Labor Day 1950, there was nothing about the races, nor in 1951."

"1949 was the last year," Miss Eugenia sighed. "But the Labor Day Boat Races were quite a thing here that year. All those long, fast wooden barrel-back speedboats, GarWoods, Hackers, lots of Chris-Crafts, and fancy homemade ones too, with their mirror-bright varnished hulls of mahogany—it was a stunning sight."

"Were you down there on the boat, watching the races?"

"No. I was aboard another boat, with friends." Miss Eugenia looked wistful. "Geneva had begun to avoid me when she was with that—with Maxwell. I had seen him with a—" she broke off, then carefully continued, "—a woman of ill repute, and he looked right at me! And when I told Geneva about it, she confronted him, and of course he denied it, and of course she believed him. Minding my own business was out of the question. I had to tell Geneva, because he was fondling the woman."

"Fondling her!"

"Exactly," Miss Eugenia sniffed, "either that or checking her for ticks."

Virginia raised her eyebrows. "Of course you had to tell her. There's nothing worse than an unfaithful man."

"And woe to the messenger," Miss Eugenia said. "Well. Enough of that." She brightened. "Those things of Geneva's are out in my truck. Pictures of her, pictures of her boat, maps of the bay out here and the islands, and boating clothes, hers and mine. And some more junk and treasures from my attic."

Virginia went out to Miss Eugenia's truck and came back in carrying a small but heavy cardboard box. She began opening the top.

"That's all old keys—Geneva's things are in the other box, the hatbox."

"Oh good—old keys came with the Savannah shipment too. But—these are so ornate!" Virginia looked closer. "Some of them are shaped like animals, and characters." She slid the box of keys to the other end of the counter and went out to Miss Eugenia's truck again. This time she came back in carrying a large hat box.

"Open it, my dear!" Miss Eugenia clasped her hands together gleefully. "You'll be surprised." She sat down in the big rocking chair by the counter.

Carefully, Virginia worked the snug lid off the box.

On the very top was a stiff, faded white cotton captain's hat with dark cord piping. Above the short black front brim, in bold script, was the legend *Chris-Craft*. Beneath that hat was an identical one.

"Mine and Geneva's boating hats," said Miss Eugenia.

Virginia picked them up, one in each hand, and turned them about. "I didn't know any of these still existed," she said. "I've seen them in early photographs and advertisements, usually on the heads of Chris-Craft models."

Miss Eugenia smiled, cupped her hand, blew on her fingernails theatrically, and pretended to buff them on the front shoulder of her dress. "Yes," she grinned mischievously.

Virginia gasped and pointed at Miss Eugenia. "You!"

"Yes—Geneva and myself. When we went to the Chicago Boat Show in 1949 to buy her boat—she had just inherited that money from her mother's estate—I told you we had different mothers?"

Virginia nodded. "My boat originally was bought at the Chicago show in 1949, too."

"Well, when we decided on that big forty-foot Chrissy, the Chris-Craft representatives there had a field day. They gave us ladies' sailor suits, white with sailor collars, and the captains' hats you're holding there. I wasn't stout then like I am now, you know. They had us pose, and pose, and pose. Of course we did, we loved it, and that summer—the boat show was in February, so we about froze—the print ads were in boat magazine and travel magazines all over the country!"

"Do you still have any of the ads?"

"In this box," Miss Eugenia leaned forward. "At the bottom, under the clothes."

Virginia carefully pulled out two folded sailor outfits, each consisting of white pants and white blouses with sailor collars. Underneath were several magazines. Virginia picked up the first one.

"Turn it over," Miss Eugenia said.

Virginia looked at the back of the magazine, which contained a full page ad for Chris-Craft. From the mahogany deck of an enclosed-bridge cruiser identical to her own *Chaucer* except for the lack of a flying bridge, two fresh-faced young ladies clad in white sailor suits beamed saucily from beneath the narrow brims of their jauntily-angled captain's caps.

"You two are so beautiful," said Virginia, smiling. She tilted the photograph. "This boat is identical to mine, except my boat has a flying bridge."

"That's the boat Geneva bought, and that's us," Miss Eugenia nodded, misty-eyed. "We modeled for their prints ads while we were in Chicago—there are pictures in these magazines of us in sleek polka dots swimsuits and smart halter-and-shorts sets, posing on the boats and waving. Everything was perfect then. Neither of us had any idea what lay ahead. Maxwell, my sister's, ah, 'gentleman friend' who later disappeared, he was there, too."

She pulled an embroidered cotton hankie out of her pocket and dabbed the corners of her eyes. "There are more magazines and photographs underneath."

Virginia lifted out the magazines and set them on the counter. She picked up a yellowed envelope, and a sheaf of black and white photographs fell out onto the counter. "Oops," she said, picking up the one on top. She turned it right side up and studied it.

Two young women and a man beamed at the camera from the stern of the same boat in the magazine ad. "This is you, and Geneva, too?"

"And Maxwell," confirmed Miss Eugenia, "right here in George-town, the day the boat was delivered. She was carried from Chicago to Norfolk by train, then sailed down the Intracoastal Waterway to Georgetown. It was the end of February when she arrived. Geneva had her name, *Cheshire*, put on the transom in gold leaf the very next day. See?" She pointed, picking up a photograph of the boat's stern.

Virginia gasped. *Cheshire* was emblazoned across the stern in the same old-fashioned Copperplate script Remy had used for *Chaucer*, the same script she'd asked him to replicate from the faint old *Ch* she'd found on the stern.

"Just like the *Ch* I found under the old varnish on the transom last year," murmured Virginia.

"What did you say dear?" Miss Eugenia asked.

"Underneath all the old wood stain and varnish that had been put on my boat's transom over the years, I found a faint *Ch*. It made me wonder if her name had been *Chaucer*. That name fit well on the transom, the seven letters, I mean. And since I had no history of her after she was sold at the 1949 Chicago Boat Show, I figured she must have some stories to tell, just like Geoffrey Chaucer in his *Canterbury Tales*. When Remy lettered *Chaucer* on the stern for me, he used the same lettering style."

Miss Eugenia nodded. "Boats do often have stories. Especially Geneva's," she sighed. "If that boat could have talked, she could have told what happened to Maxwell and cleared Geneva's conscience as well as her good name." She looked up from the photograph.

"A beauty, ain't she?" Miss Eugenia smiled.

"Oh yes, yes," replied Virginia, not sure if Miss Eugenia was referring to her sister or the boat. Truth be told, they were both beauties. "Miss Eugenia, what happened to this boat, to *Cheshire*? How long did Geneva keep her after the—the accident?" Virginia asked.

"Not long," Miss Eugenia shook her head.

"Did Geneva sell *Cheshire* before she, ah, disappeared?"

"No, child," Miss Eugenia grew serious again. "After Maxwell's accident, Geneva stayed on that boat, nigh on a week, wouldn't hardly leave. Then one morning, early, she took her out beyond the jetties, out into the ocean, and scuttled her."

Chapter Twenty-Five

"Scuttled her?" Virginia could hardly believe her ears.

"Sank her like a stone," Miss Eugenia said. "Geneva left with *Cheshire* towing the runabout, then came back in the runabout—and no *Cheshire*. I never saw her again."

"Never saw her again—the boat or Geneva?" Virginia asked.

"Never saw the boat again. I saw Geneva very rarely. She cloistered herself at the old McKenna house, the one she inherited when her mother died, on Pawleys Island, where we'd spent so many happy summers. By this time, the house, of course, was hers. But poor Geneva was never the same. She couldn't bear be aboard the boat, aboard *Cheshire*—why else would she have scuttled her?"

"Had Geneva been living on her boat before Maxwell's accident?"

"Practically. Back then, a lady did not live with, or 'stay,' with a fellow the way they do now, but Geneva was just about crossing the line with Maxwell. Just the two of them on that boat 'til all hours—they'd anchor out, and you couldn't be sure if one or both stayed aboard overnight.

"They'd anchor off North Island and go treasure hunting. Maxwell had him a fancy underwater metal detector. He and Geneva would skin dive—I think they call it scuba diving now—and find pottery from that old Spanish colony wreck, and sometimes even gold doubloons and pie-slice-shaped pieces-of-eight from pirate days. But the real treasure they found wasn't underwater. It was on North Island, where our great, no, *great*-great-grandparents lived all year-round, not just in the summer, like other plantation folk of their day did. Their rice plantation was over on the mainland, but they lived on North Island. You see, our great-great grandmother was from Rothesay, on the Isle of Bute, in Scotland. She missed her island home and North Island reminded her of it, so it was there her husband built their cottage."

Miss Eugenia paused. "Our great-grandmama on our daddy's side—named Virginia, just like you are, it was a popular name in those days—was born there. After our great-great-grandfather was widowed and his daughter married and moved to the mainland, he lived there the rest of his days. He was the one who was great friends with George Trenholm, the last Secretary of the Confederate Treasury, and donated heavily to the Cause." Miss Eugenia paused again.

"Remember me telling you about that a little while back, Virginia?"

"Yes, you told Remy and me, but please tell me again," Virginia said.

"Our great-great-grandfather," Miss Eugenia continued, "not only contributed monetarily, but invested a huge cache of gold, late seventeenth or early eighteenth-century pirate gold that he'd dug up on North Island years before. When Richmond fell at the end of the War Between the States, Trenholm spirited the treasury out of the city and down further south. He managed to return to his old friend—our great-great-grandfather McKenna—all that he had contributed, including the pirate gold dug up on North Island years before. Our great-great grandfather re-buried it somewhere on the island, and rumors of its existence and whereabouts had floated around Georgetown for years. Well, Geneva and Maxwell, with that fancy underwater metal detector, found it."

Virginia leaned forward, nearly speechless. "You never mentioned that part before!"

"Didn't I?" Miss Eugenia laboriously repositioned herself in the rocker. "Maxwell began making plans with 'his half' of the treasure. Geneva, who had put it away for safe keeping, was less than enthused with his talk. Then I saw Maxwell fondling the, ah, woman of ill repute. I could hardly believe it was Maxwell, but I got a good look at him. He was dressed in a careless, trashy manner, and Maxwell was usually so dapper and proper, but there was no mistaking it was him. Geneva didn't want to believe it, so she was upset with me for telling her, but I know it must have influenced her trust in him."

Miss Eugenia paused. "Geneva avoided me after that, and a few weeks later, on Labor Day night, after the boat races, they quarreled. I'm sure it was either over the treasure, or the woman I saw him with, or maybe both. Nevertheless, they quarreled loudly enough to be heard by people on other boats."

She drew a lavender cotton hanky from her dress pocket, dabbed at her eyes, and folded her hands. "You know the rest."

Virginia was respectfully silent. Miss Eugenia's pain, even now was obvious.

"I went out to the island—Pawleys Island—to see her on a number of occasions. She was not the same. She was only twenty-two, but she was old after Maxwell's disappearance—or his death. I'm sure she'd have had some measure of peace if his body had ever been recovered. After that terrible night she never was never completely herself again. She didn't want any help or companionship. She was preoccupied and distracted," Miss Eugenia swallowed, "but not so much so that I thought fit to have her committed to a sanitarium. Her hair turned white before she was twenty-three."

"I'm so sorry," Virginia said, not knowing what else to say.

"Once when I went out there, she looked, well, like she was expecting."

"Expecting—pregnant?"

"Yes. I asked her if she was—it had been too long since Maxwell's disappearance for it to be his—and she looked as if she'd seen a ghost, and she screamed at me to leave. I did, of course. She was very secretive after that, wouldn't let me in the door. I went out there, oh, every month or so, then a few times a year. Easter, Thanksgiving, Christmas...I took a full dinner every time and left it with her at the door. She never would let me in, always acted skittish. A few times I was sure I heard a baby cry, or a child whimper, and she always had an answer—she told me it was her puppy, her dog, one time she said she had a parrot—and I never got in to see."

"Didn't her neighbors see anything?"

"I'm sure they did—but the houses on either side of hers were rentals, vacant in the winter and with a new family every week or two all summer. She was well off, from her mother's inheritance, so she wasn't wanting for money, and I didn't want to make her reputation any worse by trying to get her professional help. I left well enough alone and hoped she'd get over it. Now I wish I'd barged in."

"How did Geneva disappear?"

"When Hurricane Hazel came through, her house was flooded from the storm surge and nearly collapsed on the foundation. Her body was never recovered. Her house was condemned and the property sold. The new owners salvaged and restored the house."

"I'm sorry," Virginia said.

"If I had known she didn't leave before the storm," said Miss Eugenia, sadly shaking her head, "I would have gone there and dragged her away."

When Miss Geneva left, Virginia unfolded the sailor outfits. She held up first one pair of trousers, then the other. Each appeared to be about a size six. They would be perfect for her mannequins, when she got two of them finished. She refolded the sailor outfits then picked up the photographs.

One showed Geneva posing prettily in a three-quarter profile on *Cheshire*'s bow. Geneva was wearing a dark strapless dress, no doubt to showcase the stunningly ornate, dark jewel-encrusted cross hanging from her neck. *The dress might have been silk,* Virginia thought, wishing the photographs were color instead of black and white. Maybe the dress was a deep red silk to bring out the cross necklace's dark, glittering stone—stones that might have been garnet or even ruby.

There were more close-ups of the stern's lettering, then one showing *Cheshire* at a close-up, three-quarter angle from the stern. That boat had certainly been a ringer for her own *Chaucer*—except for *Chaucer*'s flying bridge. If Geneva's *Cheshire* had a flying bridge she would almost wonder if they had been the same—

Virginia gasped. The next photograph showed *Cheshire* full-length from the starboard side, right behind the town clock right down the street here in Georgetown. Unlike the Chicago National Boat show picture of the boat, this photograph showed a flying bridge. Geneva's *Cheshire* did have a flying bridge, just like her own *Chaucer*! But that was impossible—this must be a photo of a different boat. Maybe Geneva had snapped this picture because the boat was so similar to her own new vessel.

Virginia studied the photo. The rounded curvature of the bow nose and stem was the same, unlike the sharp angles of later models. There were two portholes forward, marking the boat a forty-footer. Virginia held the photo closer. There was a name on the bow, just forward of the first porthole. She reached under the counter, hunting for her big magnifying glass. She brought it out and held it over the photo, focusing on the name on the bow.

Cheshire! This boat was *Cheshire*, but *Cheshire* didn't have a flying bridge—at least not when Geneva bought her. Could Geneva have had a flying bridge added on?

Biting her lip, Virginia dialed Miss Eugenia's phone number.

Chapter Twenty-Six

M iss Eugenia's phone rang and rang.

Virginia knew Miss Eugenia did not have nor want an answering machine. She had no cell phone, either. Virginia felt ready to burst. She wanted to ask her about *Cheshire* now, not later. She finally put the phone down when the bell on the front door jingled—and in walked Charisse. Where had she met Charisse before here in the shop? At the marina, maybe?

"Hey, neighbor. G'morning." Charisse drank deeply from the mug she was holding.

"Morning," said Virginia, looking up from the photographs. "Good coffee, huh?"

"The best. I grind it myself." She glanced appreciatively around, one hand smoothing the slim skirt of her crisp yellow linen summer suit. "You open early. That's good," Charisse said. "It's nice you have a lot of small things, too. So many of the visitors here are on motor coach tours from up North, and they don't have room to take much back."

"I didn't realize that," Virginia said. "But it does make sense. So many nautical items are big, like my ships' figureheads. I want to fill up the store with pieces of all sizes and have lots of antiques that are small and affordable."

"That's smart," said Charisse, taking a sip from her coffee mug. "Lots of visitors come onto Front Street after a tour of the Historic District. They're eager to find something historic to take home, but they might not want a great big antique."

"Do you have a cat?" Virginia asked, looking at Charisse's hands. The backs, wrapped around her coffee mug, were scratched. "I bring mine to the shop with me sometimes."

Charisse looked at the back of one hand. "No—I was pruning some rose bushes near one of my real estate signs. Gorgeous roses, but they were thornier than I realized. I ought to have been wearing gloves."

"I thought sure you were a cat person," Virginia said.

"No, I don't like cats," Charisse replied, shaking her head, her shiny dark hair swinging.

Virginia grimaced and smiled. "Sorry, I didn't know. I guess my shop sign is not the best scenery to have outside your apartment door."

"No, no," Charisse smiled. "I love your sign."

"I'm going to frame some of these," said Virginia, picking up one of the photographs Miss Eugenia had brought. "They're small. A friend of mine brought them in for consignment. They were all taken in the late forties. Want to look?"

Charisse set her coffee mug on the counter and carefully picked up the photograph closest to her, one of the photographs of *Cheshire*. She picked up the next photograph, a striking three-quarter-length profile shot of Geneva and Maxwell in swimsuits, posing aboard *Cheshire*, the Georgetown lighthouse behind them. She studied the photograph.

"Who are these people? Did the person who brought the pictures know their names?"

"Yes," answered Virginia. "The woman's name is Geneva, and the man's is, ah—oh it's on the tip of my tongue. It's two syllables, and it starts with an M."

"Malcolm?" asked Charisse.

"Almost! It's Maxwell. That's it. Do you know— "

Charisse started, knocking her coffee mug over. "Oh, I'm sorry, I'm so clumsy." She set the mug upright.

"No, you're not clumsy—you ought to see the messes I make. Just a sec." Virginia sprinted to the bathroom. "Don't worry about it—I'll get it up," she called over her shoulder.

There were no paper towels open, so she took a roll off the shelf above her head and tore the plastic wrapper off.

When she came out, Charisse was standing up, looking down into her shoulder bag. She looked up apologetically. "I thought I had some tissues, but they were all gone."

"That's all right," said Virginia, wiping off the counter. "I spill stuff all the time. Besides, none got on the pictures." She glanced up at Charisse. "I'd love to hear some more about those historic tours."

"Sure," said Charisse. "My office has moved—now it's the one with the blue door right down the street after you pass the town clock. Lots of my customers who end up buying a home here 'found' Georgetown when they visited on a historic tour."

The bell on the door jingled as a couple wearing beach visors, sandals, and khaki shorts walked in, holding hands. The woman was pointing to the copper slipper tub. The man looked at it too but kept glancing up at the ship's figurehead hanging above it.

"Hi, folks," Virginia said.

"Oops, I better be getting down to the office," Charisse said, glancing at her wristwatch. "Thanks for showing me the pictures." She turned toward the door.

"Sure," said Virginia. "I'm open until five if you want to stop back in. And Charisse," she tilted her head to one side, "where have we met before?"

"I tend bar at the Riverfront on Wednesday evenings," Charisse called over her shoulder. "Maybe it was there. See you later."

"Oh, you forgot your coffee mug!" Virginia called, but the bell had already jingled as the door shut behind Charisse.

Virginia took the coffee mug in the bathroom, rinsed it out and set it on the shelf. It was light green with sea scallops etched on it—just like the mug Remy had been drinking out of this morning.

The couple stayed in the shop for half an hour, talking about boats with Virginia. They looked through Miss Eugenia's photographs, exclaiming that they had seen a boat nearly identical to the pictured boat, *Cheshire*, just a few days ago in Murrells Inlet, with a name similar to *Cheshire*. It turned out they had seen Virginia's *Chaucer*. The couple could hardly believe it was not the same boat—maybe, they suggested, the flying bridge had been added. When Virginia showed them the photo of *Cheshire* with a flying bridge, they were adamant—the flying bridge had been added on, and *Cheshire* and *Chaucer* were the same boat.

Before leaving they bought the replica ship's figurehead, saying it would be perfect above their fireplace mantel and, if Virginia could get another one, they would buy it for their oceanfront home.

After they left, Virginia gathered up Miss Eugenia's photographs, making a mental note to find frames for them tomorrow. The very first one she wanted to frame was the one of Geneva and Maxwell aboard *Cheshire* with the North Island lighthouse in the background. First, however, she needed some lunch. She got out the phone book, dialed the number of the River Room, and ordered their fried oyster platter for lunch. The River Room was so close, she could walk over and pick up the lunch and be back here in the shop in less than five minutes. It had been a long time since breakfast, and some nice oysters, crispy on the outside, juicy on the inside, would hit the spot.

After lunch, she tried Miss Eugenia's number again.

Miss Eugenia answered on the third ring. "Hello there?"

Virginia took a deep breath. "Miss Eugenia, my *Chaucer* was bought at the 1949 Chicago National Boat Show, just like your sister's *Cheshire*. They look nearly identical, except for mine having a flying bridge and hers not—at least not at first. When did Geneva have a flying bridge added to her boat?"

"That summer," said Miss Eugenia. "An outside steering console and upper decking were added on by," she hesitated, clearing her throat, " ...by Maxwell."

"My *Chaucer*," said Virginia, "looks just like the photograph of *Cheshire* after Geneva and Maxwell added the flying bridge. Is it possible *Cheshire* was raised? After Geneva scuttled her? I think maybe my *Chaucer* is Geneva's *Cheshire*."

There was silence on Miss Eugenia's end of the line.

"Miss Eugenia?"

"No," Miss Eugenia said carefully, "that can't be."

"My boat was bought in Maryland in the early 1970s," Virginia went on. "But prior to that, I can't find any records, except that she was built in 1948 and was taken to the 1949 Chicago National Boat Show. There's no record of who bought her, or who her first owner was." Virginia hesitated. "I think her first owner was Geneva."

Chapter Twenty-Seven

"That's impossible." Miss Eugenia said slowly. "They are not the same boat."

"I have my boat's hull number and both engine numbers on the brass engine plate," Virginia replied, "but not much more. The Chris-Craft records from 1948 and 1949 are in a maritime museum, and the museum archivist sent me my boat's original plans and first destination—the Chicago show. But the records end there, before she was sold."

"I'm afraid they are two different boats," Miss Eugenia said. "Geneva scuttled *Cheshire* out in the ocean, not here in the harbor. She took her out through the bay through the shipping channel by the lighthouse, and into the open sea beyond the jetties, towing her little outboard. Geneva had only to open the seacocks, turn off the pumps, and down *Cheshire* went. Geneva motored back to town in the outboard." She paused. "Of course, this heightened suspicion toward Geneva. Even though *Cheshire* had been thoroughly searched, it appeared Geneva was getting rid of evidence of killing Maxwell."

"*Chaucer* was nearly scuttled yesterday, right in the marina," Virginia said. "She nearly sank in her slip, and would have if no one had been around. If she had sunk, she would have been raised."

"Oh you poor child," said Miss Eugenia. "I know that was an ordeal."

"It was," agreed Virginia, wondering if she should tell Miss Eugenia about the bouquet and the snake. "Miss Eugenia, could Cheshire have been raised, after Geneva scuttled her? I mean by someone else, since she was abandoned?"

"No." Miss Eugenia was adamant "We are talking about the open ocean, even though it was just outside the harbor. All that's left are the photographs. Surely I would have known—" She broke off and cleared her throat. "Dear, I must water my garden. I'll see you tomorrow. Tah-tah."

"'Bye." Virginia replaced the receiver. *I hope this wasn't too much of a shock for Miss Eugenia,* she thought, especially after going through

Geneva's photographs and clothes after all these years. But I did tell Miss Eugenia I would frame some of these pictures for the shop window. Maybe seeing them will give her some sort of peace.

Three small groups of customers came in after the first couple. Virginia sold several copper keys, two ice-fishing decoys, and a captain's chair. Elated with her sales and the shop's new-found popularity, she went back to the photos on the counter. The first one she would frame would be the one of Geneva and Maxwell aboard Cheshire with the lighthouse in the background. She looked through the photos one by one, then again, then a third time.

The photograph of Geneva and Maxwell aboard Cheshire in front of the lighthouse was gone.

*****

Driving back home to Murrells Inlet from Georgetown that afternoon, Virginia ripped into a rollicking tune on her harmonica. She was in high spirits. The possible *Cheshire-Chaucer* connection was tantalizingly mysterious and would have piqued her sense of intrigue even if her own boat was not involved.

She could scarcely wait to share this with Belinda. She had so much to discuss with her. As soon as I get home, thought Virginia, I'll give her a call so we can plan to have lunch.

Could her own *Chaucer* have been *Cheshire*, where Geneva and Maxwell's drama unfolded? Did Maxwell come to an untimely end while Geneva was passed out, just as Miss Eugenia believed? Or did Geneva kill Maxwell? If so, did she kill him in anger? By accident?

Did she push his body over the stern, leaving blood on the aft starboard cleat? Did he die on the boat or just disappear? No wonder Geneva secluded herself on Pawleys Island for years afterward, to get away from the unspoken accusations and cruel gossip.

Or was she hiding from guilt?

Virginia laid her harmonica on the passenger seat, deep in thought, and geared down as the traffic slowed, nearing Pawleys Island.

Virginia scowled. On a darker note, Geneva's scenario reminded her uncannily of Gordon's death, and the questions that must have gone through the minds of Sheriff Bone and everyone else around, including her neighbors. While she had no reason to feel guilty, sometimes Virginia heard snide remarks about making a marriage last forever and was sure she could feel accusing eyes on her.

She picked up her harmonica and began playing again. It was good to be working in Georgetown now, where not everyone wondered if she had killed Gordon, except perhaps the creep who put the horrible cut-and-paste "Virginia you're next" in that newspaper.

Miss Eugenia, of course, knew about Gordon's death, but she believed in Virginia's innocence, the way she still believed in Geneva's.

Hearing about Geneva's saga makes me feel as though a weight has been lifted from me, she thought—someone else suffered an experience similar to mine.

But—while the experience had led inadvertently to Geneva's demise, it was making Virginia more resilient, with renewed determination to find out what really did happen to Gordon.

Approaching the south causeway leading onto the island, Virginia felt her spirits lift even higher. Aside from being thrilled to at last have her own antiques shop, she loved being in Georgetown. Miss Eugenia's proximity and daily visits were quite pleasant, and Charisse dropping in from upstairs was nice, too. Other Front Street merchants had stopped by this week, welcoming Virginia into their midst.

All this gave Virginia a sense of community she had been missing. The steady influx of tourists, no matter how friendly, at the Murrells Inlet store, had left Virginia feeling a little lonely. She felt lonely at the marina, too. Living aboard in town would be a so much better.

I can't wait to move Chaucer *to Georgetown,* she thought.

She turned off Ocean Highway 17 onto the South Causeway leading to Pawleys Island. Having finished fine-sanding and painting the mannequin she took to the shop this morning, Virginia was ready for another. Now was the best time to stop pick one up, as she might not have time tomorrow morning. Hopefully she could finish it tomorrow and dress the pair in Miss Eugenia's and Geneva's vintage sailor outfits.

She pulled into Remy's empty driveway. *He must still be in Little River,* she thought, *or on the way back.* She loaded up a mannequin, the one with an original painted-on necklace, and was climbing back into her Porsche when a delivery truck roared up. The driver hopped out, a box in one hand and a clipboard in the other.

"Sign for this?" he asked, handing her the clipboard.

"Certainly." Virginia signed her name and gave the clipboard back. She placed the box on the front seat. She did not have a key to Remy's place and did not trust leaving the box unattended on his steps, so she would give it to him tonight or tomorrow, since she knew she would see him. She depressed the clutch, put her car in first gear, and glanced down at the label on the box as she waited for the delivery truck to leave so she could get out.

She gasped and when she saw the label. The box was addressed to Cameron Jamison, in care of Remy Ravenel. Why would Cam receive mail at Remy's home?

Hmmmnn, she thought. *Am I being reasonably suspicious or merely jealous? How will this sound to Belinda's professional ear?*

*****

She heard the gate creak and looked over the starboard side of the flying bridge. Remy was walking down the dock. His face lit up when he saw her.

"Look who's peeping over the side," he called. "Honey!"

Virginia immediately bristled. This morning he had a coffee mug just like Charisse's. This afternoon a package addressed to Cam arrived at his house, in care of him. *Remember, you catch more flies with honey than vinegar,* she told herself and smiled.

"Remy," she greeted him, with more cheer in her voice than she felt. She climbed down the bridge ladder and gave him a big hug when he came aboard. "I was so worried."

"What were you worried about, honey?"

"Well, I stopped your house to get another mannequin, and you weren't back yet. I just got a bad feeling."

"The traffic was terrible up in North Myrtle Beach," he said. "You must have heard about that wreck. The traffic was backed up for miles, with only one lane open. What with the wreck, plus the regular rush hour traffic, commuters going back to their inland homes after work, it took me forever."

"No," Virginia said carefully, "it wasn't that." Suddenly she felt sheepish. Surely lots of people had the same coffee mugs. But was this a coincidence? She took a breath. "It's probably just a coincidence, but the mug you were drinking coffee out of this morning? Charisse came by after you left, and she was drinking out of one just like it."

"Oh, that," Remy laughed. "Honey, I can put your worry to rest. She saw me down there, painting your window, and she brought me down some coffee. She said she likes you and wants to get to know you better."

"And she's known you a long time," Virginia pointed out.

"Charisse is just a friend, honey, and she's not interested in any kind of relationship other than as friends, I promise. I've known her a long, long time. She's been married and divorced twice, and widowed once. She taught me to dive. She helped me find my house—did the title search and everything herself. And, like I told you, she's a few years older than me."

More than a few, he said before, thought Virginia. "I'm not prone to jealousy," she said, "not unless there's reason. Is there?"

He lowered his head, looked Virginia in the eye, and smiled. "No. I'm yours. You know how I feel about you. Charisse is no threat."

"Well, after Cam——"

"Ah, speaking of Cam—I still feel bad about that night, and I feel like it's my fault. She's totally generous, never asking for anything—she asked me to bring her some more business cards to the florist shop. You just wouldn't believe how many people she meets who need a sign," Remy said. "And she asked how you were doing. She's happy for us. She mentioned what a great name you'd chosen for your store—she loved your Cheshire cat sign——"

"She saw the sign?"

"Yes! I had a picture of it with me. You know I take pictures of all my signs, and poor Cam, I felt so sorry for her when I saw her hands—they were all scratched up from helping an injured cat, even though she doesn't like cats. Cam is very kind-hearted."

Raising her eyebrows, Virginia folded her arms. "I stopped by you house to get another mannequin, and the UPS man got me to sign for a package addressed to her."

Remy looked down, shaking his head. "I'm sorry. I really was never serious about her, and I feel bad because she thought she was moving in with me. She was around all the time, when my divorce was pending. I was glad of the company and never realized she was so serious. She was just a friend, and it became a friendship that got out of hand. I never meant for her to think there was *anything* more than friendship."

"Are you sure?" Virginia asked. "I mean, unless she's mentally disturbed, she wouldn't think there was a permanent relationship there unless you'd, ah, reciprocated in some way."

"You mean physically reciprocated?" Remy sighed. "Yes. It was a mistake."

"Not just that but—did you ever tell her you loved her?"

"Well, yes," he said. "But I didn't mean it," he added hastily.

"If you didn't mean it, then why did you say it?"

"I meant it when I told her, but I didn't mean it afterward. I was temporarily on the rebound." He grinned sheepishly. "I didn't even know you then. Well, not since college."

"Well—when you tell *me* you love me—"

"I mean it!" Remy picked her up and swung her around. "Now I've got cold stuff in my truck to cook you dinner—if you'll have me—and I better bring it aboard before it melts out there in the parking lot. I just wanted to check first and make sure you were not, ah—"

"—mad at you? Never."

"Good. Honey, I'm ready to grill you the best rib-eyes you've ever tasted, right out here on the dock, so we can go to bed early," he smiled devilishly, raising his eye brows. "Then I'll get up before dawn and bring back sea trout or some other delicious fish—maybe spot tail bass—for tomorrow night's dinner."

Virginia sighed. Remy was so sweet. She would call Belinda tomorrow. She was glad she had not called earlier and shared her suspicions about Remy. Poor Remy—she was taking out her Gordon-induced-post traumatic stress on him. Remy should not have to suffer for the ordeals Gordon had put her through. He had endured troubles of his own, despite the fact that he seemed to have brought them on himself. But men, she reminded herself, sometimes mature later than women, and Remy seemed to be reaching a wise, well-seasoned maturity after suffering from his earlier poor judgment.

I should not burden Belinda with any of it, Virginia thought. But, I do want to spend some time with her, and tell her about the possible *Cheshire-Chaucer* connection. Belinda will enjoy hearing about that.

*****

Much later, long after falling asleep, Virginia awakened to the creak of the dock gate. Rolling over and sitting up to get out of her berth in order to peep out the curtain, she felt Remy stir beside her. Carefully she lay back down, hating for him to think she looked out the window every time she heard a noise. A few minutes later she heard the sound of a car door closing.

Neighbors, just neighbors, she told herself, *neighbors checking on their boat. I've got to stop being so paranoid* she thought, falling uneasily asleep.

*****

When Virginia opened her eyes the next morning, Remy was gone. *He's already left for that early morning fishing trip,* she remembered.

She was an early riser, but he, she knew, had already cleared the jetty and was on his way to the sunken wreck *City of Richmond,* about thirty miles off Murrells Inlet. It was only about fifteen miles off Georgetown—maybe when she moved *Chaucer* to Georgetown he would move his boat there, too.

Turning over, she yawned and stretched happily, remembering the rib-eyes Remy grilled for them on the dock for dinner last night and the sea trout or spot tail bass he was planning for tonight.

Hopping onto the bed, Gabrielle stretched luxuriously. Recovered from whatever was upsetting her before the near-sinking, she began to purr contentedly as soon as Virginia touched her. Virginia smiled. Thinking about Remy made her want to purr, too.

Picking up her phone, she dialed Belinda's number. Belinda often went into her office early to meet a patient who had to make appointments before his workday began. If that was the case today, maybe she could catch Belinda at home before she left.

Belinda answered on the third ring.

"Hey, Belinda, when can we meet for lunch?"

"How about Friday?" Belinda suggested. "I'm leaving for Charlotte late this morning, for a Counselors of the Carolinas symposium. Keynote speaker, Dr. Belinda Bunnelle! I'll be back on Thursday. What's new with you?"

Enthusiastically bringing Belinda up to date on her new shop, Virginia made sure to mention Remy and Miss Eugenia's involvement in the shop, not forgetting her interesting new upstairs neighbor, Charisse. She also told Belinda about the possible connection between her *Chaucer* and Geneva McKenna's *Cheshire.*

"They were both built in 1948 and bought from the same boat show in Michigan in 1949?" Belinda sounded skeptical.

"Yes, but Miss Eugenia insists Geneva scuttled *Cheshire* in 1949 before holing herself up in a house on Pawleys Island for—five years!"

Belinda was silent for a few seconds. "Did this—ah, Geneva, have any children?"

"No children. No, wait. Miss Eugenia said something about hearing a baby, but Geneva said it was her puppy or something. And she wouldn't let Miss Eugenia inside the house. Maybe she did have a child."

"Sugar, I've got to go in early, but I'll call you this morning before I leave for Charlotte. What's your number at your new shop?"

Virginia told her, then looked at her watch as she hung up. She had better get going, too.

Half an hour later, Virginia was walking down the dock, coffee mug in hand. When she reached her car, it was locked, just as she'd left it—but her mannequin was gone.

Chapter Twenty-Eight

Stamping her foot in frustration, Virginia sloshed her coffee. Someone had taken her vintage mannequin—the only one with an original painted-on necklace—while she and Remy slept not five hundred yards away!

Sighing, she unlocked the driver's door and gingerly got in. She looked around.

Everything looked all right. She got out and looked behind the rear tires, remembering the cement block incident. Nothing. She breathed another sigh, this one of relief.

She debated whether or not to call the sheriff's department and decided not call. The last time Sheriff Bone had been down here to talk to her was to question her about Gordon's demise.

Grimly, she drove up the winding road toward Ocean Highway 17. The sun dappling through the overhead canopy of trees did not cheer her as it normally did. On impulse, she drove across the highway, heading east instead of turning south. This detour would not take long.

She drove up into the restaurant parking lot overlooking the inlet and the small marina where Remy docked his sport fishing boat. Pulling up beside his Range Rover, she took out of the Porche's console the sticky-note pad she always carried and wrote a quick note.

Remy, I love you, and dinner was delicious. V.

Beside her initial, she added a heart with an arrow through it, then got out of her car and stuck the note to the glass underneath his windshield wiper.

Her heart felt a little lighter as she entered the highway's tree-lined drive south. She still had time to pick up another mannequin from Remy's before heading for the shop.

The drive down the North Causeway, bordered on both sides by the vast marshes separating Pawleys Island and the mainland, brought a refreshing salt breeze through her open windows. As she got out of her Porsche in Remy's driveway, a movement from the window above caught her eye. Looking up, she saw nothing was but the window and the open shutters within.

Is someone up there, with no vehicle here and Remy gone? Virginia wondered. Not taking her gaze from the window, she stepped several feet to one side, then the other. All she could see beyond the reflected sky on the windowpanes were the thin, gauzy curtains.

Probably, she thought, *I saw the reflection of a gull flying by.*

Driving away with her mannequin, she looked back over her shoulder at the window.

The curtains moved ever so slightly, and she caught a glimpse of yellow as what might have been a face disappeared.

Virginia sighed, facing the road ahead. It couldn't have been a face. It was probably just the ceiling fan stirring the curtains. She took her harmonica out of her console. She was a little jittery and needed to play some music to loosen herself up. A dozen bars of a Scottish aire later, she was back on the highway and feeling more relaxed. When she got to the shop, she promised herself she would concentrate on framing those old boating photographs Miss Eugenia had brought her—and maybe edge a bit closer to understanding the *Cheshire-Chaucer* connection.

When she opened the shop door, Virginia smiled. The shop smelled so good. The leftover candle-wax smell from the previous shop blended nicely with the aroma of the furniture polish she used early yesterday afternoon on every wooden piece in the shop. The latex paint she used late yesterday to finish the first mannequin smelled good, too.

Setting the finished mannequin's stand in the window, she put one of the sailor outfits on the mannequin as she put the body together. For a crowning touch she set one of the Chris-Craft captain's hats jauntily on the molded hair. Not yet satisfied, she went out on the sidewalk and surveyed the window, then came back in and moved the mannequin a little to the left. The window display would be perfect after she'd hung the vintage photographs and ads—and finished the next mannequin.

At nine-thirty, the phone rang for the first time that morning.

"Cheshire Cat Maritime Antiques," Virginia answered, wondering if she would ever get over the thrill of saying that.

"Can you talk for a minute?" Belinda said.

"Surely," Virginia answered.

"I like hearing you answer the shop phone—'Cheshire Cat Maritime Antiques' has a good cadence to it. But how did you choose that name?"

"Remy's house has a Cheshire cat door knocker, an old copper one."

"Where is his house?"

"Pawleys Island."

"Oh." Belinda was silent for a few seconds.

"Belinda?"

"Virginia," Belinda said slowly, "I don't normally discuss my patients, past or present, but, well, your story of Geneva sounds awfully similar to the background of one of my former patients in Charlotte."

Virginia swallowed. "It does?"

"Yes," Belinda said carefully. "I looked in my old files after we spoke this morning. She—my patient—had post-traumatic stress going way back into her early childhood, before she was school age. She was in her mid-fifties—but looked younger—when I treated her, and she was having nightmares. She'd been in foster homes since she was about three, but nothing was known about her prior to being found alone in the Charlotte bus terminal."

"She was found in the bus terminal alone? A three-year-old?"

"Yes. From her occasionally vivid memories before that time, I deduced that she had lived with her mother, isolated in some big old island beach cottage, where her mother nearly drank herself to death grieving over the patient's dead father, whom the patient was afraid of and could describe in detail. And she—the patient's mother, I mean—was obsessed with Cheshire cats—"

"Cheshire cats!"

"Yes. Cheshire cats. And she—the patient's mother—thought she had a large boat, or used to. The patient's early childhood memories, and nightmares, seemed to hinge around a catastrophic storm." Belinda took a breath. "When she was found in the bus terminal in Charlotte—it was in 1954, in October, just a few days after Hurricane Hazel."

"Was there any record, or any indication of where she came from?" Virginia asked.

"None that I know of. When I treated her, it had been over fifty years since she was found in that bus terminal, and according to what was in her records, no one was sure she'd even been on a bus. Someone could've dropped her off. All she had with her were the clothes she was wearing, and she was holding a blanket and a baby doll, a life-sized baby doll. She wasn't talking when she was found, didn't speak for quite a while, and seemed to have no memory before the bus terminal. Her island beach affiliation didn't come out until she started having those nightmares and got into therapy with me."

"Belinda, this is disturbing." Virginia shivered.

"Yes, it is," Belinda agreed. "Listen, I'm on my way to Charlotte, for a few days, you know, to speak at that conference. I'm going to run this file to the marina and leave it in your boat. I have to go through Murrells Inlet anyway, so it's no trouble. There's a photograph of the patient in it, plus notes on what I told you just now, from my sessions with her."

"You know where the key is," Virginia said. "And Belinda—thanks."

"*De nada*. While I'm in Charlotte I'll get the tapes of my sessions with her out of storage and bring them back with me so you can hear what her voice sounds like—in case you recognize it."

"Belinda—you don't usually take photographs of your patients or tape their sessions, do you?"

"Tape their sessions with the patients' permission, sometimes, yes. But photographs, no." Belinda sighed. "This was different. I didn't take the photograph. This was a police department mug shot."

Virginia swallowed. "What had she done?"

"She was charged," Belinda said carefully, "with kidnapping and assaulting her former fiancé's new girlfriend."

Virginia swallowed. "Assaulting her—how?"

"Tying her up at gunpoint, cutting off her hair, cutting her face. It was nasty."

"Oh." Virginia, swallowed, feeing almost dizzy. "Was she sentenced to prison?"

"She probably would have been." Belinda's reply was terse. "She was out on bail—heaven knows why—and her attorney had her seeing me, hoping to get her off on an insanity plea."

"What happened to her?"

"She skipped out on her bail, disappeared without a trace. My guess was, she was heading for the Outer Banks, since she was obsessed with her dreams and memories of an old island beach cottage. We were in North Carolina, so the Outer Banks was logical."

Virginia drew a shaky breath. "Yes. Old island beach cottages— Oak Island, Hatteras Island, Ocracoke Island—it could have been any of them."

"I certainly thought so. I made some phone calls, made a couple of trips to the Outer Banks, took the ferries, talked to a lot of locals.

Do you know, a lot of those old beach homes—some of the ones that made it through the storm—have their Hurricane Hazel waterline marked on the wall? I spent about ten days altogether."

"You were really determined. I'm impressed. What did you find out?"

"Nothing. It was in the fall, in the off season—anybody from off would've stuck out. She would've been remembered. But nothing. Nothing."

"How long ago was this?" Virginia asked.

"A few years before I moved down here."

So a few years before Gordon died, thought Virginia.

"Now," continued Belinda, "in retrospect, I think she might have headed down around Charleston—Sullivan's Island, Isle of Palms, James Island, old island beach cottages galore. And when she struck out probing her memories down there—"

"—she might have headed on up the coast a few miles—" Virginia mused.

"—to Pawleys Island," Belinda finished. "Now sugar, this file will be waiting for you when you get home, so study it, then put it away, 'cause I'm not supposed to do this."

"Yes, I will," Virginia said. "And Belinda, be careful. They're calling for a storm. I take it you're riding to Charlotte?"

"Absolutely! By Thursday that ol' storm will have come and gone. Now watch your back, hear me?"

"I hear you, Belinda. Godspeed."

Virginia put the receiver down slowly. Cam. Cam was obsessed with Remy. She broke into his home—his old island beach cottage—or at least invaded it when he was away. But Cam was younger than Belinda's former patient, or at least *looked* younger. She swallowed. There was a photograph in the file, Belinda said. *I need to stay busy,* she thought, *until I can get home and look at it. Otherwise I'll worry myself silly.*

In between customers, she set to work taking apart old, framed, water-spotted lighthouse prints from the store in Savannah. Long ago she had discovered that most customers loved to talk to her while she was working on a project. She put aside the prints in case they were valuable, then cleaned the frames and glasses to ready them for the Chris-Craft photographs and the magazine ad. After framing the magazine print ads and enough small photographs to create a striking backdrop, she hung all the pictures on the street-facing side of her closed-back window.

As an afterthought, she placed a coil of red cotton rope in the mannequin's hand—*let her be about to throw a line!* She didn't have white rope in the shop—was colored mooring line used in the forties as it was now? She'd have to find out. In the meantime, far be it for anyone who was not there back then to say red mooring lines were not used during the late 1940s.

*****

Belinda wound her gears out one by one on the curves going up Waccamaw Road away from the marina and toward Ocean Highway 17. She loved driving this road and was looking forward to her ride to Charlotte. The weather was perfect for riding up there today and hopefully back on Saturday. In between, though, there would be plenty of foul weather from that pesky storm brewing out in the Atlantic.

She smiled knowingly behind her face shield. For all the preparation and evacuation that would go on down here in the next couple of days, the hurricane would, as usual, turn out to be just another tropical storm by the time it reached the South Carolina coast.

Belinda gunned her motorcycle, happy for her work-related road trip. Her exuberant, adventurous mood was tempered only by her concern for Virginia.

She still felt uneasy about having left the manila file folder on the beautiful antique-lace-covered map table in the salon of Virginia's boat. She hoped she was not causing Virginia undue worry, but dammit, everything Virginia told her about Remy, his beach cottage, the Cheshire cat door knocker, the Chris-Craft coincidences—if they were coincidences—was all too much to ignore.

That patient had been downright spooky, starting off each session as a jaded, world-weary adult, then talking in that halting, little-girl nightmare voice when she got all wound up.

The storm she talked about, now *that* was a hurricane. It had to have been Hurricane Hazel, Belinda reasoned, because the patient had been found at the bus terminal not long after that storm.

The Patient had been Belinda's reference for the patient, since she had not been allowed to reference her by name on official documents. For simplicity's sake, and so the patient's name would not inadvertently be spoken on their session tapes, Belinda had never, even in passing, used her name.

Turning onto south Ocean Highway 17, Belinda never left first gear, turning after about one hundred yards into Fox's Lair Antiques, the shop Virginia had managed. There was something for sale there she wanted to get for Virginia.

Belinda parked her bike and went inside.

Mr. Kimbel looked up. "Well, hello! Belinda, isn't it? Virginia's friend?"

"Yes—and there's something I want to get for Virginia. She'd been talking about it and admiring it for about a year, but she didn't have a good place for it aboard *Chaucer.*"

"Ohhh—you mean the clipper ship anchor?"

"Yes. That's it. It will make a nice shop-opening present for Virginia."

"And it will fit better in the shop than it would have on the boat," Mr. Kimbel laughed, "unless she had kept it in the water!" He opened a drawer and got out a SOLD tag. "Let's tag that anchor right away."

Belinda walked outside onto the shop's porch with Mr. Kimbel.

Right beside the huge ancient joggling board, upon which generations of plantation children had bounced, sat the magnificent clipper-ship's anchor.

"She'll love it," Mr. Kimbel said. "And it'll be a great permanent piece for her maritime theme. We are, you know, primarily fox-hunting here."

"Yes," Belinda smiled. Virginia had told her that 'we're primarily foxhunting here' was practically Mr. Kimbel's motto for Fox's Lair Antiques.

Back inside, Belinda paid for the anchor. "Can you have it delivered?"

"Absolutely." Mr. Kimbel smiled. "It would be hard to fit that on your motorcycle, or in Virginia's Porsche. Perhaps after this hideous weather front comes and goes. Be careful on that motorcycle, dear."

"I'll be in Charlotte by this evening, and at a conference there until after the bad weather front has passed," Belinda said.

Mr. Kimbel put a hand to his chin. "Hmmmnn—you'll be heading west from Georgetown? Are you planning to drop in and see Virginia's shop?"

"I hadn't planned to," Belinda admitted, "and I've already taken the package I had for her by her boat. But I will. Then I can give her forewarning of the new decoration that will be arriving at her shop."

"She'll be thrilled," Mr. Kimbel assured her. "And give her my best—it's not the same around here without her."

*****

By the time the window was done, Virginia's stomach was growling loudly. After devouring the rib-eye sandwich she had brought from last night's leftovers, it was mid-afternoon and she was ready to begin on the mannequin she had brought from Remy's this morning.

The bell on the door jingled, and Charisse walked in. Instead of one of the crisp linen summer suits Virginia had seen her in, she was wearing shorts and a halter top. The ties of a bathing suit top peeked out from the neck of her halter. Her tan was deepened since yesterday, her shoulders a dark mahogany, brown with undertones of red.

"Great window!" Charisse said admiringly.

"Hey! Day off, huh?" Virginia greeted her.

"Yeah, I worked a half-day Saturday and Sunday showing houses, so today's my day off."

Virginia peered at Charisse's face, framed on either side by parentheses bracket-shaped marks from above the sides of her eyebrows to below her cheekbones. "You must have been snorkeling—I go in the creek at the south end of Pawleys sometimes, if the water's not too murky.

"I—yeah, that's what I did, right off the beach, to cool off in between lying in the sand reading." She laughed. "I just have to make sure and get all the sand out of my library book before I take it back."

"I love the library here," said Virginia. "I love to read, and do historic research, but I've only been to the library here once so far."

"Oh it's the best," Charisse answered. "The archives are awesome, and all the old *Georgetown Times* and census records are on microfilm. I spend a lot of time there, what with all the research stuff in local history and the rare book room."

"Census records? Are you researching family genealogy?"

"I did when I first moved here," Charisse said. "Now I mostly research the histories of properties my company has for sale." She glanced at her watch. "Got to get ready for tonight—we've got two live bands, and I'm earliest bartender. See you!"

"See you," Virginia replied. *Hmmnn,* she thought. *One day I will think of where I saw her before meeting her here. She wasn't a customer at Fox's Lair. It wasn't as far back as college—it was more recent than that. Could it have been at the marina?*

Ten minutes later the bell on the door jingled, and Belinda walked in, resplendent in brown distressed leather. "How do you like my new light leathers?" She asked, twirling. "Those black ones were cool, but they clashed with my hair." She ran a hand through her long blonde locks.

"Belinda!" Virginia came over to embrace her. "What a treat! Was the symposium cancelled because of the storm? Can you come with me to Remy's for dinner tonight? He went fishing this morning, so we're probably having spot tail bass—they're running right now, you know."

"Oh, I'd love to—and I want to meet the handsome devil, too, but I'm on my way to Charlotte as we speak—just stopped by to tell you in person that Fox's Lair will, one day soon, be delivering you your grand opening present from me."

"From Fox's Lair? What is it?"

"Well, it was too big to bring on my bike, and it used to hold a whole clipper ship in one place."

Virginia clapped a hand over her mouth in delight. "No! You didn't! It costs the earth!"

"Yes. I did. Let me treat you to an extravagant present before I get tied down with a gorgeous husband and a bunch of rug rats like you're about to!"

"Than you, Belinda." Virginia felt tears in her eyes,

"You're welcome, sugar. See you when I get back," Belinda said, her hand already on the door knob. "Oh, I almost forgot—I left that folder inside your boat, like we planned, before I decided to come here. Otherwise I would've brought it straight here. Watch your back, girlfriend." Then she was gone.

The phone rang. "Cheshire Cat Maritime Antiques," she answered.

"Honey!" Remy enthused. "Are you all set for seafood tonight?"

"Grilled spot tail bass?"

"Fried sea trout. You'll have a dinner fit for the queen that you are."

"I can hardly wait—my mouth is watering. Was it rough out there?"

"No, pretty calm. I got a little sunburned, though."

"Remy—was anyone at your house this morning?"

"No, there shouldn't have been. I locked up before I went to Little River yesterday, and I just got back here myself." He lowered his voice an octave. "And I like keeping stuff at your place, so I don't have to go home every night. Last night was nice."

"I like you keeping stuff there, too," Virginia said. "But Remy, when I stopped by for another mannequin to take to the shop this morning—"

"Didn't you pick up one on the way home yesterday?"

"Yes, but it was gone this morning."

Remy sighed. "I finally started locking my house, and you leave your car unlocked."

"It was locked. I had to unlock it with the key this morning. But what I was going to tell you is that I thought I saw someone in your house this morning. It looked like they backed away from the upstairs window, and the curtain moved." She hesitated. "I saw something light yellow—maybe blond hair."

"Or a yellow headscarf?"

"Well, maybe—" Virginia said.

"No maybes," Remy said, "and no worries. That was my cleaning lady. She sometimes wears a yellow bandanna on her head. I forgot she was doing my house this morning."

"Oh." Virginia hated being distrustful. "Charisse stopped by."

"Gordon and all his womanizing left you paranoid, honey," he teased. "I'm surprised you didn't think it was Charisse in my house."

"No, silly, she'd been at the beach. She had sand all in her library book."

"She did? Well." Remy cleared his throat. "Can you be here for dinner at, say, six?"

"How about seven—I have to go by the boat."

"What? Don't you have stuff at my place? Seriously, maybe you need to move in."

Virginia gulped. So soon! So far all she'd left there was her favorite long cotton batiste nightgown. "Seven's okay?"

"Sure, honey. Seven's fine. I love you. 'Bye."

"I love you too. 'Bye."

*****

Twenty-five miles west of Georgetown, Belinda cleared the out-skirts of the town of Andrews. It was beautiful out here in western Georgetown County. The gently curving two-lane bridged swamps and wound between rolling pastures filled with cattle and horses. Coming down over a rise, Belinda entered a long, straight high-banked stretch of road with swamps on either side—the perfect place to tach out. She opened up her throttle, then clucked her tongue. *Dammit,* she thought, watching a car pull out a hundred yards down the road in front of her.

Glancing in her rearview mirror, Belinda slowed back the throttle and prepared to poke along behind—or go around. She came up behind the car just as a slightly crooked brake light came on in the back window. Why was this person applying brakes? Belinda clucked her tongue again and shook her head as the car continued to slow. Why pull out onto a busy state road then put on brakes? Some drivers seemed to *want* to cause an accident.

Now the car was slowly pulling onto the right hand shoulder.

With another quick glance in her rearview, and a clear road ahead, Belinda swung out into the oncoming lane to pass the car. Still behind the car, she saw that it was no longer paralleling the edge of the road but pointing, hood forward, down the steep embankment.

Belinda slowed. Was the car about to go down the embankment into the swamp?

Rear end high and still on the highway, nose pointed down the embankment, the car rocked to a stop.

Passing alongside, Belinda looked over.

The driver's door was opening slowly to the halfway point. Then it teetered, and, with the weight of the downward swing, flew fully open so hard that it bounced against its hinges.

Glancing first in her rearview then ahead to make sure no traffic was coming, Belinda slowed even more, looking to see if the driver was in need of help—or perhaps not. She tensed, hand ready on the throttle, ready to take off if necessary.

The car's driver, a woman holding a tiny baby wrapped in a pink blanket, climbed shakily out and fell face down beside the car—on top of the infant. The woman did not move again.

That's it, I'm stopping, Belinda thought. She wheeled her bike over to the shoulder, and unable to find a spot in the soft shoul-

176

der hard enough to support the kickstand, reached back into her saddlebag and pulled out the six-by-six square of wood she carried for such occasions.

Though hating to waste precious seconds, she knew her bike might be the only means of getting help if it was needed. If she laid the bike down, or if it fell over, she would waste much more time getting it upright again by herself.

Running to where the motionless woman lay sprawled, Belinda crouched down and winced. A baby's tiny hand, partially covered by a frayed pink blanket corner, stuck out from beneath the T-shirt-and-jean-clad torso of the motionless woman.

That baby will smother if I don't get this woman off her, thought Belinda, grabbing the woman under her armpits and pulling her up off the baby. To Belinda's relief, the woman put her hands on the ground and pushed herself up on her knees.

"Are you all right?" Belinda asked, craning her neck to see around the woman to the baby on the ground.

The woman stood up, leaving the baby where it lay.

"Is the baby all—" Belinda broke off and screamed. The baby's mottled blue-white eye stared up at the sky with an opaque, unseeing gaze. Not a baby, but a baby doll, a very old one.

Belinda leapt to her feet. Tensing with recognition, she backed up.

"You!" The woman was on her feet, eyes blazing. "Why couldn't you leave well enough *alone*?"

Turning abruptly, Belinda ran for her bike. Thank heavens it was only a few feet away. Thank heavens she hadn't laid it on the ground it in her haste to be a Good Samaritan.

Then she felt the woman's arms go around her knees, tackling her from behind. She tried to twist backward as she hit the ground, but something hit her in the back of the head.

Then there was nothing.

Chapter Twenty-Nine

"Remy, I'm thinking about going inland before this hurricane gets any closer."

Virginia stood just behind Remy's house at the stone outdoor fireplace, where Remy was scraping the iron grill he kept on the hearth. The surf purred rhythmically behind the low sea oaks anchoring the huge sand dune that separated the house from the beach. It was hard to believe a hurricane was headed this way.

"Ah, another one," Remy shook his head. "This house has stood through hurricanes, both large and small, since it was built, way back in the 1850s." He laid the grill back over the driftwood piled there. "Back then they built beach cottages behind the dune line instead of on top of it. If this hurricane actually comes our way, we'll be safe and sound here in my house. You don't need to worry, honey." He lit a match and held it under the driftwood.

"The storm's predicted trajectory has us right in its path," Virginia said. "Miss Eugenia told me about it this afternoon. She's worried. I haven't seen the news in a couple of days."

"Miss Eugenia—her home ought to be pretty safe too," said Remy. "Ever get a look at that foundation? It's ballast brick—brick that came across the Atlantic in the holds of British ships, then was left here when the ships' holds were loaded with heavy lumber to take back to Britain to build more ships. That foundation, with Miss Eugenia's house built on top of it, has been withstanding storms and floods, like a lot of those houses down in Georgetown's Historic District, a hundred years before my house was even built, since way before the Revolutionary War."

"You have a good knowledge of the architecture and history here," Virginia said.

"A working knowledge," Remy said. "When I was looking for an old house, I researched Georgetown's Historic District, on my own, planning to buy there, but Charisse brought me straight out here, the day I walked into that office. That's how I met her, did I ever tell you?

"She's a smart real estate agent. I said, 'Beachfront? No way!' But Charisse really knew what she was doing. It was almost like she was waiting for the perfect person for this property—me, even though I didn't know it until she made me look at it. This house was a bargain—it was flooded during Hurricane Hazel and never really repaired properly. Ever since then, it was a low-price summer rental—no insulation at all. No heat, no AC. You've heard Pawleys Island called 'arrogantly shabby?' Well, my house was shabby and homely. It looked like a tall, rambling, historic shack. But I fell in love with it at first sight—just like I did with you." Remy turned to her and smiled. "Twice."

"I fell in love with you, again, at the Wooden Boat Festival, although I didn't realize it. Your cooking perpetuates my feelings," she grinned. *His cooking actually does help the fact that our re-involvement happened way too fast for me,* she thought.

She looked at the grouper lying on the platter on the picnic table, cleaned, herbed, bathed in olive oil, and ready to go on the grill. It had a quarter-inch hole going through its side.

She turned the fish over.

"Did you spear this grouper?" she asked.

"No. I gaffed it to get it in the boat." Remy looked up from the grill. "Why?"

"The hole in this grouper—it goes clear through the other side, like a spear gun hole."

"Oh—I gaffed it really hard. Gaff went all the way through. I didn't dive at all today."

"But the mask marks on both sides of your face—I thought—"

"Oh—yeah," Remy rubbed the sides of his face. "This afternoon I put on a mask and three-foot snorkel to go a few feet under and untangle one of the aft lines from the prop."

"Oh." Virginia smiled, picturing him in the water. *Remy is so handsome,* she thought.

With the driftwood smoke and its rainbow sea-salt sparks rising behind him, he looked positively devilish. It was no wonder Cam had taken his disinterest so hard. She stood on tiptoe to kiss his cheek. How could she ever have doubted him?

She wished she could mention her conversation with Belinda and her own suspicions that Cam might be Belinda's former patient to Remy, but it was confidential. Belinda had placed a great deal of trust in her by sharing the file.

Ever since she had expressed to Remy her initial worries about Cam, and her concern about his relationship with Charisse, he had been endearingly attentive, constantly phoning, and best of all, cooking—all to overcome the legacy of distrust Gordon had left her. She was not ready to mention this new suspicion to him, not yet.

It's natural, she told herself, to be cautious about Remy, considering how Gordon destroyed her trust, and how very fast her relationship with Remy had progressed. *Fiancée.* It was way too soon to be engaged, but, she was almost ashamed to admit, she did not want to risk losing him. If he wanted to say they were engaged, she would continue to go along with it.

Chances are, she thought, *things will be just fine and I will want to marry him—after a year or so of serious trust-building.* In the meantime, she was glad they were not living together, at least not yet.

*****

Tuesday morning dawned beautiful and clear. Virginia usually enjoyed getting up before sunrise, but not this morning. She had not slept well at all.

All during dinner at Remy's last night, she anticipated looking at the photograph in the folder Belinda left for her. When she got home and went aboard *Chaucer,* there was no folder.

Her spare key was exactly where she left it.

Making coffee, Virginia brooded. It was not like Belinda to forget or change her mind—Belinda was dependable. Besides, when Belinda came in the shop yesterday, she said she left the folder inside the boat.

With vague misgivings, Virginia headed for Georgetown.

She was only at the shop a few minutes before she heard the unmistakable rumbling rattle of Miss Eugenia's diesel engine. She immediately put her copper tea kettle on the burner behind the counter. She had decided to keep all her coffee-and tea-making supplies behind the counter so she could avail them without leaving the front of the shop. Her copper tea kettle, Liberty Blue and Blue Willow teapots, silver tea balls, and assortment of hanging antique tea accessories were functional as well as good conversation pieces—and some of them were for sale.

The antique keys from Blockade Runner Antiques in Savannah were hanging up near the front of the shop, but Virginia had hung the copper animal keys Miss Eugenia had brought amongst the hanging tea accessories.

"Morning, Miss Eugenia. Did you see where I hung your copper animal keys?" Virginia smiled at her as she walked in. "I thought they'd look good with the sterling tea balls." She reached up to tinkle some of the keys together. "There were three of each animal, all literary—three cats playing the fiddle, three cats in boots, three cows jumping over the moon, but only one Cheshire cat."

Miss Eugenia squinted up at the keys. "You're right, there was only one Cheshire Cat key left. These were all at our house long before I was even born. There was a little locking copper box with a corresponding animal for each set of keys. All the boxes are long gone. Geneva, of course, got the Cheshire cat box, and two of the keys. The other key was still with the rest of these." Adjusting her purple-rimmed glasses, she tilted her head back, searching the hanging keys. "I *know* I brought it in. I picked it up and looked at it the day I brought them here. I meant to show it to you."

"I saw it—I hung it up," said Virginia, "right here." She fingered the empty hook. "It's gone."

Miss Eugenia shook her head, giving the keys one last look. "It'll turn up. We have more urgent fish to fry. Do you know that the weather people just upgraded that storm to a hurricane? It's headed directly for us. We're under a hurricane watch."

"Oh, Miss Eugenia, I've evacuated unnecessarily so many times since I moved to the coast. When I was living up in Myrtle Beach, engaged to my late husband, he owned a beach service. Every time they said a storm was coming, he had to drag all the lifeguard stands off the beach, while his roommates boarded up windows, and while my roommate and I stocked up on enough ice and batteries and canned goods to see us through a week without electricity! Once, the Myrtle Beach airport even moved all their aircraft to another state! All that, and the power didn't even go off. Ever since I started living aboard *Chaucer,* I don't even leave. Sure, there've been some rough storms, but I double up the lines and—"

"Virginia." Miss Eugenia interrupted. She folded her arms. "Except for Hurricane Hugo in 1989, there hasn't been a major hurricane to hit this coast since Hazel in 1954. Those of you too young to remember Hazel are not respectful enough of the forces of nature. You need an evacuation plan."

"I suppose you're right," Virginia conceded. "But the chances of another direct hit here are slim, and I can't leave my boat unattended when a hurricane is forecast. And I can't leave the shop either—not now."

"You certainly are a faithful shopkeeper," said Miss Eugenia, "day in and day out."

Virginia brightened. "Would you like to keep the shop sometimes?"

"Love to," Miss Eugenia said. "In fact, I'd be honored. But when there's a hurricane, dearie, neither of us should be here. You'll *want* to be closing—all the Front Street merchants will be closed."

The kettle began to whistle.

Virginia took it off the burner, opened her wooden tea box, and scooped some loose tea into one of the silver tea balls. She hung the tea ball down in her blue willow teapot and picked up the kettle. "Let's have a cup of tea."

Miss Eugenia clapped her hands together in delight. "I'll just wash up," she said, heading for the bathroom.

As Virginia emptied the kettle into her teapot, she saw, through the steam, a man outside the window looking at her mannequin in the sailor outfit. She put the kettle down and looked up to see that he had turned his attention to the framed photographs behind the mannequin.

Virginia tilted her head to one side. The man seemed so familiar. The light brown tailored linen sport coat he had on looked familiar too. *Maybe he'll come in*, thought Virginia. Folks who took that much interest in her displays usually ended up buying something.

"Virginia, your restroom is precious, with the pedestal sink and the period water taps," Miss Eugenia began, emerging from the bathroom. She spotted the man. Her voice dropped. "Oh, my."

The man turned, put on the brown fedora hat he was holding, and began walking away, limping slightly as he favored his right leg.

That is the man, thought Virginia, *who was on the dock the first time Remy came to see me on the boat.*

Miss Eugenia looked pale and shaken.

"Miss Eugenia, are you okay? You look like you've seen a ghost."

The older lady raised her eyebrows and nodded toward the man's departing figure. "I feel like I've seen one."

"That man has been at the marina," Virginia said. "About a month ago he was down on my dock, then he left in a float plane."

"If I didn't know he was dead," said Miss Eugenia, "I'd think I had seen Maxwell, or what Maxwell might look like today, had he lived."

"Maxwell?!" Virginia gasped. "Geneva's—"

"Yes, dear," Miss Eugenia replied. "One and the same."

Chapter Thirty

That night, Virginia roused from a deep sleep in Remy's cozy rice bed.

She heard him talking quietly in the hall. *Who is he talking to,* she thought. Raising her head, she looked at the clock. Twelve forty-five. Could something be wrong? They had both gone to bed nearly two hours ago.

She got up and sleepily padded to the bedroom doorway.

"You're just going to have to accept it," Remy was murmuring softly into the telephone mouthpiece. "I need more time."

Virginia tiptoed to the open hall closet door and stood behind it, listening.

Remy rubbed the back of his neck, his hand under his hair making his unbound tresses ripple and shimmer in the dappled moonlight filtering in from outside. "No, of course it's not permanent. But for the time being, until we find what we're after, it's the way things are."

Virginia backed away from the doorway. Who could Remy be speaking too? Cam? She padded back to the bed and climbed in. She pulled the sheet up around her but did not lie down.

Remy came back to the bed a moment later. "Aw, baby, that woke you? I'm going to get an unlisted number—man and his wife take turns calling me, think I can produce their sign out of thin air. They need permits, and it's a sandblasted sign, no way will I start on it 'til after they get their permit." He sighed and kissed Virginia on the top of her head. "Baby, let's go back to sleep."

Baby, thought Virginia. *Baby?*

She lay awake in Remy's arms for half an hour as he snored softly. *Baby*—he had never called her "baby" before. He had always called her "honey."

Virginia woke up and sat straight up in bed. How long had she been asleep? Remy lightly snored beside her. The carved rice heads on the tall posts of Remy's nineteenth century bed were silhouetted in the moonlight shining through the wide shutter slats. A light breeze filtered in between them from the open window, up here on the top floor high above the dunes and sea oats. All seemed normal. She rubbed her arms through the thin sleeves of her cotton batiste nightgown. What had awakened her?

Crunch, crunch. Something was walking on the gravel drive below the window. She was sure of it. The ocean side of Remy's house faced east and only picked up surf sounds, but the west-facing windows up here in Remy's master bedroom were nearly over the island road and picked up sound from the paved road and gravel drive below.

Carefully swinging her legs over the side of the high bed, she felt with her toes for the bed steps. Lightly touching the three steps as she made her way down to the floor, she picked up her thin cotton robe and pulled it on over her nightgown. She crept to the open window and peered out.

Below, an opossum trotted along the drive. She breathed a sigh of relief. Suddenly it froze. It was "playing possum"—something must have frightened it.

Wide awake now, Virginia took care not to wake Remy. She padded out of the bedroom and into the hall. *This is what it will be like,* she thought, *when we have a child and I get up to check on him or her—Remy sleeps so soundly, he will never wake up.* Passing the open door of the east bedroom across the hall, Virginia was attracted by the light of the moon reflecting off the water. She walked in. *How many women,* she wondered, *have done this in the century and a half since the house was built? How many since Remy has lived here? One? Two? None?*

A crash from the across the hall shattered the peace of the night. She rushed out of the east bedroom, across the hall and stopped, grabbing the doorframe of the master bedroom.

Remy was standing by the bed in a pool of moonlight, the wide planks of the heart-of-pine floor around him glittering with shards of glass. Behind him, in shadow, lay the stone that had broken the window glass and burst open the unlatched shutters.

Virginia reached inside the door and turned on the light.

Raising a hand above his eyes to shield them from the overhead glare, Remy glanced up at Virginia. "Stay there—I already stepped on the glass when I jumped out of bed." Limping, he gingerly picked his way through the glittering shards to the edge of the bed, then sat down to examine his right foot.

When Virginia started toward him he looked at her and held up his hand. "I'm all right, you just keep yourself keep from getting cut."

She turned and headed for the stairs. Down in the dark kitchen, she turned on a light, grabbed a broom and dustpan from the broom closet, and pulled some paper towels off the roll over the sink and dampened them. As an afterthought, she grabbed the paper towel roll, too. About to head back up, she paused on the bottom step. The un-curtained kitchen windows gaped darkly.

Could who ever have done this still be out there? A flash of red out in the marsh caught her eye.

She stepped over to the window. Halfway across the marsh, over on the creek bridge linking the island and mainland spans of the South Causeway, a car was stopped. Two tail lights and a crooked rear window brake light formed a three-point triangle. She heard an engine accelerate.

The rear window brake light went off, and the car headed across. With a shiver, she turned and headed back upstairs.

She came back to the bedroom door just in time to see Remy wince as he pulled a piece of glass out of the sole of his foot. "Be careful," he grimaced, "It's not all flat on the floor. This piece," he held up a bloody triangle, "must have been lying upright, or else I landed on it just right."

Sweeping the broom gently ahead of her, Virginia made her way into the bedroom and passed Remy the roll of paper towels. She leaned down and swept glass fragments onto the dustpan, then cast the broom all about under the bed to make sure no shards landed there.

Crouching down, she wiped the floor with the wet paper towels to make sure no glass particles remained to pierce a bare foot. She looked up at the window.

No wonder there was so much glass—the stone had gone right through both the fixed upper window panes and the raised lower ones. The stone remained where it had landed.

To her surprise it was not grey or dark but light pink. Gingerly, she picked it up. "This is strange."

Remy glanced up at the stone. "That rock—it's pink," he said, pressing a wad of paper towels against the sole of his foot. "That's weird."

"It's a rose quartz," Virginia said. She turned it back and forth. "It's almost just like the one I have at the boat on the galley table." She turned it over and gasped.

Remy looked up. "What?"

"It says 'Glastonbury' on the back of it. My big rose quartz at the boat—I bought it in Glastonbury when I went to England and Scotland with my parents last spring."

Remy stared at her. "I've looked at yours before. I've picked it up—the pink rock on the galley table. It doesn't have anything written on the back."

"Well it does now—and I didn't write it."

Remy shook his head. "Virginia—"

"I've never told anybody where I got that rose quartz," Virginia said. "No one's ever asked. But it's written in my travel journal from that trip. Someone's been in my boat."

"Are you trying to tell me," Remy said, raising his eyebrows, "that someone went aboard your boat, found and read your travel journal, got a marker and wrote 'Glastonbury' on your rock, then threw the rock through my window?"

Virginia blinked. "All kinds of weird things have been happening lately." She hesitated.

"Ever since that night you had to call the sheriff's department over Cam breaking into your house."

Remy narrowed his eyes. "When the rock came through the window a few minutes ago and I woke up, you weren't in the bed."

Virginia stared at him. "No, I was across the hall."

Remy tilted his head to one side and raised his eyebrows. He sighed. "Well?"

She gulped. This couldn't be happening. "I think I'd better leave." She turned and grabbed her clothes off the dressing table chair. Without a backward glance, she headed for the bathroom down the hall.

A moment later she was headed down the hall toward the stairs. As she passed the bedroom door she heard Remy call her name. She stopped, poised for flight.

"Virginia," he repeated.

Despite his even tone, she heard underlying pain in his voice. Putting her hand on the door frame, she looked in.

Remy sat on the dressing table chair, the empty paper towel roll on the floor beside him. He held all of the blood-soaked paper towels pressed tightly to the bottom of his foot.

A single drop of blood fell from the lowest corner of the paper towels and another formed right away.

He looked up at her. "It's deep. Can you drive me to the emergency room?"

Chapter Thirty-One

D awn was breaking when Virginia opened her Porsche's passenger door in front of the sliding glass exit of Georgetown's hospital emergency room. Wincing, she silently watched Remy limp over the threshold, awkwardly lower himself on his right leg until he was seated, and ease his bandaged left foot into the low-slung car's passenger boot.

The silence between them had been barely noticeable during the two-and-a-half hour wait in the hospital ER. Nearly everyone there was abuzz with the latest weather updates on the tropical-storm-turned-hurricane that devastated Puerto Rico and was now whirling toward the South Carolina coast. By six a.m., the hurricane watch was officially changed to a warning, with the governor ordering evacuation of all barrier islands. Hurricane Harvey, now a Category Four hurricane, was expected to make landfall on the South Carolina coast within forty-eight hours.

The cut on the bottom of Remy's foot required stitches both inside the wound and out. Not only was the gash much deeper than he thought, it contained more glass. The piece Remy pulled out at his house was only a splinter of the shard that had broken off deep in the sole of his foot.

Wincing, Remy settled into the passenger seat. Finally, after a deep breath, he spoke.

"Virginia, I'm so sorry about what I said back at the house. I know you would never do something like that. I'm ashamed I even suggested it. I guess these hurricane warnings give everyone the jitters, and people can end up being rude and saying unkind things."

Resisting the temptation to remind Remy that his 'being rude and saying unkind things' to her at the house had more to do with the rock coming through his bedroom window than the weather, Virginia decided to accept his apology.

"You'd just gotten glass in your foot," Virginia said. "It was the pain talking." She hesitated. "I guess. And we were under hurricane *watch* at the time, not warning."

Remy's eyes filled with tears. "I love you so much. You're the best thing that's ever happened to me."

"I know. I mean, I love you, too," Virginia quickly corrected herself. If Remy's rudeness was the pain talking, his change of heart must be the pain*killers* talking.

"And you know, baby," he went on, "that hurricane's either gonna make landfall further north, like they always do when they're 'sposed to hit here, or it's gonna whirl itself out, you know? You heard the TV in there say it had gone down from a Category Four to a Three? There's no use to evacuate. Leave your boat, stay with me, we'll be fine."

Turning out of the hospital parking lot and onto Black River Road, headed for Ocean Highway 17, Virginia glanced over at Remy.

Settling back into the low bucket seat, he gave her a sleepy smile before closing his eyes. "We'll be fine," he murmured, falling fast asleep before they reached the river bridges leading north out of Georgetown.

On Pawleys Island, Virginia helped Remy into his house and assisted him in getting settled on the couch. Once he had gotten some rest, the ER doctor had assured her, he would be able to amble around carefully.

After making sure Remy had everything he needed, she drove toward Murrells Inlet and *Chaucer*. Once she was aboard the boat, she would have just enough time to change clothes—and check one thing—before heading for the shop.

According to the radio's last weather update, the hurricane was not expected to make landfall until tomorrow night, or early the next morning. *Where* it would make landfall was the important question now.

Walking down the dock, Virginia breathed a prayer of thanks that *Chaucer* appeared undisturbed after last night's mischief. Once inside, she quickly fed Gabrielle, changed clothes and brushed her teeth before venturing forward to the galley, breath held.

She stepped down into the galley and gasped. The spot on the galley table under the porthole, the place where she always kept the rose quartz, was empty.

Driving to Georgetown, Virginia tried to remember the last time she had seen the rose quartz in its usual spot in the galley. She had not noticed it missing, but then on the other hand, she did not look at it every day. It was definitely there last time she dusted. It could have been gone for several days. It could have been taken the day the boat nearly sank, the day the bouquet and the snake—Virginia grasped the wheel tighter. That was it—that crazy Cam must have taken it. Remy had said, just a day or so after the boat's near sinking, that she had scratches on her hands from trying to rescue a cat—and hadn't Gabrielle acted strange and clingy but did not want to be touched the night of the near sinking? Added to the fact that Cam, as Virginia had pointed out to Remy, worked in a florist shop where she would have easy access to flowers—and to landscapers, who would often come across snakes?

Virginia gulped. Cam was surely the one who put the blocks behind her tires. Virginia narrowed her eyes. If Cam's car had a crooked rear window brake light like the one she seen the night those blocks were put there—Virginia clenched her teeth. She could feel her nostrils flaring.

By the time she reached Georgetown, Virginia was certain: Cam had done all of these things. Cam was trying to wreak havoc on their lives, and Remy was terribly naïve.

Riding down Front Street, Virginia noticed several shop owners already on the premises.

The Thomas Café and the Coffee Break Café across the street seemed to be busier than usual for breakfast—there was not a parking space empty within a block of their front doors.

Early as always, she unlocked the door of the shop and took a deep breath. Normally she left the door unlocked after she arrived. Today, however, she needed a little time to herself before facing anyone, except possibly Miss Eugenia. Locking the door, she looked up at the clock—forty-five minutes until she opened at nine. No doubt she would be closing early, with the hurricane warning.

She put the tea kettle on, filled the silver tea ball and put sugar in her china cup. A nice cup of tea would be settling. She would take it to the back of the shop and work on her second mannequin. When all of this hurricane nonsense was over, she would display this mannequin in the other window with the ships' figureheads and the copper slipper-backed tub. This particular mannequin was made with her arms folded across her chest and her weight resting on one leg.

I can pose her holding one of my antique linen sheets around herself, thought Virginia, *so she can appear to be about to step into the tub.*

The tea kettle whistled, breaking into her thoughts. Virginia picked it up off the burner and poured boiling water into the teapot onto the tea ball. As she lifted the lid to place it on top of the teapot, a sharp rap sounded at the door and startled her, causing her to nearly drop it.

Glancing toward the door, she started again. A man in a rumpled light brown tailored linen sport coat smiled at her through the glass door. He was wearing a brown fedora and—yes, he dipped as he moved to the right, favoring his right leg. It was the man she had seen, yesterday, or the day before, looking in the window—the same man Remy had seen looking at *Chaucer* through binoculars the first day he came to her boat—right before she had her lettered and all this craziness began.

Virginia bit her lip. She had not turned her '*Closed*' sign around to '*Open*' yet. It was too early. Legitimately she could point to the clock and her posted hours, telling him to come back when she was open—when there would be other businesses open and other people around.

He smiled again and raised his eyebrows.

Virginia sighed and mustered a pleasant expression. Hoping she was not making a grave mistake, she went to the door and unlocked it.

Chapter Thirty-Two

"Good morning," Virginia smiled, opening the door a few inches. "We actually open at nine."

"I apologize for being so early," the man said, taking off his fedora, "but I wanted to catch you before you get busy."

"With the hurricane warning, I can't really gauge how busy my shop will be," Virginia said, slowly opening the door, "but the other merchants will be down here preparing for the storm, as I will be." She did not expect many, if any, customers this morning, but she did not want him to think she would be alone, either.

"That's my reason for urgency," the man explained, holding his fedora with both hands in front of his chest. "You have a 1940s Chris-Craft up in Murrells Inlet, yes?"

"Yes—*Chaucer*," Virginia replied.

"People with boats too large to trailer sometimes sail them out of the area to avoid a hurricane and then can't bring them back to the same dockage, because the dock is gone," he said soberly. "Of course, everything may be the same after the storm, but I was hoping to talk to you about your boat before the storm hits, you know, just in case."

"I understand. But I'm keeping *Chaucer* right where she is, in Murrells Inlet. The marina I'm in is very sheltered, being over on the waterway." Virginia tilted her head to one side, waiting. He knew where *Chaucer* was docked—he'd been there! If he wanted to buy *Chaucer,* he ought to stop dancing around the subject long enough for her to tell him no.

"I was hoping to interview you about your Chris-Craft for a national boating magazine. A 1948 like yours, in decent condition, is a bit rare. And live-aboards," he cleared his throat, "*successful* live-aboards, like you, are of great interest to readers. Living aboard a boat sounds like the ultimate utopia to many readers, and they love to read about those who pursue that dream and realize it."

Virginia listened skeptically. The man seemed legitimate, but he was talking too much and running on nervously. Why would he be nervous?

"What boating magazine is it?" she asked. "I have several favorites."

"I'm freelance," he said quickly and held out his hand. "Malcolm Trapier."

Freelance, thought Virginia. *Unemployed?*

As if reading her mind, he drew a boating magazine out of his canvas satchel and held it out to her. "I write for several. The article about your boat will be for this one."

Virginia reached for the magazine. "This one is my favorite—"

"Keep it. My business card's in there too," Malcolm smiled. "The managing editor and I have become good friends, and I write quite a bit for them. This article will probably be in our December, or possibly January issue. That is," he added quickly, "if you allow me to write it."

"Well, yes, of course," said Virginia. This could be excellent publicity for her shop, especially if he could take photographs after she had *Chaucer* docked here, right behind the shop. "It would be an honor to have *Chaucer* featured. Her restoration has been a great deal of work, and I am very proud of her. After this storm—"

"Could I go ahead and take photos of your boat today? I hate to put it this way, but Hurricane Harvey is supposed to make landfall tomorrow night and your boat might, ah, be—"

"Damaged?" Virginia was surprised. "Surely not. The Waccamaw River section of the Intracoastal Waterway, where *Chaucer* is docked, is the safest place for her. Folks with saltwater dockages sometimes *bring* their boats to our marina when a hurricane is expected—I certainly wouldn't take *Chaucer* away from there."

"Well, yes, you're right, of course. I was just thinking of the high winds and flying debris…" His trailed off, as he raised his eyebrows.

Virginia tapped her chin with her forefinger. He did have a point. "I suppose it *would* be better for you to take pictures today. Or tomorrow. If the storm is fierce, my boat and all the others in the marina will have leaves and grass stuck all over them, or worse. But I must ask you not to go aboard until later, when I'm there. Today, I'll be here in the shop."

"Certainly. I can get all my outside shots today. And I thank you. May I ask you some preliminary questions?"

"Of course. And help yourself a cup of tea. You don't mind me working on my mannequin while you—"

"—not at all. The mannequin in the window—the Chris-Craft girl—is excellent. That display brings back—memories." He cleared his throat. "Can we begin with how you decided to name your boat *Chaucer*?" He brought out a small spiral-bound notebook.

"Surely," said Virginia, relieved. And she had thought he was so sinister.

*****

Malcolm had just left when Miss Eugenia opened the front door of the shop. She stood, hand on the doorknob, watching him disappear around the corner of Screven and Front Street.

She tapped the toe of one purple rain boot nervously on the hardwood floor.

"I came to talk to you about your plans for the storm, but who was that man? He's the one who looks like Maxwell...he was just here, what was it, yesterday?" She asked.

"He's a magazine writer, working on an article about *Chaucer*," Virginia answered, holding up the boating magazine.

"I didn't get a good look at his face. It's something about how he carries himself, though. I don't recall him having a limp. Of course, that could have come later."

"His name is Malcolm...Malcolm...oh, I forgot his last name— things have been kind of hectic. He told me what it was—Trimmier, or something like that. And he said he left a business card in the magazine, but I can't find it." She flipped through the entire magazine, then turned pages until she reached the editorial page.

"He'll be listed on there," Miss Eugenia looked over her shoulder.

"Maybe not," said Virginia. "He works freelance."

"You mean he's unemployed," Miss Eugenia sniffed.

Virginia rolled her eyes and smiled. "Remy's freelance, and he's not unemployed."

"Well, that's different," Miss Virginia cleared her throat, "er, I suppose."

Virginia scanned the bottom of the editorial page for a telephone number. "He left so quickly, with the urgency of getting pictures before the hurricane, but I need to be able to get in touch with him."

She leaned on the counter, dialing the number of the boating magazine.

"Hello, yes, I was calling about one of your freelance writers—"

Virginia listened for a few seconds, her eyebrows rising. "Never?"

Miss Eugenia looked at her quizzically.

"Yes," Virginia said, "eight-four-three is the area code for coastal South Carolina. Oh, yes—we are bracing for Harvey. You take care, too. Thank you."

She hung up the receiver slowly and looked at Miss Eugenia. "They don't employ freelance writers. Ever."

Chapter Thirty-Three

A surprising number of out-of-town vacationing customers, all buzzing excitedly with hurricane news and good-natured laments of their interrupted seaside week, kept Virginia busy for the rest of the morning. During a quiet half hour, with grave misgivings and visions of sticky tape residue, she taped a heavy duct-tape X on every window in the shop.

She was taping the front door from the outside when Charisse appeared at the bottom of her apartment stairs. Virginia started.

Barefooted, in cut-off jeans and an old T-shirt, her straight dark hair escaping from a ponytail, and a bandanna tied lengthwise around her head, Charisse was disheveled and cross.

"Do you have a crowbar," she frowned, "or a big screwdriver, maybe?" Not waiting for an answer she continued, "My window, the one right up there," she said, gesturing to one of the her apartment windows above their heads, "it's stuck, painted shut. It might even be caulked shut, under all that old paint."

Virginia looked at her watch. She should call and check on Remy. He had not called—he was probably asleep from those pain pills. He could wait a little while, and Charisse looked like she could use a hand.

"All my tools are at the boat," Virginia told her, "but I'll come up and help you open it. Remy had it open the day he hung my sign, so we ought to be able to open it together."

Charisse did not move. She looked up toward the sign.

Poor thing, thought Virginia, *she's so worried about this storm, she's almost petrified with delayed reaction.* "I can come up now and help you open it, Charisse," she repeated. "Together we ought to be able to raise it."

Charisse's eyes widened for a fraction of a second, then she blinked. "No, no, that's okay, we would have to have tools to pry it loose. Remy never opened the window. He looked out the window, to make sure the sign was hung straight. My other window opens, but this one, the one near your sign, never has."

Oh." Virginia frowned. Didn't she see the curtains moving in *both* open windows the evening she rented the shop?

"I've got to get back up there," Charisse said, turning to put one bare foot on the stair above the one she was standing on.

"Okay." Looking down, Virginia pulled more duct tape off the roll. "Where are you going for the storm, if it gets bad?"

That bandanna tied around her head like a headband, thought Virginia, *that's how I met her before. She was wearing a wreath of gardenia flowers around her head when she sketched my boat, and then asked me all those questions on the dock over a year ago. I wonder,* she thought, *why she was so interested in my boat?*

*****

No customers came in after three o'clock. After noting that several other Front Street merchants were doing so, Virginia locked the shop, put the Closed sign on the door, and left.

Driving down Front Street, she noticed that while a few shopkeepers seemed to be conducting business as usual, most others, like her, had closed up and left. Some had even taped a big *X* on their windows like she did.

On impulse, she turned onto Queen Street and headed for the library, hoping it was still open.

It was. In fact, the library was filled with patrons selecting books and murmuring anxiously about the storm.

"I need plenty to read in case we have to stay in, if that storm comes," she heard one elderly lady say, "and the library's closing early today, because of it."

No one was in the local history room.

Virginia headed for the microfilm reader, switched it on, and opened the file cabinet drawer to look for the reel containing the *Georgetown Times* issues of 1954. "January-July 1954," she read aloud. "August-December 1954."

She took out the *August-December 1954* box, opened it, removed the reel, and put it on the spindle. Laying the film across the reader to thread it through the other side, she saw, illuminated on the reader, a photograph of a hunter holding up a deer by its horns. She read the caption—*First Day for Deer Season.*

Virginia tightened her mouth. In the weeks leading up to Hurricane Hazel, people in Georgetown were going about their daily business, never knowing a hurricane would devastate their county, and for some, their lives, before the year was over. She had heard someone say, just moments ago out in the library, that this Hurricane Harvey was 'another Hazel.'

She turned the knob several times before reaching October.

October 1, 1954 was a Friday. The Georgetown Gators won their home football game, according to the caption under a photograph of jubilant cheerleaders in long-sleeved sweaters, knee-length flared skirts and saddle-oxford shoes. Happy times.

The next bi-weekly addition told a completely different story. The mid-week edition came out on Thursday. Hurricane Hazel had come in on Tuesday, and the *Georgetown Times* featured photographs taken on Wednesday, the morning after.

The front page featured a photograph of a row of seaside lots on Pawleys Island. One of the lots was bare but for pilings that had once held up a cottage. Another lot held a cottage collapsed like matchsticks beside the bare pilings that once supported the structure. Another lot was bare but for a lone commode.

Virginia shivered and began to read one of the accompanying articles.

Hurricane Hazel made landfall at high tide, but not just any high tide—it was a lunar high tide. The hurricane struck on the full October moon, during the highest tide of the year. A rambling inn, built on top of a huge dune, was completely destroyed, as were many houses built during the 1900s.

Although the entire island was flooded with the storm surge, the oldest section of houses on the island, according to the paper, fared the best, since the houses were built directly behind the protective line of sand dunes.

That's where Remy's house is, thought Virginia, *in the oldest section.* She swallowed uncomfortably. High tide for *Chaucer,* at Waccamaw Marina, was late tonight, at around two-thirty in the morning. Pawleys Island high tides ran three hours earlier—around eleven-thirty p.m. Would Hurricane Harvey make landfall during high tide?

*****

Driving over the South Causeway to Pawleys Island, she reflected that Remy would probably spend the next twenty-four hours in a haze of pain medication and come out to find his foot healing and the hurricane warning, like his foul mood, was just a memory.

Instead, he was awake, awkwardly pacing the kitchen floor, limping and cursing under his breath. He looked up when the outside kitchen door opened.

"Remy," Virginia came in and put her purse down. "You must be in terrible pain."

"Nah," I've had my foot up most of the day, like I'm supposed to, to keep the swelling down. And the pain medicine helps a lot."

"Good," Virginia nodded. "Good." *Thank goodness,* she thought.

"It's just that—" Remy stopped and leaned on the old trestle table. He shook his head, running his hand worriedly across his forehead. Pulling a captain's chair out from the table, he eased himself down onto it. Wincing, he carefully placed his bandaged foot up on the table. Leaning back, he looked at Virginia.

"What, honey?" *He looks feverish, or terribly worried,* she thought.

"It's just that I can't," he hesitated, "—I can't reach Cam. I can't get in touch with her."

Virginia felt her body tense. Cam—would Remy ever let them be free of her? He had no idea how dangerous she might be.

Remy sighed "I know, I know, you're sick of hearing her name, and I don't blame you. But she called me, and left this weird, weird message."

Oh, no. Virginia folded her arms and shifted her weight to one leg, never taking her eyes off Remy. "And?"

"And I can't reach her. She doesn't answer." He bit his bottom lip. "She sounded scared, really spooked."

Virginia sat down. "Remy, this hurricane has got people on edge. The moods in the shop today ran a gamut of emotions from very excited to extremely worried to barely controlled panic. Most folks seemed to be, if anything, erring on the side of caution by cutting their vacations short and leaving the beach. Some were panicky—but not too panicked to stop in and hunt for antiques in their way back inland. Others were almost giddy, you know, planning hurricane parties and such."

"*I* wouldn't mind a good hurricane party if I wasn't so worried about Cam." Remy smiled a crooked one-sided smile.

"When did she call?" Virginia asked.

"Oh, it was on my phone when we got back from the hospital," Remy said, easing forward on the seat and settling his shoulders down in the rounded chair back. "I didn't take my phone with me when we left."

"She wasn't who you were talking to on the phone late last night when I woke up?"

"Huh? No. No, like I told you, that was a customer." He shook his head as if to clear it. "A damned disgruntled customer."

"Oh—I saw Charisse right as I was closing up the shop."

"Oh yeah?" Remy raised his eyebrows.

"Yeah." Virginia nodded. "She had a case of storm stress. Trying to get a window open."

"Charisse." Remy leaned his head back and closed his eyes. "Damn."

Virginia watched Remy a moment, until he started to lightly snore. Then she took out a frozen container of the homemade vegetable-and-venison stew she'd made last week and left in Remy's freezer. After microwaving it, she ate a bowlful while standing at the counter by the microwave. She poured Remy a bowlful and placed it on the table near his sleeping form, then went upstairs and fell asleep watching the Weather Channel.

*****

When she woke the next morning, the Weather Channel was still on, and Hurricane Harvey had picked up speed and was now a Category Four hurricane.

Virginia had a quick bath and hurried downstairs to the kitchen.

The untouched bowl of stew was still on the table, but Remy was gone.

Chapter Thirty-Four

Virginia looked out the kitchen window. She breathed a sigh of relief. Remy's Range Rover was still in the driveway. *At least he was home, and not driving around, worried and taking pain pills.*

I hate to leave him hobbling around here, she thought, *heading up the stairs, but I have to secure the boat, and I should go to the shop too.*

Opening her car door to leave, Virginia saw Remy coming slowly around the corner of the back garden. She stared quizzically at him as he limped along, carrying four birdhouses that minutes earlier had hung in the garden.

At her look of surprise he, shook his head good-naturedly. "Anything not tied down will be a missile."

Virginia quickly set her purse on the seat. "I'll carry those, and the rest of—"

Remy firmly shook his head. "Go ahead. I can do most of this, no problem. If we both work here now, then you may not have time to secure the boat. The later it gets, the harder it may be to drive. And," he had added grimly, "they may close down both causeways this afternoon. So go now. And come back soon as you can, hear?" He grinned and kissed her.

Virginia had to ask. She swallowed, then said quietly, "Did you ever hear from Cam? I know you were worried."

Remy shook his head, his smile gone. "No. But I've decided I'm not going to be responsible for her any more. I didn't make her emotionally needy. She was like that before I met her, and I can't help her. She was a friend to me when I needed one. I tried to remain her friend, but she needs more. I can't be her savior."

Virginia, saying nothing, nodded. *Good decision, Remy,* she thought.

"Virginia, I believe we have a future together. I hope Cam will be all right, now and in the future. But she needs fixing, and I can't fix her."

*****

Virginia shivered, walking down the dock in the windy early morning. Each boat she passed pulled hard against its lines in the stiff breeze. When she reached *Chaucer*, she could hear her telephone ringing inside.

She did not need to pick up a stern line to pull the big craft over. *Chaucer* was little more than a foot from the dock, held tightly at the ends of her lines by the wind.

Stepping quickly aboard, she drew back the folding screen, unlocked the door, slid it open, and hurried down the two steps to pick up the phone just as it stopped ringing. With a sigh of exasperation, she put the receiver down. Her caller ID showed Miss Eugenia's number. Biting her lip, she picked up the receiver and began dialing. Miss Eugenia was often hard to reach by telephone and might have headed for Virginia's shop to talk to her in person as soon as she replaced the telephone receiver. *Please answer,* Virginia thought— *phone service might be out later.*

"Virginia!" Miss Eugenia answered in the middle of the first ring. "It is *certain* the hurricane will make landfall in Charleston, or above. And now it's a Category Four! And the wind is still picking up."

Virginia swallowed. "I—I know. You're not planning to stay there in your house, are you? Come stay with Remy and me. I'll come and get you."

"Absolutely not. I'm going to the high school. It's on high ground, and set up for a storm shelter. You should come there, too."

"I can't," Virginia said, exchanging waves with her neighbor, who was walking down the dock, headed for her car with an armful of clothing from her boat.

"Why can't you?" Miss Eugenia asked. "Surely you and Remy are not staying aboard, out in the water. Or at the dock, which might be worse."

"We're not staying aboard at all. I'm staying at Remy's. His house has withstood hurricanes on Pawleys Island for over a century and a half and—"

"*My* house has withstood hurricanes in Georgetown harbor, on this bayside peninsula that is now the Historic District, for over *two* and a half centuries, and I'm not staying there! Have you thought about what it will be like out on Pawleys Island, with the force of the storm and the storm *surge*?"

"Remy's house can handle the wind," Virginia said, hoping to convince herself of this. She glanced up at her cabin ceiling as the tin roof high above the dock rattled. "It's in the Pawleys Island historic section, with the really old houses from before the Civil War. These houses were all built behind those huge dunes, not over them or in front of them like nowadays. The dunes protect the houses."

"My dear, the wind is only *half* of it," Miss Eugenia said. "If the hurricane makes landfall at high tide, there will be a raging storm surge to rival Noah's flood, plus the wind. The old McKenna house, Geneva's, was in that same historic section and it was flooded during Hurricane Hazel."

"This house, Remy's house, is strong, Miss Eugenia, and high enough to be above rising water. And besides, I can't take Gabrielle to the storm shelter."

There was silence on the other end of the line. Virginia heard shouting at the far end of the dock. *Hurricanes,* she thought, *certainly get people on edge.* "Miss Eugenia," she said, "you come out and stay with Remy and me. We'd love to have you."

"Virginia—" Miss Eugenia began, "Virginia, dear, thank you, but no. If you change your mind, just come to the high school and leave Gabrielle in her carrier inside my truck tonight."

"We'll be fine at Remy's house," Virginia said, "and I almost forgot to tell you—Remy cut his foot badly last night, and I took him to the emergency room for stitches. He'll be better off at home."

"Well," Miss Eugenia sighed, "all right. Be safe. I'll see you after the storm, Lord willing. 'Bye."

"'Bye." Virginia held the receiver in her hand after Miss Eugenia hung up. Finally replacing it in the cradle, she climbed the ladder up to the bridge and began pulling long coils of rope from the built-in mahogany seat storage box.

I wonder how many hurricanes Chaucer *has weathered since 1948,* thought Virginia, *and how many owners have done just what I am doing now—preparing to tie extra mooring lines, hoping their boat will withstand a fierce storm?*

Remy's words rang in her head. *"Anything not tied down will be a missile."* She glanced about the boat, making sure nothing stayed on deck that could be flung projectile-like through the air.

She set to work doubling up *Chaucer*'s lines, tying a sister line to each of the two stern lines, forward lines, and spring lines, after giving each one more length than usual.

It was impossible to predict at this point exactly when the hurricane would most effect Murrells Inlet, but if it struck at high tide, as predicted, *Chaucer* would need extra line, even in the center spring lines, to ride the high water.

Virginia hoped the long bow lines, always held taut by cement blocks on pulleys, would keep *Chaucer*'s stern from smashing against the dock if the hurricane struck between tides, when all but the bow lines would be slack.

She unzipped the canvas Bimini cover from its metal frame overhead in the bridge. If left in place, the Bimini would be ripped loose, perhaps tearing the frame from the bridge before the heavy canvas gave way.

Still dwelling on Remy's grim warning, Virginia then climbed back up to the bridge. She removed the shining old chrome bell and the brass swinging cup holders from their brackets, along with the long metal-tipped mahogany boat hook.

As she was heading below, Derek pulled up in the marina's Boston Whaler, crabbing sideways against the wind and the wind-driven water.

"Hey, Virginia! Want me to set your anchor across the marina?" He offered.

She looked up. Across the marina from *Chaucer* was due east, the direction from which the heaviest winds would probably come, she knew, considering how the cypress and maple trees lining the marina were leaning hard from the east wind.

"Yes!" Gratefully, she gave him the anchor off *Chaucer*'s bow and stood on deck watching as he dropped it in the water forty feet across the marina. She then cleated the anchor line off on the keel-attached Samson post on the bow. This anchor would keep *Chaucer* from going under the dock at low tide, or against the dock at high tide.

*****

Forty-five minutes after boarding *Chaucer*, Virginia began her last task—removing the mast. *Chaucer*'s mast was a six-foot mahogany fixture rising from the deck above the saloon to hold the white central masthead light above the bridge. As the highest point on the boat, it risked being crushed against the inside ceiling of the huge boatshed when the water reached its highest level in the storm's surge.

Having previously stripped, sanded, and refinished the mast in place, she now strained against her screwdriver to twist out the last of the four large, deeply driven brass screws she had so carefully re-caulked against leakage only a few weeks earlier.

At last, the screw began to turn. When Virginia finally lifted the mast off its base, she felt a twinge of alarm. A clump of brightly colored plastic-coated wires still held the mast to its fixed base. The mast's twelve volt wiring ran directly from deep inside the mast into the boat. She knew it could take her a long time to chase down the ends of these wires and disconnect them properly.

Virginia gnawed her lip. It was time to leave—the wind was increasing steadily, making it harder to move around the outside of the boat. She was running out of time, but she could not leave the dismantled mast here on top of the deckhouse! Even if she lashed it down securely, it would probably be whipped and dashed to pieces, ripping loose the wiring in the process.

Sighing, Virginia climbed below and snatched a pair of wire cutters from her large red metal toolbox. She hurried back to the mast and quickly cut through the all the coated wire, releasing the mast. This was a sorry way to disconnect wires, she knew, but the clean cuts would be simple to wire back.

She lifted the mast over the windshield and into the bridge, climbed over the windshield, then carefully carried the mast down the ladder to the aft deck, where she put it through the open rear hatch and onto her bed.

After securing Gabrielle in her cat carrier, Virginia put two days' worth of foul weather clothing in her back pack. Before zipping it, she went to the top drawer in the saloon bulkhead and pulled out her birth certificate and car and boat titles. Underneath was a DVD.

Virginia's nostrils flared—it was the DVD the private investigator made of Gordon and that *woman*. The one she had never watched. Maybe during this hurricane crisis, provided there was power, she could watch it and get Gordon out of her system once and for all. Virginia sighed and stuck the DVD into her pack. Watching this might help, but Gordon's memory would continue to haunt her unless she could uncover the events leading up to his death.

She locked up, lifted Gabrielle in the cat carrier carefully up onto the dock, then climbed up. Hating to leave, she took a long look at *Chaucer*.

The old yacht looked grand, gracefully straining against her lines. *Will she still be afloat this time tomorrow?* Virginia steeled herself to turn and walk down the dock toward her car. With Gabrielle yowling from the cat carrier, Virginia reluctantly drove away. She took her harmonica from the console and played a few bars.

Heading south on Ocean Highway 17 toward Pawleys Island, Virginia put the harmonica in her pocket. She had to constantly compensate with her steering for the buffeting action of the wind despite the Porsche's low, heavy build. Virginia noticed vehicle after vehicle loaded down with grocery bags piled high enough to show out the windows.

Did she and Remy have enough food? She knew Remy, a soup lover, kept a hefty supply of a wide variety of canned soups in his pantry, but may not have stocked up on other essentials.

She pulled into the grocery store at the entrance to the North Causeway to load up on non-perishable foods as well as ice, cat food, cat litter, bottled water, and whatever else she might see to get them through the impending storm, should it strike hard here.

She breathed a sigh of relief to be off the highway, then found a parking spot. She opened her door, only to have her breath nearly sucked away when the gale whipped her car door fully open against its hinges.

With some effort she got out of the car and swung her door shut, hurrying toward the store. She held her whipping hair out of her eyes as she dodged earnest-faced, camo-clad men and nervous, grim-faced women rapidly exiting the store steering unwieldy, top-heavy, overloaded carts of groceries, ice, and beer.

The men are enjoying this, she thought, *almost like it's a survival game.*

Upon entering the bustling grocery store, Virginia heard her name and turned to see Remy limping toward her from the check-out counter.

"Honey, am I glad to see you," he said fervently, kissing the tousled hair on top of her head. "They're not leaving the causeway open much longer."

Seeing that the cashier had at least two dozen more of his items to ring up, Remy gently pulled Virginia aside and said quietly, "The island is being evacuated. They've already closed the North Causeway, and this one," he inclined his head toward the South Causeway, "will be closed soon."

"Do we have to leave?" Virginia's calm voice belied the alarm she felt as she looked into Remy's eyes. Securing *Chaucer* and leaving her had been hard enough. Now Remy's house was not safe either? With the causeways closed, they would be marooned at the edge of the Atlantic, with a quarter-mile of marsh and creek separating them from the mainland.

"It's a mandatory evacuation," Remy said. "But in our case, I think we'll be all right if we want to stick it out. I don't think we have to leave. The house can take a hurricane, and it may not even strike here."

"Remy, it's just that your house is right on the ocean, and if they're evacuating the island, well, your house is so—" Virginia struggled for a non-offending word to convey the frailty of his eighteenth century home, "—so old," she finished lamely.

His mustache twitched as he tried not to smile at Virginia's discomfort, but he gave up, throwing back his head in delightful peals of deep laughter.

"Honey, the house got old, remember, because it was built *behind* the sand dunes instead of in front of them—or on top of them. Now these folks," he swept the crowded grocery with his eyes, "are not staying *on* the island. All of our on-island neighbors and tourists renting from our neighbors headed for the hills hours ago."

"But Remy, all of these people in here buying groceries and supplies—"

"—are from Georgetown. They came to stock up here because stores in more populated areas are running out of beer and bottled water."

"Are we the only ones staying on the island?" Virginia asked.

"Probably," Remy nodded.

"Some of the other old houses on the island are built behind the dunes."

"Sure they are." He grinned. "But their owners don't live there. We do."

Virginia returned his grin nervously. Even if she could talk Remy into evacuating inland, she did not want to be far from *Chaucer* when the storm ended. Remy was adventurous, but not foolish. She trusted his judgment. If he was staying, she was staying.

Chapter Thirty-Five

Virginia awoke late in the afternoon to the shrill whistle of Remy's kettle. Raising her head from the comfortable arm of the overstuffed sofa in the second floor sitting room where she had fallen asleep, she peered over the sofa back's smooth golden oak frame and out of the east window to the ocean below.

Grey and churning, the water rose up to crash in great curling breakers on the huge grey rocks of the granite-and-timber groin that stretched from the dunes out into the Atlantic just southeast of the house.

Resting her chin on the back of the heavy sofa, she once again breathed a sigh of relief that two of Remy's next-door neighbors had transported everything moveable, except for the kitchen table and chairs, from the kitchen up to this floor before they left. Thank goodness the kitchen, midway between the ground and the twenty-two-foot high first floor, was the only low part of the house.

After getting Gabrielle settled and stowing away all of the supplies from the grocery store, she and Remy had nestled down on the sofa to watch the Weather Channel. To her dismay, the mandatory evacuation orders were repeated with alarming frequency.

Mentally and physically tired from the strain of preparing for the hurricane, Virginia lay her head on the soft arm of the sofa as she and Remy had watched the two o'clock p.m. hurricane update. Hurricane Harvey would make landfall sometime during the night, somewhere on the lower Carolina coast.

If it made landfall anywhere near here at high tide, Virginia knew, with it would come a storm surge that would crash and roll across the areas of the island not protected by sand dunes.

High tide is late tonight, she remembered sleepily. *It is hard to even imagine the Atlantic, rolling and crashing a hundred yards away, surging and roaring up under the house,* thought Virginia, rubbing her eyes and yawning. She reached for Remy, but his spot beside her was empty. Had she been asleep? She had to have been. How *long* had she been asleep?

Virginia looked at her wristwatch and rubbed her eyes again. It was close to five o'clock. Had she really slept that long? Maybe her watch was wrong. She looked at the television for the digital time read-out on the screen, but there was none.

"It is *beyond* the last minute for evacuations from all outlying islands and property east of Ocean Highway 17," the announcer was earnestly stressing. "All island causeways are closed, as mandatory evacuations for all barrier islands and property east of Ocean Highway 17 have been in effect since—"

Virginia sat up. It might get worse, but she'd made her decision and the causeways were closed. Come what may, she was here for the duration of the storm. She padded over to the television and switched it to DVD. Reaching into her backpack, she pulled out the private investigator's DVD and popped it into the player. Biting her lip, she pressed play and concentrated on the screen, preparing herself for the true-life adultery scenes from nearly two years ago.

The porch-light-lit front doorway of Gordon's pre-Revolutionary home—at the time of this video, *her* home, as well—came onto the screen.

Virginia smiled. She had told the PI that Gordon *always* used the front door.

There was movement to the right as Gordon's head appeared, then rose, as he climbed up the front steps. Apparently the PI had cropped the excess footage, or he had not started filming until Gordon appeared.

Virginia grinned. This PI was *good*. The video cut right to the chase.

A smaller, dark head appeared after Gordon's.

Virginia swallowed and leaned closer to the screen. Was this someone she would recognize? Someone she had run into at the post office or grocery store? Maybe the camera would show the woman's face.

Long dark hair swung gently on a tall, slender female frame as Gordon's companion climbed the steps onto the porch.

Virginia bit her lip hard. Of all Gordon's dalliances, this was the one that was proven. The PI assured Virginia he kept constant surveillance all night, until the pair left the next morning. That was all the more hurtful...Gordon had this woman in *their* home, in *their* bed.

Gordon's companion turned at a three-quarter angle toward the camera. Her face was still in shadow.

Virginia leaned closer. Something about the way the woman moved, the way she stood, looked so familiar.

The woman reached up and flipped her long hair away from her face. As she did, she turned her face up briefly so the camera caught a full frontal view.

Virginia gasped. There was no mistaking who Gordon's companion was. The woman was Charisse.

"Hey, honey." Remy limped around the corner with a steaming cobalt-blue mug in each hand.

Virginia started. "Oh!" Her heart melted at the sight of Remy. "Bless your heart—you walked all the way up those stairs with your injured foot. I don't want you straining your stitches in this storm, Remy Ravenel."

She ejected the DVD. Remy did not need to see this now. Later, definitely, but now, no.

Remy grinned. "It doesn't hurt much—good medicine." He sat beside Virginia on the sofa and placed the mugs on the trunk in front of her. The steam rose, bringing a delicious scent to Virginia's nostrils.

"Mmmmnnn—coffee. Ah, Remy, you do know how to soothe a lady's hurricane nerves." Closing her eyes, she savored the rich dark scents of the coffee before taking a sip. "Wow, that's good—and there's a big shot of something else in there too."

Remy grinned. "Coffee liqueur—it's my own recipe," Remy said, leaning back and holding his cup with both hands. "Freshly ground dark coffee, vanilla beans, dark brown sugar, and vodka—I make a big batch a couple of times a year."

Virginia took a sip. "So very, very good—it tastes as wonderful as it smells." She took another sip. "With pain medicine, is it safe for you to be drinking this? And aren't you supposed to keep your foot up to it won't swell?"

"It's okay."

Virginia raised her eyebrows but decided not to pursue that subject.

"Well, it's delicious," she said brightly. "I didn't mean to sleep so long! Actually, I didn't even intend to go to sleep at all at a time like this."

Remy put his mug down and reached over to smooth Virginia's tousled hair. "We're safe here. And you must have needed to sleep, the way you went out. You weren't asleep that long, anyway. According to this grand gift you gave me, you were out for one hour and ten minutes." He chuckled. "Unless it lost time."

"What gift?" Virginia asked, surprised.

"What gift." Remy rolled his eyes and gave Virginia his most charming smile. "The elegantly wrapped gift you placed on my bed when we got back this afternoon. After you fell asleep, I went into the bedroom to make the bed, from which we were so rudely awakened last night, and what did I find but that you'd crept into the bedroom this afternoon, made the bed, and left this awesome watch on my pillow." He glanced fondly down at the familiar-looking timepiece on his right wrist. "Honey, I have to tell you I was shocked when I opened that box, shocked and delighted. An antique Rolex, almost like the one that was stolen, or lost. Virginia, where on earth did you find it?"

Virginia could scarcely believe her eyes. It looked so much like the one her dad, and his dad before him, had worn for years, the one he had given Gordon. She swallowed, staring at the smooth, well-seasoned leather band and the old silver watch it held. She had seen it hundreds of times after her dad gave it to Gordon because Gordon had worn it almost everywhere. It couldn't be the same watch—yet, here it was.

"Remy," she said slowly, "I didn't put that watch on your bed. I didn't make the bed, either. I haven't even been in the bedroom."

"So who came here while we were gone, made our bed, and left me an expensive gift-wrapped watch as a major hurricane approached? Virginia, I love the watch. Stop joking."

Virginia took Remy's hand and looked closely at the old timepiece. The face of the watch bore no name, but the shape of the case and the design of the red-and-black numerals were unmistakable. She had not seen an old Wilsdorf & Davis Rolex like this one since Gordon wore the one her dad gave him—the one he had bought in the pawn shop in Belfast when he was in the RAF and stationed in Ireland during World War II. But it melted into a lump of metal, when Gordon died in that fire. She had the lump of melted metal to prove it, didn't she?

Chapter Thirty-Six

"May I hold it?" Virginia asked.

Wordlessly unbuckling the watchband, Remy handed it to Virginia.

She turned over the timepiece, warm from Remy's wrist and silken smooth from decades of use, and opened the hinged back second cover. Besides the London Hallmarks of WS, for Wilsdorf and Davis, and Rolex, their new name, inside was etched in old-fashioned script *To Roderick from Mother*.

Virginia sucked her breath in. It *was* the watch that had belonged to her grandfather, the one her dad gave Gordon. She bit her lip and blinked back tears of frustration.

"Remy, the watch you had when we met looked like my grandfather's watch, but I was sure it wasn't, because that one burned up, melted, when Gordon died. I have that melted lump. I never even looked inside your watch to see. But this one *is* my grandfather's watch. He wore it nearly always. My dad bought it in a pawn shop in Ireland during World War Two. I know it's the same watch because of this inscription from the first owner. My grandfather always meant to have the inscription removed, but he never did, and he finally decided it was part of the watch's history and let it stay."

Virginia ran her finger over the words inscribed inside the watch. She drew a ragged breath. "My dad gave this watch to Gordon right after we were married."

"When you and Gordon were divorcing, it seems like Scotty would have wanted this back, since it was his father's, and it had been in your family that long."

"Well, yes," Virginia said slowly, turning the watch over. "After we separated, I asked Gordon for it back because it was a family heirloom, but he said he lost it. I was sure he was lying, because he wanted to keep it. Then when he died, I was sure he was wearing it, because the melted metal was—was where the watch should have been.

Remy rolled his eyes. "Virginia, surely he had other watches. People do, you know."

"Not Gordon. Before this one, he never even wore one. But it *must* have been some other watch, because this *is* Gordon's. The inscription and markings are identical. After this storm is over, I can verify the serial number, too."

Remy frowned, looking at the inscription. "You're sure it's the same inscription?"

Virginia nodded. "Even without the inscription, these watches are pretty rare. This is a trench watch, made when most men still carried pocket watches. But soldiers in the World War II trenches needed a watch they could glance at, so as to not waste valuable time pulling a watch from a pocket. Wilsdorf & Davis made this with the hinged back to help keep out dust and dirt—they hadn't perfected waterproof yet. And they wanted a name that was easier to pronounce, in any language. The name 'Rolex' is an onomatopoeia—it came from the way a watch sounds when it's being wound up. See, look—inside it says *Rolex* and it says *W&S* for Wilsdorf & Davis—they were still using both names."

"Gordon said he *lost* it?"

Virginia shrugged. "That's what he told me. But apparently he didn't tell anyone else he'd lost the watch. His sister listed it as a way of identifying him! Sheriff Bone asked me several times if I knew where it was."

"Did you?" Remy asked quietly, one eyebrow raised.

"No." She paused and swallowed. Her mouth felt dry. "You're the one who has the watch, Remy." Virginia felt anxiety rising within her. "And your only explanation is that it just turned up *gift-wrapped* in your bed?"

"Honey, I'll *show* you the gift-wrap—it's right here in the waste paper bin." Remy narrowed his eyes. "Gordon said he lost it? And you didn't believe him?"

"Maybe," said Virginia, struggling to keep her voice even, "he left it somewhere he shouldn't have been and didn't want to tell me where."

"Left it at some woman's home, maybe?" Remy raised one eyebrow. "During the time you were hiring a private investigator, putting a voice-activated tape recorder under the desk in his study—"

"Remy? What—" Virginia gulped. How did Remy know she put a voice-activated tape recorder under the desk in Gordon's study?

She told Remy about putting it in Gordon's truck, but she never told anyone except Gordon about putting it under the desk in his study—she told him after she taped his incriminating calls. Who had *Gordon* told that could have told Remy?

Remy folded his arms. "If I didn't know you better—or if this was a movie on the Lifetime Channel instead of our real lives—I'd be betting *you* did Gordon in."

Virginia stood up, looking disbelievingly at the man with whom she had planned to stay through the hurricane despite the warnings and mandatory evacuations.

"It's usually the wife who—" Remy began, stopping when the voice on the Weather Station abruptly ceased and was replaced by a loud and constant bleeping.

Remy and Virginia looked at the television. The entire screen was flashing red. Then the screen went blank.

Remy picked up the remote and quickly flicked to several local stations. The screen registered a blank each time. "Well—the cable is out."

That's obvious, Virginia thought, biting back the urge to say so. She walked stiffly out of the room to the alcove that opened onto the west porch. She opened one of the French doors just enough to slip outside into the whipping wind, then shut the door behind her.

Leaning on the smooth, weathered railing and looking out across the beach road to the marsh and the creek beyond, Virginia felt tension rise in her throat. She had been calm throughout the preparations for this impending storm. Now her suppressed fears were surfacing—all because of the watch.

There was a click behind her and the French door opened wide. The floor-length raw silk drapes flew back into the alcove in a flurry of crimson, then floated down as Remy limped onto the porch and closed the French door behind him.

He looked out towards the creek then down toward the weathered floor boards. One hand on the railing, he turned his good foot sideways to study the treads of his leather hiking boot. "Creek's whipping up pretty good, huh?" He inquired companionably.

Virginia kept her gaze toward the marsh.

"Virginia, I had to ask," he said humbly, his voice barely audible above the gale-force wind. He put one hand on her shoulder, then took it away. He took a deep breath. "How else could Gordon's watch have gotten here?"

"*Someone brought it here,*" Virginia replied, her voice flat, her eyes never leaving the marsh. "And that *someone* was not me."

Remy curled his upper body against the house to light a cigarette, then turned back and exhaled smoke into the wind.

"Who would have even *had* Gordon's watch? And what's more, who would have wanted to put it in this house, on *my* bed?" Remy queried.

"Was the house locked?" Virginia asked, turning to face Remy.

"I was only gone a short time," he replied. "Anyone trying to sneak in would have had to wait for me to leave. Besides, who would take the time to do something foolish like that with a hurricane on the way?"

"A mentally unhinged person," Virginia hesitated. "Like Cam."

Remy shook his head. "You can't blame that poor girl for every unexplained thing that happens."

Virginia felt her nostrils flare. Looking down, she caught her breath. Blood was seeping onto the deck from beneath Remy's bandaged foot. "Remy——" she began, looking up at him.

Remy narrowed his eyes and looked into hers. "Mentally unhinged person?" he asked carefully, slowly tapping his chin with his forefinger. "Hmmnnnnn. . . didn't you tell me Sheriff Bone questioned you *multiple times* about Gordon's so-called *accident?*"

Overhead an engine droned.

Virginia looked up to see a red seaplane, a biplane, flying low, making its way painstakingly south. *A seaplane evacuating,* she thought, *and there's no way to land on water in this weather.* She bit her lip. *I should have moved* Chaucer *inland, upriver.* Now it's too late.

Remy looked up in disgust. "Idiot. Nice old Stearman like that ought to be in a hangar. Both wings and floats will tear off in this storm." He shook his head. "Not many Stearmans with bi-wings *and* floats—pilot ought to take better care of it."

Remy pulled open the French door and limped inside, leaving Virginia alone with his innuendoes.

She fought back tears. What did Belinda tell her? *Don't listen to what he says—watch what he does. How could he even* infer *that she had something to do with Gordon's death?* The tears slid unheeded down her cheeks and were dried almost instantly by the wind.

She gulped back a sob. If she could only see Gordon one more time! If she could only ask him what had happened that night. *If only someone had known what was going to happen and warned him,* she thought.

Her sobbing nearly inaudible in the wind, Virginia gulped, wishing she had never even met Remy Ravenel. Being involved with him was turning out to be almost as bad as being married to Gordon was.

*****

Snuggled on the thick down comforter that draped the four-poster in Remy's guest bedroom, Virginia stroked Gabrielle's dark chocolate ears. The big Siamese quietly purred now, paws kneading the comforter like biscuit dough, but Virginia knew it was only a matter of time before the willful feline resumed her restless pacing again, spoiling to go outside despite the gusting wind.

Outside in the near-darkness, the wind howled. Virginia, acutely aware how much closer to the ocean she was on this side of the house, was sure she could hear it roaring. She cringed as the whole house seemed to shudder.

She heard Remy limping down the hall.

"Can't trust any of 'em," she heard him mutter. She heard him opening the hall closet door, then rummaging around inside the closet. What on *earth* was he doing?

Seconds passed.

Virginia heard an unmistakable click, and another. She frowned, biting her lip. Remy was loading a firearm.

Virginia scowled. She should never have agreed to stay here.

Why was Remy so nervous—other than from the storm—and how *did* he get the watch? Could he have known Gordon? How else would he have gotten it? Why was it wrapped in a package?

Dread began creeping over her. Maybe Remy did not fare well under stress, and now, he was also drinking, taking pain medication, and walking around bleeding instead of elevating his injured foot.

And here *she* was, stranded in the face of an approaching hurricane, alone on an evacuated island with a man who was more untrustworthy by the minute.

Without a break in her purring, Gabrielle began switching her tail.

Virginia sighed. Tail-switching was a sure sign. Gabrielle was becoming uneasy and spoiling for trouble.

A gust of wind whistled loudly over the house, rattling the cover high atop the chimney flue, sending an echo down the chimney and rattling the French doors.

One of the French doors burst open and Gabrielle leapt up, hissing and spitting, back arched. Without a backward glance, Gabrielle dashed out onto the balcony.

Virginia bounded onto the floor and was out the door and on the balcony in seconds, but Gabrielle was already gone. "Gabrielle!" She shouted into the wind, leaning over the wooden railing.

Gabrielle never looked back. Barely visible in the shadows not reached by the outdoor floodlights, the top of her fluffy dark chocolate tail disappeared over the window sill of Remy's potting shed.

Horrified, Virginia saw the surf, glistening from the outdoor floodlights, surge past the edge of the potting shed.

"Gabrielle!" Virginia shouted, as another gust of wind whipped her hair across her face. She flung her hair back, casting it off her eyes just in time to see the potting shed shudder and collapse. *Remy, damn him, said they were protected behind the high dunes.* "Gabrielle!" She screamed, running back inside, out into the upstairs hall, and down the stairs into the kitchen.

"Remy, the potting shed collapsed on Gabrielle! And the water is rising into it!" She headed for the kitchen door.

Remy looked up from radio he was working on at the old trestle table. One of his rifles, a World War Two Browning Automatic Rifle, lay beside him on the table along with three lit kerosene lamps. He laid the cigarette he was smoking on the edge of an ashtray full of cigarette butts and stood, screwdriver and cloth rag in one hand, then limped toward the door after Virginia.

She did not wait for him but raced, barefooted, out of the back door and across the garden to the wreckage of the potting shed. "Gabrielle, Gabrielle!" She shouted, pulling at the fallen roof as the surf surged around her feet.

A plaintive loud mewing came from the debris, then silence.

"Virginia!" Remy was nearly breathless from hurried limping. He held the screwdriver he had been using on the radio. "We can unscrew the door hinges and get her out." Leaning down toward the fallen door, he touched the tops of the screws, barely visible in stormy twilight.

"But not with this." He held up the Phillips-head screwdriver. "I have to get a flathead." He turned toward the house.

"I'll get one." Virginia sprinted back across the garden to Remy's workshop beside the breezeway under the house. She pulled open the door of the workshop, where some of Remy's tools remained and where her mannequins were secured for the storm.

The wind flung the shop door against the wall. She stepped out of the brightness of the backyard floodlight into the near-darkness of the shop and reached for the second drawer of the red tool box where she knew Remy kept screwdrivers.

At first touch she recoiled from the screwdrivers—they were wet and sticky. Cringing, she picked up several, feeling the ends to make sure they were what she needed.

She ran out of the shop and across the garden to where Remy knelt in the shadows by the potting shed door.

"Here—there's oil or something on them—" She wiped the screwdrivers on the cloth Remy had dropped. In the stark floodlight juxtaposed with dark shadows, the cloth showed smears of crimson.

Remy took one of the screwdrivers, feeling for the end. He put it on the first screw of the fallen door. "Perfect."

Virginia crouched by him as he unscrewed the remaining screws. As he freed the hinges and lifted the door, she reached down below the door and slid her hands under Gabrielle's wet stomach.

Spitting and hissing, Gabrielle unwillingly allowed Virginia to hold her tightly and carry her across the garden and up the steps through the fierce wind.

Not daring to let go of Gabrielle with either hand, Virginia stood by the open kitchen door. Reluctant to leave Remy outside alone with his injured foot, she looked back, waiting for him to limp up the stairs. When he was a few steps behind her, she went into the kitchen ahead of him and stopped abruptly.

Behind her, Remy shut the door and looked at his hands in the even kitchen light.

"This is blood—or paint!" He exclaimed, holding up his red-streaked hands. "Was all this mess in my tool b—"

He stopped short.

Virginia backed into him, unable to speak, still holding the hissing Gabrielle.

Propped up in the chair, where Remy had been sitting only moments before, was one of Virginia's mannequin torsos.

Chapter Thirty-Seven

The mannequin's head was gone. The jagged neck, like a bloody stump, was topped with something thick and red trickling down the neck and between the breasts. Barely visible through the redness was a painted necklace—the unmistakable original painted necklace of the mannequin that disappeared from Virginia's car at the marina two nights before.

One of the kerosene lanterns Remy had left on the table top was smashed, its metal crushed and glass lamp broken, with kerosene leaking off the tabletop onto the floor. The remaining lantern flickered eerily, despite the electric light overhead. The third lantern was gone.

"I left my BAR on the table," Remy said. The rifle was gone.

A manila file folder lay where the rifle had been.

Gabrielle gave a mighty kick against Virginia's ribcage, took a flying leap onto the floor and bounded up the stairs.

Virginia walked over to the table and, with trembling fingers, turned open the front cover of the folder—Belinda's patient folder. She swallowed. This was the folder Belinda said she left at the boat, the folder that was not there when Virginia got there. Silently she turned over every page, scanning for a patient name.

The patient was referred to only as 'the Patient.'

When Virginia reached the last page, she closed the folder. There was no photograph.

What happened to the photograph Belinda put in here for her to identify? *Still,* she thought, *'the Patient' is undoubtedly Cam.*

The lights blinked once then went out, leaving Virginia and Remy, but for one flickering lantern throwing shadows over the kitchen wall and floor, in the dark.

"We've got to get the other lanterns now," said Remy grimly.

"Where are they?" Virginia shuddered, tearing her eyes away from the grim scenario.

Remy gagged momentarily, then shoved the mannequin torso off the chair with his injured foot. It hit the floor with a thump, chipping one of the points off the jagged neck. "Down in the shop," he grimaced, holding his injured foot off the floor. "Come on down there with me—I don't want to leave you alone in here. We need to get those lanterns now, in case the water rises further."

"Everyone's left the island but *us*," Virginia said. *Only God can help now,* she thought.

Remy looked sick. "Us, and whoever did *that*." He jerked his head toward the ruined mannequin torso.

Virginia looked at Remy's foot. Blood was seeping from the edge of the bandage. "You need to stay off your foot. I'll get the lanterns. It's just right down there—I'll leave the door open."

Remy glanced at his foot and bit his lip. He cast his eyes around the kitchen, straining to see by the light of the single lantern on the table. He pulled open the drawer by the sink and took out a flashlight.

"All right. Take this." He handed her the flashlight. "And this." Pulling a huge butcher knife from the knife block by the sink, he handed it to her, then pulled out another and held onto it. "I'll be right here. The lamps are on the top shelf." He slid a chair out from under the kitchen table, and dragged it to the kitchen door. "I promise—I'll be right here. Now hurry. And be careful."

Virginia gulped, tore her eyes from his face, and walked to the door. She pushed the door open against the wind and stood in the doorway holding it open.

Remy, wincing, lowered himself down onto the chair in front of the open door.

"Remy—" she began.

"I'll be right here," he breathed.

Virginia walked slowly down the dark steps, knife in one hand, flashlight in the other, the wind tearing at her clothes. At the bottom of the steps, she paused, looking toward the ominously closer sound of the ocean. The ocean had already risen higher than even a lunar high tide ever rose—and it was not even time for high tide yet.

Virginia hurried across the breezeway, the wind whipping her hair. She stuck the knife in her belt and, flashlight in one hand, opened the shop door awkwardly against the wind. As soon as she got the door halfway open the wind snatched it and flung it against the wall with a loud bang. Leaving the door open, she stepped inside.

"Are you okay?" Remy called down, his voice nearly lost in the wind.

"Fine!" Virginia called up, scanning the light beam across the upper rows of shelves. She rolled the wooden track ladder toward three kerosene lanterns on the top shelf. She climbed up, hanging on with one hand, flashlight in the other, and brought down two lanterns, holding their wire handles in the same hand as the flashlight. She climbed back up for the last lantern.

The lantern's handle was lodged against the wall, and Virginia reached behind the glass globe to get it. When she brought the handle over the top of the lamp, she saw broken fingers and a disembodied hand.

Chapter Thirty-Eight

Virginia screamed and jerked back, losing her balance. She tumbled backwards, and with a thump, landed on her back on the wooden floor below, just missing the two lanterns she had set down. The third lantern crashed to the floor beside her. Still grasping the flashlight, she clambered to her feet, the light's beam making giddy patterns on the shop ceiling. Gasping to get her breath back, she aimed the flashlight at the floor where the broken lantern lay.

One of her mannequin's hands was wired to the lantern handle. What looked like blood dripped from the broken, hollow fingers. She shone the light across the floor, stopping where a bucket of crimson paint lay on its side. Slowly, her hand shaking and her breath coming back in rasps, she shone the light shakily across the shop.

Her remaining vintage mannequins stood in a row, all splattered with the blood-colored paint. Some were smashed in places as though smacked with a hammer. Painted on the heart-of-pine wall behind the mannequins, in dripping blood red, was *VIRGINIA, YOU'RE GONE.*

She froze in place, her heart pounding.

"Virginia! Virginia! Answer me! Are you all right?"

"Yes!" She called, knowing Remy should not come down to help her. "I—I'm coming back in!" Reaching out shaky fingers to pick up the lantern handles and still hold the flashlight, she took a shaky breath. She put one lantern in each hand so her trembling and the fierce wind would not bang the lanterns together and break the globes.

"Have you got the lanterns?"

"Yes!" Virginia was surprised her voice sounded so normal. Taking one deep breath, then another, she began making her way across the breezeway and up the steps.

Remy stood, holding open the door at the top of the steps, one hand braced on the chair.

"Honey, what happened down there?"

"There were three lanterns," Virginia felt her voice begin to shake. "I reached for the third one and it had a bloody mannequin hand behind it. It startled me so much I fell. All the mannequins were smashed, or hammered, or something, and they look like they have blood on them. A can of red paint was turned over. Somebody painted *VIRGINIA, YOU'RE GONE* up on the wall. There are five mannequins down there, and two at my shop in Georgetown—and this one," she nodded toward the floor by the kitchen table, "is the one stolen out of my car at the marina. And Remy," she paused to get her breath, "I think it was Cam because—"

"Cam!" Remy was incredulous. "Why? How can you imagine—"

"Because she's crazy! Remember the night she called us at the boat when she was here in your house tearing up things—remember? And the snake—remember the snake?"

Upstairs, Gabrielle shrieked, followed by a thumping and bumping sound on the staircase.

Virginia started and looked up into the near darkness to see a large bundle roll roughly down the last three stair steps and land on the floor. "Gabrielle!" What was wrapped around Gabrielle? A blanket and sheets? She ran forward. "Gabrielle!"

"Wait—Virginia," Remy started forward, then leaned down to pick up his lantern.

Virginia reached the bundle. "Gabrielle?" She tentatively felt the bundle, touching wet ropes and cloth. It was far too large to be Gabrielle—or was she tangled in all of this stuff?

Virginia began tugging at the ropes. Over the wind she heard Remy stop behind her. In the wavering light of his lantern, she saw dark red on the ropes and cloth. "More red paint," she prayed, her heart hammering against her ribs, both hands pulling at the ropes as Remy came closer with his lantern. Virginia stepped back. "It's another mannequin torso, only this one was wrapped in bed sheets, tied with ropes and," she swallowed, "less...ah...rigid."

"It's another mannequin, Remy," she repeated uncertainly, hoping somehow it was.

Remy brought the lantern closer. He held the light over Virginia's shoulder so that it shone light down onto the bundle. The torso had shoulders, and its arms were bound tightly.

"It's not a mannequin," he said, his voice hoarse.

Virginia's eyes grew large, watching the flickering lantern light illuminate the neck of the figure, where grisly bone protruded.

Virginia began to shake.

Remy cast the lantern in a circle so that it shone around the headless bloody form. He stopped the light over one of the hands. "It's Cam," he said hoarsely. "That's Cam's ring."

"Cam—Cam? If this is Cam then who—" Virginia broke off, swallowing hard against the bile rising in her throat. First *VIRGINIA, YOU'RE GONE* painted in red, then her mannequin beheaded, and now Cam was beheaded. Was Remy behind this? All the time she had been blaming Cam.

"You—" Remy's face was ashen. "Virginia, I *knew* you were behind all that fool craziness—the snake, trying to sink your boat, throwing your rock through my window, putting Gordon's watch on my bed—*you killed Gordon, didn't you?*"

Tears poured unchecked down Virginia's cheeks. She shook her head wordlessly.

The howling of the wind grew more shrill, and the ocean sounded distinctly closer.

Virginia could hear water licking and splashing under the kitchen in the breezeway.

Remy, nostrils flaring, turned away. He pulled a lighter out of his back pocket and lit the two lanterns she had brought up. This done, he wordlessly picked up one of the flickering lanterns and settled down disconsolately at the kitchen table. Not looking up, he adjusted and re-adjusted the wick height of first one, then the other.

Virginia shivered. Remy looked almost evil in the lamp-light, his face close to the lantern as he focused on the tiny flame. She walked over to the window. Below, in the darkness, the ocean was audibly smashing the underside of the kitchen floor. She swallowed. The tide—with the storm surge—was coming in faster than she ever imagined. She walked back across the kitchen, cringing as the floor trembled beneath her. She dared not go upstairs.

Poor Cam's headless corpse lay at the foot of the stairs, and whoever killed her, whoever killed her so horribly, could still be up there—with Gabrielle. Virginia swallowed and bit her lip, hoping Gabrielle had found a good hiding place.

Forcing herself not to panic, she walked over to the old trestle table and sat down in one of the captain's chairs opposite Remy. Carefully, she put her elbows on the table and rested her chin on them, praying for Remy to perceive her as nonchalant.

Remy did not look up. He raised one eyebrow, readjusting the wick of the lantern flame he was focusing on. "What?"

"Who do you think is up there?"

Remy swallowed. "I don't know." He shook his head, his gaze not wavering from the lantern flame. "I just don't know."

Tearless now, Virginia was oddly calm. *I could die tonight, unless I do something.*

Taking the knife out of her belt, she got up and walked over to the base of the stairs, steeling herself not to look down at what was left of Cam. She cast her eyes up the dark staircase. "Who's up there?" She shouted up into the upper story.

"Virginia, don't." Remy raised up out of his chair, supporting himself with one hand on the table and the other on the chair back. "Just leave it alone. Come sit down."

Virginia strained her eyes to see into the darkness above her. If anyone was moving around up there, she could not hear them with the wind howling around the house and the ocean surging underneath. Swallowing, she looked down as the house swayed on its pilings. She jerked her head up when a glimmer from the hallway above caught her eye.

A golden glow of light was moving unsteadily from side to side. Someone was up there, coming down the hall with a lantern—and whoever it was had killed Cam.

"*Now* look what you've done, Virginia," Remy screamed at her, staring up at the stair landing as the light approached. "Why didn't you just keep your mouth shut?"

Across the kitchen, the back door latch shook in its hasp, and the door glass rattled.

Virginia turned to see a stream of water dash under the door sill then flow back, leaving a dark gleaming stain on the floor planks.

"I'm here, Remy," a voice floated down from the top of the stairs.

Chapter Thirty-Nine

Turning back to the stairs, Virginia looked up. A bitter scream rose in her throat.

Remy opened his mouth then closed it.

Charisse stood at the top of the stairs, holding Remy's missing lantern. Her dark hair, crowned with a wreath of gardenia blossoms, flowed wildly around her shoulders, and Virginia's long white cotton batiste nightgown floated ethereally down her body. Her pale skin and the paler nightgown juxtaposed starkly with the dark blood caked around her fingernails. Remy's missing Huguenot cross glistened at the base of her throat.

I knew Charisse was the woman who sketched Chaucer, Virginia thought, *God help us. She is the woman with the hair-wreath of gardenias, the woman who said only the owner could have a copy of her sketch. Could she have known Gordon?*

"Cam was trouble." Stepping slowly down the stairs, Charisse nodded solemnly down to the headless, rope-bound corpse. "She was staying out here on the island for the storm, planning to bother you, Remy." Charisse looked at Remy and smiled. "But I caught her."

Stopping on the bottom step, she turned her smile on Virginia and narrowed her eyes.

"Cam the florist—she met your husband landscaping one of those properties he was representing."

She gestured with her toe down to Cam's wrapped torso. "He had his fun with *her*," she said, poking Cam's torso with the point of her toe, "then told her to hit the *road*. He tried that with me, and he paid *dearly.*"

Lifting her foot to delicately rub her toe on the hem of the nightgown, she wrinkled her nose. "She met Remy landscaping a new business where he was painting the sign. When he was done with her, she whined and clung like a leech." She grinned at Remy. "Cam won't be bothering you any*more*."

She raised her other hand from behind her, lifting Remy's BAR from the folds of the nightgown. Delicately, she placed the lantern on the landing next to her bare feet and raised the heavy rifle to her shoulder. It looked huge against her tall, delicate frame as the barrel rose, then stopped, aimed at Virginia.

"I'm sorry, Virginia," she said regretfully, "truly sorry." She eyed Virginia down the barrel. "But Remy and I, we have *plans.* Just us. Oh, and I cut your boat loose."

Virginia froze. What could she say to keep Charisse from killing them?

"You can have him," Virginia said.

Charisse cocked the BAR.

Keep her talking, thought Virginia. She reached for Remy's wrist, to which the watch was still strapped. She held up his wrist, with no resistance from him. "But tell me—where did you get this watch?"

Charisse lowered the BAR a few inches, keeping it pointed at Virginia. She looked at Remy, her eyes wide and guileless. "Baby, you let her see it?" Her voice was filled with incredulous disappointment. "That watch was from me to you, just *between* me and you."

Remy looked ill.

Charisse slowly shook her head. Her face looked mournful as she raised the BAR back up to her eye level, aiming at Virginia but talking to Remy. "You better not have told her about the Cheshire cat, Remy Ravenel."

Charisse caught her lower lip in her top teeth and closed one eye, the other eye sighting Virginia down the barrel. Her finger touched the trigger tentatively.

"No, I never told her. That was for *us,* baby," Remy said, swallowing hard.

Baby? Virginia had never heard Remy call anyone 'baby' until two nights ago, when he called her baby—right after that late-night phone call. Virginia stared at Charisse, unable to hear her next words over the howling wind, which seemed to be getting louder. She started and looked down as cold water swept across her bare feet—water that was now washing across the planks of the kitchen floor.

"Virginia!" Charisse shouted. "Look at me when I'm talkin' to you!" Charisse raised her chin, smiling calmly down the BAR's barrel at Virginia. "I wasn't the first woman your husband went off with."

"Went off with?" Virginia bit her lip. "What do you mean, 'went off with?'" She winced as the water surged over her feet again, this time a little higher.

"How stupid are you, little girl?" Charisse demanded, walking slowly down the stairs, keeping the barrel of the BAR trained on Virginia.

"H-how did you meet him?" Raising her chin, Virginia struggled to keep her voice even. She flinched as something slapped up against the house.

"Your husband was *so* easy to own. All I had to do was ask him about a property, and the rest was history. The first place he took me was 'his' boat—my mama's boat. That's all I wanted from him, at first, before I started getting attached to him. He was good lookin,' that Gordon. He loved real estate almost more than he loved women. And I thought he loved me more than *anything*. But then he changed his mind about me and wanted to crawl back to you, so I made him suffer and die. You didn't deserve him *and you don't deserve Remy!*"

Virginia clenched her teeth, her nostrils flaring.

Charisse raised her chin. "Then I was going to marry Remy until *you* got in the way. And Remy *let* you!" Her voice rose as she glared at Remy, her eyes blazing.

"Baby," Remy crooned, "I did that for us."

Charisse, keeping the BAR pointed at Virginia, narrowed her eyes at Remy. Her glare focused on his wrist, then his face. "I took your watch back, the one I gave you, because you wore it around *her*." She gestured at Virginia with the barrel tip, then cast her gaze back on Remy.

"That's okay, though. This afternoon, I left it for you, gave Gordon's watch back to you, because you're gonna die too—just like Gordon!" She aimed the BAR at Remy, then pointed it at Virginia.

Virginia gulped. "But why Gordon? And why Remy?"

Charisse's face softened with crazed pity. "You are too stupid to understand, aren't you, little girl? Gordon had the boat—my mama's old boat. At least I *thought* it was my mama's, until Remy started thinking it wasn't, after Miss Eugenia told you *Cheshire* was sunk in the ocean."

"But *Cheshire* did sink in the ocean. Geneva scuttled her, out past the jet—" Virginia broke off, watching Charisse's fingers tightening on the BAR.

"*Shut up.*" The ice in Charisse's voice chilled Virginia to the bone. "I *seduced* Gordon," Charisse continued, "because he had the boat—he was so, so easy, like I said. Us both being in real estate,

I called him all the time, asking for his expert advice, meeting for drinks—he just fell into my hands, and I could go to the boat anytime, as long as *you* weren't there. Then as soon as he got rid of you, you *moved* there! And he gave my mama's boat to *you*. You didn't deserve it."

"That's all over baby," Remy soothed. "It's just me and you now."

"And Remy." Taking her eyes off Virginia for a second to give Remy a withering look, Charisse continued as though he had not spoken. "I waited on his table one night—and I give every new customer of mine my real estate card. He was eating all by himself, and over his Alaskan King Crab Leg Plate he told me he was looking for a house. I 'found' him *this* house—at first he didn't even want to see a beach house—so I could come and stay here with him, in my mama's old house, the house where I was born!"

"Oliver's Lodge," Virginia murmured.

"*What?*" Charisse demanded. "What *about* Oliver's Lodge?"

Virginia flinched as cold water washed across her instep. "You *worked* there. That night—you took the picture of my boat off the wall upstairs at Oliver's Lodge, after you tripped the breaker and made the power go out. "

"Your boat? My *mama's* boat," Charisse corrected, tickling the trigger with her forefinger. "My mama," she went on, "crazy as she was, had enough presence of mind to give her attorney something to keep for me 'til I was old enough, in case something happened to her. He never got to give it to me—after Hurricane Hazel tore up so much down here, I ended up in foster homes upstate. Being so little, I didn't know my last name, and with my mama gone, I guess nobody was looking for me."

Nostrils flaring, Charisse glanced at Remy, tightening her grip on the BAR.

"When Mama's attorney died three years ago, his son found Mama's file in storage and advertised for me all over the state. I answered the ad—I wasn't even sure it was me he was looking for—and sure enough, I was the offspring of Geneva McKenna. What my mama had left for me was an old sealed envelope with two old pictures inside—one of this house and one of my mama's old boat—*your* old boat, Virginia—" She narrowed her eyes at Virginia, "—and this old copper key with a cat on it. On the back of the house picture she wrote, 'My darling, here lies the key to your treasure.' On the back of the boat picture she wrote, 'Here lies your treasure.' The key had a note tied to it that said 'Cheshire.'"

Carefully keeping the BAR trained on Virginia, Charisse pulled a copper key out of the nightgown's pocket. The handle of the key was shaped like a cat—a grinning Cheshire cat. "I lost my key," Charisse said, glaring at Virginia, "so I got yours. *You* should not have had it."

Virginia stifled a gasp. The cat looked just like the one on Remy's door knocker—and the one missing from Miss Eugenia's key collection at the shop.

"When I was little," Charisse said, her voice beginning to quaver, "I remember Mama talking about the Treasure Cat, how she and my daddy lived on the Treasure Cat and hunted treasure and found it buried on an island. I thought later it was a dream, or me remembering things wrong, but it was '*Cheshire* cat,' not 'Treasure Cat.'"

Keeping the BAR pointed at Virginia, Charisse, oblivious to the cold water, stepped over Cam's torso down into the salty brine on the kitchen floor at the base of the stairs. Remy backed up to let her pass. She backed slowly toward the door, the hem of the nightgown dragging in the salt water. Her eyes blazing, she never took her gaze or the direction of the BAR's barrel point off Virginia.

"How did you remember all that, from when you were just three years old?" Virginia asked. "How did you know enough to answer the newspaper ad?" She gulped, glancing at Remy. He was no help at all.

"Dr. Bunnelle—your friend *Belinda*," Charisse sneered, "helped me remember. She's sorry now. And I was almost four, not just three."

Belinda. "What do you mean, 'sorry now'?" Virginia asked, trying to keep panic out of her voice.

"Mama had a Cheshire cat door knocker on the front door," Charisse went on, ignoring her, "that same one that's on the front door now—I thought sure she called it the Treasure Cat. It was only after—"

The knob of the outside kitchen door turned and the door flew open, just missing Charisse. Straining against its hinges, it slammed against the wall, driven by the wind and water.

Charisse screamed, whirling toward the door.

Remy lunged toward her on his uninjured foot, and Charisse whirled back toward him and Virginia, discharging the BAR as Virginia dove to the side.

Remy, falling back against the wall, gasped and clasped his left hand over his right forearm. He looked down, watching blood appear between his fingers where he clutched his wound.

"Stop, Virginia!" Charisse screamed, re-cocking the BAR while staggering back to regain her footing in the ankle-deep water.

"No, *you* stop!" A wild-eyed man stood in the kitchen doorway clutching a handgun, the storm raging behind and below him.

Charisse turned toward him, her face contorted with rage.

"Char*risse*," the man caressed her name, grinning.

Chapter Forty

Virginia stared. The Stearman biplane—the seaplane. *Malcolm*. Kathy had said 'Mr. Malcolm' would fly down from North Carolina in his float plane.

Wild-eyed, his ever-present fedora gone and his linen sport coat torn, Malcolm Trapier limped into the kitchen. Ignoring Virginia, he looked from Remy to Charisse, then back at Remy. He shook his head.

"I can't believe you two fools, wasting time diving for an old wreck that never was!"

Remy, leaning against the wall and clutching his arm, raised his eyes from his blood-covered fingers and glared at Malcolm.

Charisse gulped and clutched the BAR tighter.

"Yeah, I knew you two went out and dived that old wreck day before yesterday—but that's not Geneva's boat!"

Virginia gasped. Remy and Charisse *had* gone diving! And both lied about the mask marks around their eyes, claiming to be snorkeling, at different locations.

"That wasn't *Cheshire*?" Charisse said weakly.

"No!" Malcolm laughed. "There's all kindsa old wrecks out there past the jetties! I raised that boat three days after Geneva scuttled her, cost me a right pretty penny too, and a sorry mess that boat was. Went to Wilmington to see about my sick wife, came back, and the damn boat was gone, sold for back dockage. Nobody knew who bought her or where they took her."

Virginia swallowed. She squinted at the gun in Malcolm's hand. It was undoubtedly a Walther PPK. It looked awfully like the Walther PPK Remy had shown her when they first met, the one that had gone missing from his Range Rover a short time later.

Malcolm turned his gaze on Virginia, "You've got that *Cheshire* boat, so you know where it is! It should have been mine years ago! You and this other bitch are going to get it for me." He looked pointedly at Charisse, then at Virginia. "Soon as this water goes down," he gestured with the Walther at the water flowing over their ankles, "we go. You," he gestured with the Walther toward Charisse, "you have Geneva's look. You must be our daughter. Geneva thought I was her precious Maxwell come back to life—else she wouldn't have let me near her!"

Charisse stared at Malcolm in horror.

The wind howled even louder, making the house shudder and groan.

Virginia looked anxiously up at the ceiling over the rear half of the kitchen, where the groaning was the loudest.

"Don't mind that," Malcolm grinned, following Virginia's gaze. "If this house withstood Hurricane Hazel, it can handle anything. And I would know—I was here."

"You're insane!" Remy looked up from his bloody hand.

"After the Labor Day Boat Race," Malcolm said, looking pleased with himself, "Geneva and Max were staying on her Chris-Craft in Georgetown, sitting at that same table in the saloon of that boat drinking cognac, just like you and your lover do, Miss *Virginia*," he said, grabbing Virginia's hair and twisting her head back so she could see his face.

He grinned. "Just like you and old Remy here didn't even know I was on this little island with you all this evening, Geneva and my ill-fated twin brother Max didn't know I was following them that night." He shoved Virginia away.

Virginia nearly lost her balance and grabbed the edge of the trestle table. The wood-grain edge felt so reassuringly normal. Gripping the table edge, she eased herself down onto a chair, one wet foot tucked beneath her. How long could the floor hold up under the weight of the ankle-deep water?

Out the corner of her eye, Charisse saw Remy, his back against the wall, sliding slowly towards the floor as he held his arm. Her face fell. "Baby! I'm sorry, so, so, sorry."

She started toward him, still holding the BAR.

"Don't *move!*" Malcolm shouted, sliding back the bolt to cock the Walther.

Charisse stopped and swallowed. Clutching the BAR, she stared at Malcolm.

Malcolm looked at Charisse. "You remember me, don't you?"

Charisse gulped, her eyes wide.

"You want to know what happened to your mama?" He demanded.

She nodded mutely, oblivious to the water slapping around her ankles.

"She and Max had finally found out where her great-great-granddaddy re-buried his treasure at the end of the War Between the States—but Max made the fatal mistake of bragging about it to me. Geneva had had an idea of where it was since she was a little girl, but she'd never tried to find it. It was supposed to be the McKenna's ace in the hole, never to be used unless they were desperate. And they had never been truly desperate—but Max was. His gambling debts were overwhelming, and I was leaning on him pretty strong to keep him buying my silence about his wife down in Miami." He laughed. "I just knew pretty little Geneva didn't know anything about ol' Max's wifey down Miami way.

"Geneva *also* didn't realize at first that high-living Max was not wealthy because he had certainly made out to be. She didn't know he had a twin brother neither, because ol' Max wasn't exactly proud of me. I never put on airs like he did. But Max had run out of money and luck *and* owed a *great* deal of money for gambling debts down in Miami. Geneva was well off and smart, too—she refused to lend him any more money because she knew he'd waste it. She had begun to realize their treasure-hunting jaunts to North Island looking for pirate treasure with Max's metal detector were serious rather than just for a lark, and when they actually did find and dig up the treasure, Geneva told Max she'd keep it in a safe place. But—she kept one necklace out to wear. Had her picture-portrait taken wearing it. She wore it to the Labor Day boat races, and Max hit the *roof.*

"Max bragged to me Labor Day morning that they'd found the McKenna stash, and dug it up, and Geneva re-hid or re-buried it—he just had to get her to tell him where. That's what they argued about, late that night, on the boat...Geneva's boat, *Cheshire.* Geneva shot Max," he snorted, "shot him rather than let him get at her family legacy."

Charisse lowered the shotgun. "My mama shot my daddy?"

"Your daddy—that's a good one. Geneva was a *lousy* shot," Malcolm laughed, oblivious to the rising water swirling across the floor. "She thought she killed Max, but she didn't do any better than you did to old Remy here." He nodded in Remy's direction. "And girl, Max weren't your daddy."

Remy, sitting in the water with his back against the wall, moaned softly and clutched his arm tighter.

A high-pitched creaking sound began under their feet.

Charisse looked down at the floor, her eyes huge, then looked back at Malcolm.

Malcolm glanced down, unconcerned. "Geneva passed out that night on the boat," he continued, "and never saw me come in and finish off ol' brother Max. I drove up to Myrtle Beach and went to Max's rented room at the Ocean Forest Hotel to get the written information Max had told me he had detailing where the McKenna treasure was. Didn't have trouble getting a key from the front desk neither—me and Max was *identical.* The only thing I found was a handmade map showing where on North Island they found it, not where Geneva moved it to. I drove back down to Georgetown and went back to the boat, only to find Max's body had disappeared, and Geneva was gone, too. On a hunch, I came here to Geneva's house on Pawleys Island, and here she was. I was hoping to persuade her to tell me where the treasure was. She was right here, at this same house, covered with dried blood, pacing up and down, right here in this kitchen."

Malcolm laughed, "She took one look at me and started screaming, 'I buried you! You're dead!' Of course she thought I was Max come back to life. Remember, she didn't know ol' Maxwell had a twin brother. There was no getting any information out of her in that condition, so I drove up home to my wife in Wilmington."

Drawing a deep breath, he continued, lost in the memory of 1949 and apparently not hearing the shrieking of the wind or the thunderous pounding of the waves just below the door.

Remy gave a little moan. Virginia looked at Charisse, who was staring at Malcolm, transfixed, her knuckles white where they gripped the BAR.

"I came back a few days later, and Geneva wasn't here. She was staying on that boat, and boy, did she ever scream when she saw my face at the window that night. I thought she'd never go near that boat again—but she did, one last time. Next time I came back, the boat was gone—Geneva had scuttled it then holed up here in this house. For four years, I kept paying her little visits late at night, here at the house."

Turning to Virginia, he grinned. "I'd land in that wide creek behind the island, like I did today."

236

He turned back to Charisse. "Poor Geneva. She didn't leave here much, didn't see people—except for me, and she didn't think she had much choice there. Guess she figured if old Max had come back to life and could visit her at the boat *and* the house, there was no use to run. Nobody ever saw me but her—I landed in the creek on the south end of the island, anchored the plane, and walked in.

Finally she got to where she'd talk to me. One night, early on, we even got *intimate*—" he gestured with the handgun toward Charisse—"and here *you* are. But," he gave a deep sigh, "she never would tell me where she hid the treasure.

"Then she birthed you! And a few years later, she apparently decided she had to move Max's body! I surprised her right when she was digging up old Max, right here, smack in the middle of Hurricane Hazel's approach. Everybody was gone from the island but her and you, and she'd just uncovered what was left of old Max when I showed up. When she said she buried him I figured she meant she'd shoved his body off the boat but noooooo—she'd dragged him off the boat the night it happened, brought him here, and buried him right under this house. And then lived here, holed up in this house by herself, and then with you! No wonder she acted so crazy."

And no wonder Charisse is crazy, Virginia thought, her stomach tightening as the dull roar of the ocean became louder. She looked from Remy, to Charisse, and then to Malcolm. None of them seemed to notice the storm *or* her.

"Maybe seeing his remains after five years right next to me, alive and healthy, gave her some clarity," Malcolm went on. "All I know is when she saw me, she finally realized I wasn't him come back to life. She *never* knew me and Max was twins, though. She just knew right then I'd been fooling her. She came at me with that shovel, and when she swung it at me and sliced my kneecap in two, I grabbed that shovel, and she fell back and busted her head on that bottom stone step. I buried her right down there with her precious Max—she had the grave ready! My knee hurt so bad, I wish I could've killed her again."

"You killed her? You buried her, and nobody knew?" Charisse screamed, a strange disoriented look in her eyes, her hand clenched tightly around the BAR.

"Yeah, but I never found out where Geneva hid the treasure. I took you back to Wilmington with me, bought us both bus tickets to Charlotte, then slipped off in the next town while you were asleep."

"You are *vile*," growled Charisse. "I was only a little child and—"

Struggling to keep her balance, Charisse gasped, and looked down, horrified, at the floor wrenching apart at her feet.

Chapter Forty-One

The rear part of the kitchen at the door where Charisse was standing gave a mighty, rending groan, beginning to collapse as the stairs leading down to the ground ripped away.

Charisse leaped forward across the tilting, separating floor as Malcolm lunged forward to snatch the BAR from her hands.

Malcolm was a second too late.

Charisse fired off a round toward his outstretched arms. Her shot missed.

Unscathed, Malcolm started, letting go of the Walther. He snatched at the falling weapon, grabbing it before it hit the water, and slipped and fell onto the floor, splashing in the knee-deep water.

As Charisse glanced down at the fallen Malcolm, Virginia leapt on her, throwing her face-first to the floor.

Charisse came up fast, coughing and spitting salt water as she and Virginia struggled with the BAR.

The storm surge was now over two feet deep in the kitchen. The sound of the waves churning under the house was deafening.

As Virginia struggled to hold Charisse down and take the BAR from her, Charisse broke free and jumped up, holding the rifle point blank at Virginia. She cocked it, never taking her eyes off Virginia.

"It won't fire after being under the water!" Virginia shouted desperately over the wind.

Charisse, furious, grabbed the barrel and swung the BAR, baseball bat-like, at Virginia's head.

Virginia ducked and the BAR's stock hit the fireplace with a force that chipped one of the stones and caused the rifle to discharge— with Charisse still holding the barrel.

Charisse's eyes widened in shock. Letting go of the BAR barrel, she stared down at her stomach and the bloodstain spreading across the thin cotton batiste nightgown.

Virginia reached out and caught the BAR as Charisse dropped it. Standing back upright, she felt an arm close around her neck and the cold barrel of the Walther nuzzling her throat.

Malcolm turned his hand and pressed the muzzle hard against Virginia's neck. "Now you drop that piece, missy."

She let go of the BAR then heard a *thunk* as it hit the floor just beneath the water. She took a shaky breath as the pressure of the muzzle against her neck was relieved.

"Your store window display gave me the idea to talk to Geneva's sister Eugenia this morning," he laughed nastily, tapping the muzzle of the gun painfully against Virginia's head.

Dear God, please let Miss Eugenia be all right, prayed Virginia.

"Miss Eugenia is my mama's sister! You better not have hurt her!" Charisse screamed, blood pouring between her fingers as she held both hands over her stomach.

A shot rang out over the howling wind, and Charisse screamed.

Standing shakily in the knee-deep water, leaning against the wall for support, Remy clutched the BAR firmly in one outstretched arm, while blood trickled from his other arm. "It *will* fire after being under the water," he growled.

Malcolm fell backward onto the slanting broken floor and slowly slid under the water, into the gaping hole where the deck had been only moments before. His blood clouded the water where he fell and washed back into the kitchen as the next surge of salt water rushed over the broken boards where he had fallen.

Horrified and gasping, Charisse backed away as Malcolm's blood flowed toward her. Her own blood, flowing from her stomach, between her fingers and down her legs into the water, mingled with Malcolm's before washing away.

A huge, heavy old brick fell from the arch over the fireplace and splashed into the water, followed by another, then another.

The cracked and broken section of floor sagged dangerously, the wooden planks groaning. Outside the house, the wind shrieked like a train whistle. The higher-pitched whine of long nails being pulled from deep inside cypress planks rose to an ear-splitting crescendo. The remaining kitchen floor, with Charisse closest to the edge, tilted and groaned.

"Baby watch out!" Remy reached toward her.

As Charisse reached out one bloody hand and grasped Remy's, the straining planks gave way underneath her feet and his.

Virginia watched, speechless, as Charisse and Remy, surrounded by shattered lumber, were sucked away by the raging receding waters of the storm surge.

Climbing up the stairs, she turned around near the top as she heard a shrieking sound. Clinging to the banister, she saw the rest of the kitchen disappear. The headless body of Cam bobbed once, ropes trailing, and was gone.

The loud howls of the wind and surf were pierced by the ear-splitting screech of rending wood as the house next door was torn from its pilings. Virginia scrambled up the last three steps and collapsed on the landing on her back beside the lantern Charisse had set there. Above her, where the ceiling met the wall, she saw the inside of the roof moving and pulling like the interior bulkhead of a jetliner flying through turbulent skies.

Shakily she stood up, taking one last look down at the floorless kitchen walls. The fireplace and chimney, missing more brick now, remained. Already the ocean surge was receding, leaving a briny, wet waterline.

One hand on the wall, the other holding the lantern, she made her way down the hall of the quivering house past Remy's bedroom. She never wanted to go in there again. She went further down the hall and toward the guest bedroom. Holding the lantern high, she looked into the room. Above the shutters banging and clattering against the clapboard wall outside, she heard a plaintive meow.

There, huddled on the comforter Virginia had slept under just this afternoon, was Gabrielle. With the storm howling on every side of the house and the ripping sound of splitting wood from neighboring houses echoing in her ears, Virginia lay down, putting her arms around Gabrielle to wait out the remainder of the hurricane.

Wishing she had her harmonica, she tried not to think about Remy and the implications of Charisse's ominous 'I cut your boat loose.'

Malcolm was crazy, she thought, trembling. *He probably never even buried Geneva, and she probably never buried Maxwell. No bodies could have remained buried under this house for decades—could they? Geneva surely disappeared in that long-ago hurricane, and Maxwell disappeared off the boat—off Cheshire-Chaucer, just like Miss Eugenia said. Just like Remy, Charisse, and Malcolm disappeared tonight.*

Chapter Forty-Two

Early October

The operator of the huge yellow excavator raised the machine's bucket. Only a few more loads of sand, and they would be ready to drive the deep timber piles for the reconstruction of this historic home. Post-hurricane Harvey construction on Pawleys Island called for foundations to be deeper than ever before, and with good reason.

He shook his head. This house was a *disaster*. If it was not so historic, it likely would have been bulldozed with dozens of other shattered, collapsed beach houses. Why even—he squinted, then gasped.

Talk about historic! Biting his lip, he lowered the bucket to the ground and cut the engine.

Snatching his hard hat off, the foreman stalked over, squinting derisively up at the operator. Wiping his forehead with his sleeve, he grimaced. "What now?"

The operator leaned down, hands on his knees. "We might have an old grave here."

The foreman rolled his eyes. "Another mannequin, you mean. There must have been half a dozen of the things. Just keep going. We're already way behind schedule."

Climbing down from the cab, the operator walked over for a closer look at what was caught in the bucket's jaws and what was still in the earth. "No. This is no mannequin. This is clothes and hair—and bones."

Late October

Virginia and Miss Eugenia stood side by side in the Prince George Winyah Episcopal Churchyard, the breeze ruffling the hems of their black dresses. Miss Eugenia's dress was actually a shade of purple eggplant so deep that it appeared black.

It was a quintessential Lowcountry October day, the kind that convinces visitors to move to Georgetown County and reassures locals that they would never want to live anywhere else.

Virginia took a deep breath of the cool dry air and looked up through the sun-dappled live oak leaves to the bright blue autumn sky. Then she looked down at the same sunlight playing breezily on the weathered and mossy gravestones from the past two centuries.

"You know," Miss Eugenia sighed, staring down at the single new grave, "the first grave was laid here in 1737. Some of these live oak trees are even older. Geneva loved this cemetery and loved these trees, with their low-hanging limbs and Spanish moss. We had picnics here as children, played here in the afternoons. She should have been resting here since 1954."

"She's here at last," said Virginia.

Miss Eugenia nodded. "Yes, indeed."

"By the grace of God, we're not burying Belinda, too," Virginia said.

Belinda was completely recovered from the concussion she received at the hands of Charisse. The evacuating motorist who found Belinda by the road noted that Charisse's tire tracks, cut into the shoulder of the road when she spun out in her haste to leave, ran within an inch of Belinda's unconscious form.

A shadow passed over Miss Eugenia's face. "I've decided not to do anything about Charisse. No memorial service."

"I don't blame you," Virginia replied, shaking her head slightly. She had debated whether or not to tell Miss Eugenia that Charisse had been her niece, finally deciding that telling her was best.

Up above them, an owl hooted from a live oak branch.

"Geneva loved owls, too," sighed Miss Eugenia. She shook her head. "I can't get over Malcolm and Maxwell Trapier being *twins*."

"That was a shock," Virginia agreed.

"When I told Geneva about seeing Maxwell with the, ah, woman of ill repute, it probably wasn't even Maxwell."

"It might have been," Virginia offered, "but it was most likely Malcolm."

"Probably so," said Miss Eugenia. "But Maxwell was bad for Geneva anyway, with the wife in Miami and that huge gambling debt. I'm glad you told me about that. I had been feeling so guilty about mistaking Malcolm for him and making a false accusation."

"You did what any good sister would," Virginia said. "You told her." She rolled an acorn back and forth with the toe of her pump. "I'd best be getting back to the shop."

"You go on back, dearie. I'm going to stay here for a while, then head back home and order that wall tent."

Miss Eugenia, following a long-time yearning to reenact the events her Daughters of the War Between the States chapter memorialized, had decided to become a Civil War reenactor. She and the Georgetown Daughters had formed a cannon crew and bought a bronze twelve-pound Napoleon, christening her *Harvest Moon* in honor of the paddle-wheel steamer whose 1865 sinking they commemorated every year. Since they would, as all good Civil War reenactors do, be fighting on the Federal side as well as the Confederate, they decided that naming their cannon after the only Federal flagship ever sunk by the Confederates would be appropriate. Their first weekend-long reenactment, complete with period tent-camping, two battles and a night-firing, was near Charleston next month, at Boone Hall Plantation.

Virginia gave Miss Eugenia a hug and walked back through the patchwork maze of eighteenth-and-nineteenth-century gravestones under the live oak canopy. She was thankful Miss Eugenia had closure at last.

Remy's body, so far, had not been recovered, and Virginia did not attend his memorial service. A service for Cam was pending, though Virginia did not plan to attend it, either.

Gordon was adulterous with both of those women—first Cam, then Charisse. Cam's rhapsodizing descriptions of Gordon's boat made Remy wonder if it was the one in the photograph Charisse's mother had left her, and Remy told Charisse. Now all four were dead, as well as Malcolm Trapier. Virginia heard that Malcolm's wife came down from Wilmington to claim his body and salt-waterlogged red Stearman biplane-seaplane.

Prince George was only two blocks from Cheshire Cat Maritime Antiques, so Virginia walked. Since she was staying with Miss Eugenia until *Chaucer* was repaired, she could walk to and from the shop and the boatyard also. Her beloved old Porsche—in which she found her harmonica, safe in the console—as well as Remy's blue Range Rover, was ruined in the storm surge. Tomorrow she was buying, second-hand, the British-racing-green Range Rover from, of all people, Renee Ravenel-Ryan, Remy's ex-wife.

Virginia reached Front Street, glad the boats remaining in the street after the storm surge receded had finally been removed. Though most shops on the lower end of Front Street were badly flooded and left with high waterlines after the surge receded, Cheshire Cat Maritime Antiques, on the higher end, had received only minimal storm damage. Virginia had already ordered a small engraved copper plaque to mark her shop's seventeen-inch-high waterline.

The Harbor Promenade boardwalk, with its boat slips and floating docks behind the shops, was being repaired, as was *Chaucer*. Soon Virginia would be able to move back aboard and live right behind her shop.

She stopped by the boatyard every day to check on *Chaucer*'s progress. Found adrift in the narrow canal behind the marina the morning after the hurricane, cut mooring lines trailing from all of her cleats, *Chaucer* spent the night of the storm tossing about in the shallow, sheltered canal. The next morning she was floating evenly with no list, the bootstripe Remy painted just above her waterline showing she had taken on no water.

Chaucer's flying bridge, however, was sheared cleanly off, no doubt when the ninety-miles-per-hour winds rushed her under the low stone flyover bridge separating the canal from the marina compound. In the saloon, Virginia found strewn dozens of wilted gardenias—undoubtedly tossed there by Charisse before she sliced free all Chaucer's mooring lines.

Minus her flying bridge, *Chaucer* presented the same sleek profile she did in Chris-Craft's 1948 pictorial specifications—and in Eugenia's photographs of Maxwell and Geneva aboard her in 1949 when she was Geneva's beloved *Cheshire*.

Virginia, unconditionally thankful her boat survived the storm, resolved to restore the damage to *Chaucer*'s upper deck according to the original plans and not replace the flying bridge.

Aboard *Chaucer*, testing the integrity of the original upper deck below the smashed teak planking of what was left of the flying bridge deck added by Maxwell in 1949, she found a partially crushed copper box. On the broken lid of the box was a broadly grinning Cheshire cat. Beneath the broken lid, the box was filled with ancient jeweled crosses, seventeenth-century gold coins, and, from a much later era—Confederate War Bonds. On top of the War bonds, resplendent with large inlaid deep red rubies, was the cross necklace Geneva had been wearing in one of the photographs Miss

Eugenia had brought to the shop. It was the necklace Geneva had taken out of the box to wear after she hid the rest from Malcolm, the necklace that had been one of the catalysts in the death of Maxwell, and, eventually, in the deaths of Geneva, Cam, Malcolm, Remy, and Charisse.

Geneva had sent *Cheshire* to a watery grave and died without revealing the hiding place of the McKenna treasure. It was a good hiding place, unwittingly sealed in by Maxwell as he built the flying bridge onto *Cheshire*'s original upper deck. Geneva accessed it by a plank she loosened for her secret use. Little did he know, by embedding the copper Cheshire cat into the newly built flying bridge, he was marking the hiding place of what he sought so fervently. Vigilant varnishing and caulking by subsequent owners had permanently sealed the loosened plank.

That cross necklace, as well as the trunk and all its contents, now resided at the Georgetown Harbor Maritime Museum on permanent display. On temporary display at the museum was the *Emily St. Pierre* figurehead, on loan from Virginia.

In a gesture that still brought tears to Virginia's eyes every time she thought about it, Miss Eugenia gave the figurehead to Virginia the day after the hurricane, when she knew at last Virginia had not perished in the storm surge. They both agreed the museum was the safest place for the irreplaceable figurehead until all storm damage repairs were completed in Cheshire Cat Maritime Antiques.

Nearing her shop, Virginia walked past the old market and glanced up at the town clock. Good—five minutes to nine. Built in 1844, the clock tower weathered many a storm before Hurricane Harvey, and the clock still worked, most of the time.

In front of her shop, a man was lifting a great brass sphere out the trunk of his car. Virginia grinned. *Yes!* Just what she'd been hoping to have in the shop—another antique diving helmet. Every day since she had re-opened after the storm, customers had been bringing in the most incredible things they found washed up on the beaches. For all of its destruction, Hurricane Harvey yielded a myriad of treasures.

She reached into her purse for her keys and let her fingers linger a few seconds on her harmonica. Somehow, she would find a minute sometime this morning to pull it out and play a few bars.

Looking up at her sign, Virginia unlocked the door of her shop and smiled. The Cheshire cat grinned down at her, having survived the hurricane unscathed.

About the Author

Elizabeth Robertson Huntsinger might wish she lived in a past era were she not so happy in this century reenacting colonial pirate adventures and the Civil War with the Charlestowne Few and the Pee Dee Light Artillery. A native of Manning, SC, Elizabeth moved to the edge of the continent to study English at Coastal Carolina University. After graduation, she spent years living aboard her first Georgetown County home, her antique wooden boat anchored in Murrells Inlet. Now a full-time storyteller with Georgetown County Library and Georgetown County First Steps, Elizabeth also conducts Ghosts of Georgetown Lantern Tours (www.ghostsofgeorgetown.com) with the love of her life, Lee Huntsinger, with whom she has a daughter, Virginia Lee. Elizabeth is the author of three non-fiction books: *Ghosts of Georgetown*, *More Ghosts of Georgetown*, and *Georgetown Mysteries and Legends*.

Waterline is her first mystery novel.